BOOMTOWN

A JONATHAN CROWLEY NOVEL

JAMES A. MOORE

This one's for Tessa, for everything. For Dan Brereton, and Joe Lansdale for the inspiration, and for Charles Rutledge for the encouragement in dark times. For Kasey Lansdale, because she's awesome. Big hugs, also, for Amanda Spedding and Geoff Brown, who read the work, liked the work, and helped with the work.

COLORADO TERRITORIES

1869

CHAPTER ONE
FROZEN MOMENTS

The Trapper

"There's something wrong with the world when it's cold enough to freeze a waterfall." The trapper spoke to himself, or just possibly his horse, but neither of them responded. The proof of his comment lay above him and to his left, a frozen wall of white ice that only two days before had still been running water.

The cold was all-encompassing, a living thing that seemed to thrive on sucking the heat from the world around man and stallion alike. He called his horse Stomper, and it was a massive thing, meant for hauling wagons. The black beast barely seemed to notice his weight or the burden of the sled behind it, but the cold sent plumes of steam from its muzzle with each breath. Covered in the thick coat he'd sewn for it, his stallion looked more like a locomotive than it did an animal. He wouldn't see his beast of burden and closest living acquaintance killed by the elements if he could help it.

It wasn't the elements, however, that had done most of the killing in the area. If he had to guess it was Indians. Someone must have driven them half mad if they were responsible for the bodies he kept finding.

The idea had been, as it always was, to shoot enough bison and foxes and wolves to load his sled with furs. Instead, he'd been gathering the dead for the last two days. He didn't have it in him to leave them frozen to the ground for animals to feast on. His mother would surely rise from her grave and beat his fool head into a new shape if he ever got that callous.

Didn't much help him get his work done, but there was enough money set aside, and as a trapper and hunter it wasn't overly likely that he'd starve any time soon.

The latest body showed itself on the left side of the trail, and he nodded his head and tugged the reins. Stomper came to a halt and snorted agreeably.

The trapper slid from his saddle with practiced ease and walked over to the latest grisly find. Nine bodies so far, each one cut, shot and in different stages of undress, depending on the sex. There were two women who had likely been of marrying age among the dead. There was also a little girl child and an old woman who should have never headed from the east to the wilds. Only the crone had any clothes on her by the time the murdering dogs were done. The others had been treated as poorly as the whores in San Francisco, and that was poorly indeed.

The man in the snow stared with dead eyes behind thin spectacles. The frost on the lenses hid the color of his eyes and made him look blind as well as dead.

That he was dead was obvious. Even if he'd not been frozen to the ground there were lacerations on his skin and shreds of meat and flesh peeking from under his tattered clothing. Like the waterfall a short way back, the trickles of blood had frozen into twists of crimson that hung suspended from his wounds. If he had to guess, the trapper would have told anyone curious that he suspected the man had been dragged behind a horse for a while. His shoes were torn apart—a pity that, as they could have fetched a few cents—and his clothing, thin and fine and no doubt very expensive, had peeled half way from his body during the long trip. Ropes still bound his hands and cut into the flesh of his wrists and forearms. He'd very likely fought hard to get away before his attackers had finished with their job.

"Well, sir, I'm sorry to meet you this way." He looked the body over again and frowned. Someone, his killers or otherwise, had turned out the man's pockets and taken everything that might have value. The cloth of his vest was split where his watch fob had been torn away. The derby he'd likely worn at one time was nearby and judging by how clean it was, he guessed it had been dropped by the killer after the fact.

"I reckon we should get to work, old boy." The wind let out a moan from the nearby trees and sent an additional shiver through him. No one else bothered to reply and he reckoned that was for the best.

He took the axe and pick from the bundle he kept on Stomper's flank and got to digging. The night before had seen a hard, freezing rain and the body was stuck in a thick caul of ice and mud.

Ten minutes later he had a rope wrapped around both wrists—new rope that had not frozen into the ground—and he tied that to Stomper's sled before urging his horse forward. The ground gave up its prize reluctantly, and for a moment the trapper thought the corpse would break like a sapling before it finally came free with a crunching sound.

Once uprooted the dead man slithered stiffly across the ice and bounced off two aspen trees before coming to a rest. He slid the body across the ice until he could wrestle the weight onto the back of the sled.

He had leather aplenty, and he used it to lash the body on top of the other corpses.

"Well, sir. You're the tenth and I pray the last. Let's see about getting you to Carson's Point. Might be we can arrange a funeral for you."

The rain started again, dropping from the sky in a half-frozen state and solidifying as soon as it touched the ground. The sound it made as it rattled to the earth was not unlike a dozen sets of teeth chattering away.

"I'd never wish a good man to hell, sir, but I reckon it just might be warmer at either end of the journey than it is here."

They rode together in silence, he and his ten companions, and Stomper carried them all without complaint.

Carson's Point stood at the edge of the woods, a dark, brooding place in the best of times, surrounded by thick lumber walls from the town's brief stint as a military outpost.

The army had abandoned the place as useless, and not long after the vermin had moved in. Seven families came into the area led by William Wadsworth Carson, who no doubt had his own reasons for fleeing from South Carolina and moving into the Rocky Mountains. Whatever the reasons—and there were rumors aplenty—he had successfully settled his family and the fools who trusted him in the abandoned encampment and made a town of it in short order. Not long after that the rumors started and the people came.

The trapper shook off thoughts of how the damned place had come to be and instead worried about beating the worsening weather.

He made it to town with only a hint of the earlier sunlight left to show that the world was not completely lost in darkness.

Well before the fortified walls were reached, he saw the growing explosion of tents and wagons that had shown themselves in the last few months. The walls barely afforded any real protection except from the wind these days and the doors that had once sealed the place against Indian attacks were gone, likely cannibalized to help build a new structure or two.

There were lights to be found, of course, fires and lanterns that did their best to fight off the cold and the night alike. He was grateful for all of them as he approached the town and twice as grateful as he pulled the sled to the side of his first stop past the heavy wooden barrier.

The house was not dark. It felt as if it should have been, but the whitewash was fresh and the lanterns near the front of the place blazed warmly even in the bitter cold of the winter storm.

What was freezing rain earlier had become snow and fell in thick flurries, obscuring almost everything. For that reason, the undertaker almost scared the trapper to death, and also damned near wound up with a bullet between his ears.

He'd never thought much of Mr. Lucas Slate, nor did he much care for the man's occupation, even if it was a necessary evil in the world. The man was as creepy as his house was pleasant.

The undertaker moved toward him in a thick black coat that covered his black suit and his pale face.

The trapper resisted the urge to cross himself and mutter a prayer.

Slate looked enough like the dead that he was unsettling. Not that he could help that part very much. His skin and his hair were white. Not pale, but dead white. His blue eyes pale enough that they were almost white themselves. There was a word for it. He searched his mind until he remembered it, because words were powerful things when you were by yourself as much as he was. Albino. The man was an albino.

He was also plain. His body was unsettlingly gaunt—and stronger than it looked as the trapper had seen for himself when the undertaker was moving bodies about. Though he was not particularly tall his lean form gave that illusion, especially if wearing his customary finery.

In his early twenties and already he looked much older. It was a sorry lot in life to have and he'd done his best with what the Lord had given him, the trapper supposed.

"Good evening, Mister Miles." Slate's voice was cultured, with a faint southern drawl. There was little doubt the man had come from money and from a well-bred family. The state of things in the lower states was not good these days. He could see why the man might want to flee there. Slate wasn't notorious for speaking of his past and the two never had so much as spent a meal together, so beyond that he knew almost nothing.

"Evening, Mister Slate." He did his best to hide his distaste.

Slate looked back, a tight, enigmatic smile playing around his lips without ever fully showing itself. "It would appear you've found work for me?" His eyes roamed over the stacked bodies and the smile slowly faded as he saw the marks of violence on the corpses.

"I'm afraid so." He looked away. The man made him feel squirmy inside. "I thought I might drop them here for you to tend to and then let the sheriff know about them."

"Sheriff Bulmer has left us. He found the weather a bit too extreme for his tastes, I fear." The undertaker began the tedious task of untying each of the bodies and much as he would have preferred not to, the trapper helped him.

"Did he now? Is there a new man I should speak with?"

"There is, indeed. You'll find him in Bulmer's house. He got the place as part of his salary. His name is Meade."

He nodded and touched the brim of his hat with a mitten-covered hand. "Much obliged."

Five minutes of hard labor saw the bodies carefully laid out on the side of the house away from the street, where fewer people might have to see them. The undertaker did his work in a basement area, and the entry to that spot was on the side of the house to ensure as much discretion as was possible.

"Come by in the morning if you'd like. I should have a proper assessment by then." Slate spoke softly, and the trapper had to strain to hear him. They had made an arrangement the first time he brought in bodies. Whatever valuables the bodies might carry had to be given to the next of kin, of course, but the merchants and the innkeepers in Carson's Point offered up a small payment for each burial that took place. Because he was the one bringing the bodies, Slate gave him a portion of the monies he earned. It wasn't much but every bit helped.

"I'll do that. Have a pleasant evening, Mr. Slate."

The undertaker allowed a full smile that was too much like a rictus for his comfort. "I suspect it shall be a busy one, my good man."

He left without another word. The undertaker wasn't right. He had no proof of the man ever doing anyone harm, but he didn't need evidence. He only needed to trust his instincts, and his every sense told him the man was not proper, or good, or decent, in any form.

Carson's Point was growing at a maddening rate. When he'd first come to the area there had been only one hotel to be found, a two-story affair called the Piedmont. There were now half a dozen hotels, every one of them attached to a tavern or saloon and most of them offering whores.

Four months earlier a man named Edwin Hooper had come to town and staked a claim for gold. That had been enough to start the problems. Within a week the first person followed with dreams of finding gold. Within another month there were sixty more. So far only Hooper had found a good strike, but others were still pouring into the area and looking for more of the stuff.

To make matters worse, Hooper had disappeared into the wilderness not long after making his claim and had not been seen again.

As a result, the small settlement had become something it was never meant to be. There were still houses, yes, and the hotels that were slapped together with furious speed, but there were also people living in wagons and tents scattered in every spot where they felt they could manage to stay without interruption. The area to the east of town was covered with the newcomers and even to the west a few people had managed to settle themselves between the trees at the edge of the forest. They were probably staying a bit warmer in the current weather, but he doubted most of them were properly prepared for the wildlife in the area. He'd never actually seen a wolf attack a person, but he'd seen what was left when a bear got done with a foolish settler and it wasn't a sight he'd likely ever forget.

The travelers were getting bolder, or more desperate. There were tents set up at the edge of a few properties that he suspected were not supposed to be there. The owners weren't likely to want strangers camping at their doorsteps and if he had to guess the new sheriff was going to be very busy trying to keep the peace or twice as busy dealing with disputes.

He made sure the ties on his holster were unfastened and the grip was in easy reach. There'd be plenty of arguments in the area, but if anyone decided to involve him in their misery, he'd see the dispute was settled his way.

The Piedmont had a room and the stable boy knew both the trapper and Stomper on sight. A quarter dollar got the horse taken care of and a promise of more of the same guaranteed that the stallion would be fed and treated properly.

He got a room and bought himself the luxury of a bath as well. Because he was a regular, he got fresh water and warmed to boot.

Afterwards, he dressed in warm clothes, wrapped himself in a duster he'd lined with fur and went off to see the sheriff. He was tired, but business was business and best tended to before the night was finished with him.

Anson Meade

Anson Meade paced along the porch of his office and waited for his deputy, Pace, to show back up. Pace Peabody came with the job. He was an able enough deputy, but not timely.

Anson was used to a certain level of efficiency from his time in Boston and then Manhattan. Apparently, that sort of timeliness died a horrid death once one crossed the Mississippi.

It was nighttime and colder than should have been possible, and still there were people walking along the streets. Most of them were either drunk or working toward a state of inebriation with a vengeance. There was nothing else to do in Carson's Point, and most of the people looking for their fortune had decided to wait out the storm in town. Those that didn't were likely going to be found dead after the world thawed again.

The stranger coming toward him was an imposing figure, draped in a well-worn duster and a wide-brimmed hat that was as weathered as the man's face. A thick, well-groomed beard and mustache hid half his features. The weapons on the man's hips were clearly shown, not as a threat but as a warning, and he walked like a man who'd used them in the past and likely would again.

The stranger looked at him and nodded. "Evening. Would you be the new sheriff?"

"That I would. Anson Meade. How can I help you mister...?"

The man's gray eyes looked him up and down quickly, taking his measure, no doubt, and hopefully not finding him too wanting.

"Miles. Name's Miles. I'm just here to let you in on what I brought into town with me. I'm a trapper by trade, and I was looking for hides and found a few bodies instead." He kept his voice reasonably low; soft enough that anyone not standing nearby wouldn't hear him. There was no one else around, not even that idiot Pace.

"Bodies? Any notion of how they might have passed?"

"Poorly. They were killed. All of them."

"How many?"

"Ten as I recall." The man looked around again, quickly, a fast scan of the eyes that said even more about him having been in combat situations repeatedly. "Found them here and there. They might have been all together once, but that wasn't how I found them."

"Do you think they were all together? Did they look the part?"

"No. They looked to have come from different camps. Hell, from different countries by the way a few were dressed."

"Where would a man have to go to find these bodies?"

"Slate's place. He's the only undertaker in town, isn't he?"

Meade pulled out his pipe and stuffed the bowl with tobacco. The good thing about a pipe was it would warm your hands. "Had a man report finding bodies last week that left them out in the cold. Said he couldn't bring himself to touch them."

Miles' face twisted into a contemptuous frown. "Hardly worth calling him a man then, is it?"

The sheriff nodded. "Can't say as I don't agree with that assessment." He raised the glass shield on the porch's lamp and then slid a twig against the flame inside until it caught fire.

The trapper squinted against the breeze and smiled briefly. "Don't much care to hold your opinions, do you?"

"I don't see a reason to, Miles. Some things need saying."

"Fair enough." He touched the brim of his hat as the sheriff brought his small brand to the bowl of the pipe and drew the flame to his tobacco.

"You know Pace Peabody?"

"I do. He still the deputy here?"

"Not for long if he doesn't get his sorry self down here to relieve me."

"I see him, I'll let him know."

"Have a good night, Mr. Miles." He watched as the trapper headed off into the darkness and relaxed a bit after he was gone. There were limits to how much he wanted to handle in a day and those limits were being tested sorely. With any luck Pace would show up soon and he could handle the rest of his work and call it a day.

After waiting an additional ten minutes, Meade surrendered to his impatience, turned toward the western side of town and started for Slate's place. He told himself the shiver he got at the notion was strictly from the cold. He almost believed it, too.

By the time he arrived at the funeral home, Slate was waiting for him. He nodded his greeting and the cadaverous figure beckoned him inside. The undertaker had set up a fearsome blaze in the furnace of his house and the heat inside was stifling. It needed to be. His skin was stippled with perspiration and the thin hair on the top of his head was wet enough to glue itself down.

The bodies he had arranged in the basement were frozen solid, all of them twisted into unsettling shapes in the light of the fire. They were thawing, but only just starting the process.

He looked from one body to the next and felt his jaws clench and his teeth rub together. It was likely that the women had been violated, even the ones too young to know of sin.

"What kind of sick savages would do a thing like this?"

Slate looked at him and shook his head solemnly. "You might be surprised by how poorly men can treat each other when the mood strikes them, Sheriff."

"What do you mean by that?"

"I've been through Georgia, Alabama and Mississippi." He turned those pasty blue eyes to look into Meade's and stared hard. "I have traveled through Texas, Missouri, and areas I suspect don't have proper names yet. I have seen exactly how vile and savage soldiers can be when they've decided to make a point."

"Union or Confederate?"

The man looked away and his long, nimble fingers worked at stripping the clothes from a dead man. "Both. More's the pity."

"Man I met, Miles, he said there were ten bodies?" Meade did a slow count and then double-checked his numbers.

"Just so, Sheriff."

Meade shook his head. "Why am I only seeing nine?"

The undertaker frowned and stared at him for a moment. "That hardly seems like the sort of jest a lawman should be making on a night like this, Sheriff."

"I assure you, I don't take murder lightly enough to joke about it."

Slate stared at him for another moment and then counted the bodied aloud, frowning as he reached nine. "There would seem to be an issue here. Either I've left a body outside, or I've miscounted." He moved around the basement room and gently lifted each corpse as if there were a chance they might be hiding another body beneath them. When that failed to produce a tenth cadaver, he climbed the stairs and moved out into the cold to examine his lawn.

Slater came back down frowning. "Apparently I've miscounted."

"You sure that's all it is?" Meade's pulse thudded heavily in his chest. The notion of the dead being stolen did not sit well.

"I have a table for belongings, those I could pry free. Let's check there, shall we?"

Slate stepped into a smaller room with a very large table, likely where each of the bodies would be prepared when the time came. On that table were several personal items, most soaked with water or still half covered in ice.

Slate moved around the table without touching anything, his eyes flicking from one collection to the next. "This one. He was on the top of the lot." He pointed to a battered bowler and two ruined dress shoes. "There were spectacles with the hat. They've disappeared."

Meade rubbed the bridge of his nose roughly, hoping the gesture might ward off the headache he felt building as it sometimes did. This night he was having no luck.

"Lock your doors, Mister Slate. I'll check the area and see if I can find signs of any bandits." He paused for a moment. "No chance that the body was merely unconscious?"

Slate shook his head and left his expression carefully neutral. "I cut the shoes from his feet, Sheriff Meade. His body was frozen as solidly as the others you're seeing. He was just a bit closer to the fire."

"Well, I suppose we can safely assume he did not thaw out and walk away."

"If he has, it will be the first time in my history in the funeral business." That thin sickly smile wavered across the man's long face for a moment.

"Fair enough. I'll be back as soon as I can, should I find anything. Can you describe the corpse?"

Slate allowed a slight smile. "On the off chance that there's more than one wandering around?"

"Something like that."

"He was remarkably nondescript. Average height, brown hair, brown eyes, a light beard, no more than a week in growth."

"I'll see what I can find." Meade left quickly, doing his best not to run screaming from the ghastly man and his missing corpses.

Behind him the undertaker moved about his facilities, carefully rearranging bodies and trying to thaw them evenly.

The Skinwalker

The winds roared, blasting between trees that shook and groaned under the arctic cold and the growing weight of ice and snow.

Carson's Point was close enough that the lights of the town could be seen reflecting from the gray expanse of clouds.

In the darkness of the woods, he watched, his lips barely moving, his nose sallow and thin.

He was hardly dressed for the weather, wearing only leather breeches and a matching vest that had been covered with dozens of strips of cloth, knotted and woven together until the leather was barely noticeable beneath them.

Ancient eyes studied the lights from the town and his withered hand touched the leather strap around his neck. The crudely formed lump of clay that dangled from the strap was crusted with small stones, nineteen of them all told. Anyone taking the time and getting close enough might have noticed that the small gray pellets were identical, and that they had been very intricately carved with symbols that only a handful of white men had ever seen.

He was not a white man. Once upon a time he had been as dark as the natives that sometimes came through the area, but these days he'd have shamed Lucas Slate with his deathly pale flesh.

The Europeans who'd come to the new land had never seen his like before. Most of the Indians had heard of his kind, but only a few had lived to recite tales of his vile ways.

He had no name, simply because he saw no reason to be called by one.

Those few who had a reason to address him simply called him by the title he had long ago earned.

Skinwalker.

He stared at the cold sky and touched the beaded clay again, feeling the slight vibrations from the stones held tightly in the crude shape.

It was almost time. He had no way of understanding how or why he knew that, but the knowledge was there as surely as the darkness hid from the sun's light.

The cold wind cut across his skin and blew his long hair back from his shoulders and neck, but the chill had no effect on him. Hot and cold meant little enough to the few of his kind that existed.

He closed his eyes and listened to the world breathe in long, ragged gasps and felt the smile that drifted dreamily across his face.

Soon.

Everything would change.

Jonathan Crowley

He shivered violently, his flesh still half frozen and trying to warm itself.

A sharp pain cut through his stomach and hip and he shifted to get a better look. The bullet that had struck him earlier was pushing itself out of him. Naturally it made a new hole instead of going through the wound that was currently shrinking at an accelerated rate.

The wounds were healing, like they always did. Like they always had. Another ten minutes and they'd likely all be closed. In the meantime they itched like mad, except where the bullets were being expelled. He felt another working its way out of the skin on his back.

Much as he wanted to stay by the fire, that wasn't a possibility. He'd heard the pale man speaking and knew that the words were about him. He was not yet discovered, but his absence had been noticed. It was now too late to pretend he had never been here.

Then again, he wasn't exactly dressed for the outside world. All he had to do was look through the frost-rimed windows to know that much.

He moved up the stairs with careful steps, placing each bare foot lightly and testing the wooden boards before he moved. There were no creaks to warn anyone of where he was.

The house was warming up nicely, but his body still felt frozen. The maddening itch was back. The one that told him he was healing, regenerating the damage that had been done to his body.

It was easy enough to remember how he'd been hurt this time. There had been over a dozen of the men and they'd acted like savages. One of the bastards had pissed on his face before they left him to die. He could still taste the urine, though he wasn't sure if that was a memory or if the damned stuff still lingered.

"Not going to be a good day for you when I find you." His voice rasped, even though he whispered the words. "Not going to go well for you at all."

Two broken ribs pushed themselves back into the proper locations and he stifled a scream at the unexpected agony. He was healing, which meant that something dark was afoot. Otherwise, he'd have surely been just as…well, just as poorly as he had been before someone found him and dragged him here, wherever here was.

Finally, he made his way to the second floor of the building and to what he guessed was the bedroom of the man he'd seen working on bodies.

They were of similar build and height. He looked in the man's wardrobe and saw nothing but the finery of a mortician. Suits; every one of them identical, with matching white shirts and three dark hats that all matched as well. His unwitting host lacked imagination.

He peeled the ruined clothes from his body and draped the pieces over the undertaker's steamer trunk. It was the only furniture in the room that would survive being soaked by the wet discards.

When he was done he quickly dressed , loathing the idea of wearing another man's clothes, his undergarments, socks and shoes, but having no choice.

The wind outside howled furiously and he resisted the urge to join in.

Five minutes after he'd watched the sheriff leave the building, Jonathan Crowley walked down the stairs and almost ran down the undertaker who stared at him with horrified eyes.

"I-I" the man's lips trembled and his pasty skin did its very best to grow even paler.

"Hello." Crowley spoke quickly and raised one hand in front of his host. "Go to sleep."

He caught the man before he could fall to the ground and hurt himself.

A moment after that, he worked his magic. They were simple incantations, as the easiest ones were often the most reliable.

After Crowley was gone the undertaker woke with an uneasy start and contemplated what had happened.

He'd been mistaken, obviously. There had only been nine bodies. It was the only explanation.

He remembered nothing of the dead man who came down from his room wearing his suit and carrying the sodden tatters he'd been delivered in. That was for the best. Lucas Slate was not a well man, and his heart might not have taken the unexpected shock of having the dead rise on him.

CHAPTER TWO
SUNRISE ON A NEW DAY

Jonathan Crowley

The dawn broke on a crystal-clear sky, and the sunlight lit the world with extra brilliance as it struck the freshly fallen snow. It was impossible not to notice the stuff, thick and hard and covering half the town in scintillating white.

At Harding's Mercantile the boy who normally swept the floors for a few pennies a day worked harder than usual cleaning away the thick crust of ice and sweeping the wooden planks around the front clean of drifts. The store was open and ready for business, though few people walked the streets as yet.

Carson's Point woke slowly. The cold was enough to make the most energetic souls a bit lethargic, and many of the folk who'd come to town were desperately hungover as they stirred from their beds.

Jonathan Crowley had not slept since his thawing out. He was not tired. He was, instead, quietly furious. Somewhere in the world beyond the town—and he did not yet know the name of where he was as he had deliberately avoided meeting anyone—a rather sizeable group of ruffians was still walking and breathing. That was a situation he intended to rectify as quickly as he could manage.

For the last three years he'd spent his time traveling past the Mississippi, examining the wonders and oddities that he could find in an effort to finish cataloging the strangeness of the North American continent. Europe held few mysteries any longer, Australia was now a good acquaintance and Africa and Asia were old friends. This place, however, still had plenty of areas that had barely been investigated.

He carried with him a trunk of journals and the supplies to keep writing for as long as he needed. That was all he wanted in the world for the present time. All he cared to see. He'd had more than enough of people to satisfy him for a long while.

And yet, try though he might, the people found him. First there was the family that showed up at his campsite: a young man and his new wife and their child, a little boy of no more than four. They seemed pleasant, harmless enough, and so despite his desire for solitude, he allowed them to stay at his campsite and even shared a meal with them.

William and Molly Finnegan came from Ireland, a place he had not visited in longer than they had been alive, and they sought a better life in the New World, a chance for prosperity that had eluded them in their homeland.

He listened to their tales and shared a few observations even as he watched the couple with their only child.

William and his son Billy could have been siblings separated by fifteen years, but they were not. The resemblance was amazing, but one look was all he needed to know that they were related in a different way. No older brother ever adored a younger sibling so dearly. Dark hair and pale skin and light blue eyes for the both of them, and Molly, wife and mother, was fairer in complexion with hair that was a bright mess of golden and red and bright orange, an autumn's worth of colors and pale skin with a heavy scattering of freckles to show she'd spent too much time in the sunlight. Despite himself, he liked the young family.

And that was surely what had caused the problems. If there was one fact that he had learned over the years it was simply that he was better off not being close to anyone. It caused no end of troubles.

To prove his point, he had but to remember what happened when the men showed themselves.

Enough. He had other concerns for the present time.

Crowley strode into the street on borrowed shoes and doffed the top hat that was all he had been able to take from the undertaker's place. He felt preposterous in his attire, but no more so than he ever did when dressed in finery.

The people on the street seemed to find him acceptable at least, though a few must surely have decided he was an easy target. He could feel their eyes on him and he made himself stifle the smile that wanted to spread across his face. His smile, he'd heard a few people say, was enough to startle a wild dog into flight. It wasn't that his face was unpleasant—in truth it was a very average face—it was merely his grin that seemed to inspire fear.

He took his time and walked several of the streets as he assessed the situation. There were three men watching him, moving with the casual grace and precision of longtime partners. Though he couldn't interpret the gestures they made, he could understand that they were speaking to each other with signs and movements. That was fine. Knowing that they talked was enough. He could guess what was on their minds.

A man who walks down the street in an expensive suit and carries no weapons in most of the frontier towns was not a man who could lay claim to much wisdom. And a fool and his money are soon parted. Of course, he had no money. He hadn't needed any for quite some while. He'd been living on the trails, hunting for himself and taking care to handle matters as he needed.

And again he was brought back to the damned family that caught him off guard and what happened to them.

He'd been better dressed for the woods, wearing a shirt that had seen better days and wool pants that he'd patched no less than a dozen times. The couple had been wearing the sort of attire that was best left for the cities, a sure sign that they had not been as prepared for the new territories as they should have been. To be sure there was nothing wrong with remaining civil, but there were occasions for wearing finery and situations where you were better off being dressed for the elements. He'd met a few people who understood that, including two women who had the audacity to wear pants, not that he'd ever consider blaming them for their outrageous attire. He'd seen far stranger over his lifetime.

The family had been off to the side of the main trail. There were few settlements in the area, but it wasn't too hard to find the paths that had already been cut into the ground by passersby and travelers heading further west. He'd come across them as William was trying to repair a damaged wheel on his wagon.

The woman, Molly, had looked at him as he was walking past and stared as if she had surely seen a ghost. Her body tensed and she drew her son closer to her body, protecting him from any possible threat.

He had every intention of letting the man take care of his own problems, but as he walked past Molly muttered under her breath. "What's the world coming to when no one will come to the aid of a stranger in distress?" The words were softly spoken but he heard them.

"And how would I know if you're in distress, unless you ask for assistance? Your man seems to know his business well enough."

A small lie. William struggled to replace a wheel that had broken against rough stones, and the load in the wagon made his job dangerous, as well as awkward.

The girl looked at him with lips pressed together into an angry line and nodded her head. Her voice, when she spoke again, carried a soft Irish lilt that had been faded by distance from her native lands. "Fair enough then. Would you be kind enough to help a stranger in distress?"

He held back a sigh and nodded. A few moments later they were working on the wagon wheel together, he and the young man, while the redheaded woman and her child watched.

He'd planned to leave as soon as he was done. There were strange plants in the vicinity, or so he'd heard from one of the local tribes, and he wanted to study his latest finds.

Instead, William insisted that he join them for a meal and somehow before it was all said and done, he'd camped close to their wagon for the night.

William was a hopeful man. He hoped to find gold or barring that he hoped to find a town that needed a good tailor. He worked with fabric by trade, and he was very good at his job. He pointed out the clothing that his family wore as proof and Crowley had to admit that the younger man was skilled at his calling.

Everything that happened to him could be laid at the feet of forgetting how vile human beings could be when they set themselves on the wrong path.

He slept near the family's camp and when he woke in the morning, he decided to make sure they were safely on their way. Instead of finding the young couple eating or supping he found them doing what comes naturally to couples in love. They did not see him, and he left quickly, embarrassed by the arousal he felt and by the notion of being spotted by the two of them.

Had he been in a better state of mind he would have avoided the skunk.

He stepped too close to a protective mother and she defended her young ones in the only way she knew how, blasting him with a cloud of her musky stench that left him coughing and gasping and half blind.

The couple found him a few moments later, both of them dressed in hastily assembled clothing. Despite the expression on his face, they laughed at him and despite his indignant anger, he laughed back.

He scoured himself in the frigid waters of the closest stream and did all he could to remove the stench that permeated everything.

Eventually he broke the rules and used his arcane knowledge to cleanse the musk from his body. Before that time came around, he spotted both Billy and Molly watching him. Mother and child alike stared with wide-eyed curiosity. He might have called them on their actions but he was guilty of voyeurism himself and hardly in a place where he could be morally superior.

His clothes were ruined. The vile skunk odor was deep in the fabric. His original plan was to sit in the water until the couple and their child were far enough away to let him get back to his camp in relative privacy— he didn't care if a bear or bird noticed him nude—but William wouldn't hear of it. He had extra suits, he was a tailor, after all, and Crowley found himself the owner of new finery.

And somehow a second day was spent with the family of strangers and if William or Molly noticed the way he looked at the lady of the family they did not take him to task for his stares. She was attractive enough, not unpleasant to the eye, but the simple truth was that he hadn't even seen a woman in over six months and despite his best efforts to ignore them, his body had urges.

The second night came around and he stayed well away from the family. By morning he was on his way back to his camp before the sun could rise and glad to be away not only from the family he thought he could grow fond of, but also from the young woman who had caught his attention and refused to leave it. If they woke and were at a loss to understand where he might have gone, that was a smaller sin than staying around them long enough to cause trouble.

The problem was that Molly had looked back. Her eyes had studied him when she thought he was looking away and he knew the signs too well. She was young and far away from home and he was older and possibly reminded her a bit too much of someone she had once held a flame for, and if he stayed there was no guarantee of troubles, but there was a strong chance, and he wanted nothing to do with that sort of unpleasant entanglement.

He put the young family out of his mind for the day and the night and then thought about the clothes he was now wearing and how much the suit should have cost him and how little William and Molly had, and dug deep into the supplies he carried with him until he could find a small gold coin that was worth far more than the suit could ever cost.

He found their campsite in ruins. William lay dead on the ground his arms still wrapped around Billy's battered corpse. Both were cut, shot, beaten brutally. Molly was not there. Instead, he found hoof prints from a half dozen or more horses and a wagon that had been ransacked.

Was there a moment when he thought of leaving well enough alone? Oh, yes. Several of them. He wanted nothing to do with conflicts or dealing out punishment on anyone. He wanted only to be left alone. He might have stayed where he was, might have simply gone back to his camp or even taken the time to bury the dead, but he heard Molly's screams and that was enough to wear past his resolve.

William had a rifle but it had been trampled, the long barrel bent out of shape. He himself had a knife. That was all.

Crowley slipped through the woods near the path and followed the sounds of Molly's lamentations until he found the girl and the men who were raping her.

He took four steps toward the gathered crowd, intent on saving her and avenging the family she had lost and his time away from people came back to haunt him.

One of the men looked toward him and let out a sharp whistle. A dozen eyes looked his way. Six men turned to stare at the stranger moving toward them with a hunting knife held in a combat grip, and four men drew their weapons and fired.

Crowley fell to the ground and tried to rise, to make his body listen to his commands, but there was no strength. Molly screamed his name and he fought to make his feet. He was almost standing when the men tackled him from behind.

Molly kept screaming as they dragged him over to their horses, tied him to the pommels of their saddles. One of the men undid the ties of his pants and took the time to urinate a heavy stream onto Crowley's face, laughing as he sputtered. Then they mounted their horses and started away from the rest of their group, dragging him between them as they went. He could clearly remember four faces. He knew them as intimately as any man has ever known a lover. He memorized them as he was hauled across the rough terrain. He couldn't say how far he'd gone before they let him go. The darkness had swallowed him whole long before then.

He saw Molly's body in the room with him when he woke again. She was mostly unclothed and the wounds on her body made clear that she had died slowly and after being sorely misused. He saw no sign of either William or Billy.

Crowley shook off his memories and tried to keep his expression calm as he walked toward the darkness near the protective wall of the town. There were tents here, scattered and settled wherever the owners could find a spot. Several of the small camps were occupied and others were empty. It was a good enough spot for his purposes.

The sun was higher, and his shadow was lost to the glare from the fresh snow. That was a pity. It meant his pursuers would cast no shadows.

The sound of the revolver being cocked was loud in the nearly perfect silence.

"Man should be careful when walking into the wrong part of town. Might get himself hurt." The voice was strong, the accent rough and crude.

Crowley smiled and slipped the glasses from his face. "My good man, I don't think you could be more right in your declarations."

"What?" He turned to stare at the puzzled gunman. His would-be attacker wore a fine hat, an adequate jacket and a matching pair of Peacemakers, one of which he pointed at Crowley's head. Two more men stood behind the gunman, both of whom could have benefited from new clothes and a bath as well as a visit to a decent barber.

"I said you're right. A man could get hurt."

"You don't have to get hurt too badly, stranger. Just hand me your purse and we can part ways."

Crowley slid toward the man, pushing snow out of his way and kicking a thick clump of the frozen precipitation toward the first of the men standing behind the gunmen. The man flinched as the snow slapped his face. The gunman watched the snow flying and forgot to pull the trigger. Crowley smiled.

His fist smashed the revolver to the side and the open palm of his other hand caught the gunman's face, fingers slashing over his eyes in a savage strike. The man forgot all about the revolver and yowled in agony, reaching for his face to protect himself.

Crowley grabbed the Peacemaker from his enemy's hand, breaking the trigger finger in the process. His target yelped a second time and he flipped the weapon over until he was holding the barrel in his grip. He was too close in to fire the weapon, but it made a damned fine hammer for caving in his enemy's forehead.

The man with the snow in his face was still trying to wipe the mess away when Crowley struck him with the butt end of the pistol. He dropped to the ground and stayed dropped, a thick runner of blood flowing down from his busted scalp.

The third man was slapping at his holster, his mouth opened in a grunt of disbelief, when Crowley broke his jaw and his nose. He screamed and kept screaming until Crowley hit him again.

Between them the men had seven dollars and a half dollar piece. He took their money, traded his hat for the one on the gunman's head, and took the heavy brown duster off the screamer before he was done with them. Their boots were in poor shape, so he let them keep them. Their weapons he took for himself. The Peacemakers he kept. The other weapons he threw into the deepest snow bank he could find on his way to the closest hotel. He needed food and a bath and a bed to lie down in. Whatever else he had to have could wait until after he felt warm and rested again.

————

Marcus Darby

While Jonathan Crowley was settling into a warm bath, the world beyond Carson's Point grew a shade more violent.

Two miles from where Jonathan Crowley had last made camp, the men who had seen to his death stood over the bodies of people they deemed to be savages.

Marcus Darby pissed in the face of the young warrior he'd shot in the head. When he was a boy he'd seen his father piss on his mother after beating her senseless. He liked the way she'd cried and cowered when the old man put her in her place and there was no one in the world who made more sense in his eyes than his father. When he was done the man's mouth was filled to overflowing. He made sure the woman who'd tried to defend her man got a good long look at how dead he was. He held her face up and made her stare at the open eyes and flooded mouth of her lover even as he took her from behind.

She was pretty for an animal. Also, she screamed a lot and he liked to hear her noises.

When he'd finished with her, he left the squaw to fend for herself while Brandt savaged her. He had other things on his mind, like finding any treasures the Indians might have. Sometimes they had silver jewelry. It was unattractive stuff but could be melted down. There wasn't much to find, just a few repeating rifles that could come in handy, especially since they came with ammunition and that was getting precious these days.

More importantly, they had food enough to let the boys eat for a night or two. They were damned hungry, and there were too many of them to make hunting an easy proposition.

They were Confederate soldiers, or at least they had been. The tide of the war was obvious and there were too many miles between them and their homes when the time came to flee. When they decided to desert there were twenty of them. Now they were down to fourteen. The six who were missing had all been killed in combat and that was as it should be. They'd all known the risks when they decided they were done fighting for a lost cause. The future was plain enough to see and it was better by far to be away from the fights that had killed not only the way of life they'd been raised with, but also the dreams they'd once had.

There were four children with the Indians. Two were old enough to have fun with. The others he killed quickly. Didn't seem right to make a child suffer for too long, even if it was just the child of a red man.

Broaddus and Dunlap had finished picking the bodies clean of treasures and were quick about making the cuts and wounds necessary to have people think it was Indians doing the crimes. They'd seen a few slaughters in their time in Arizona and Texas and they'd caught on quickly about how some of the Comanche took to torture. Not all of them, but enough to give him the idea in the first place. Ruin the bodies enough and in the right ways and people would blame the red skinned demons for the trouble. As long as they were a little careful, they got to have their fun. The trick was to make sure there were no witnesses — none who lived to tell about what they'd seen at least.

The killing was done, except for the women and the girls. Fourteen men demanded a lot of affection, especially when they had to fight for it. The younger girl was crying and jabbering away in whatever foul tongue they spoke. He rather liked the look of her. Rather than let another of the boys have her body he grabbed her arm and hauled her to the side. She fought and cursed at him and he beat her in the stomach until she could barely breathe.

By the time she was finished crying, he was as hard as an oak branch and ready to give her a reason to cry.

Fully an hour later the girls were dead and their men were deader still. The one he'd pissed on had a half-frozen pool of urine covering his face.

There had been a time when Marcus had believed in God, but that was all in the past. If God existed, he'd have to worry about going to Hell when he died, and he knew it. There was no war to fight out here, nor was there justification for the things he'd done to woman and girl alike. There was no God, no Heaven, no Hell. It was the only truth he'd come to believe since fleeing the Confederacy and heading on his current path. It was all the comfort he needed aside from the flesh he claimed when the mood struck him.

Two hours after the attack began, the men rode away from the carnage they'd sewn and headed back for the camp they'd made for themselves in the foothills.

Four hours later the bodies were all well on their way to freezing solid.

The Skinwalker

The figure that came for them was almost as white as the snow. There were some who might have seen the Skinwalker and thought he bore a passing resemblance to Lucas Slate. Aside from the stark paleness of their flesh they had little in common. The shaman's eyes were as black as coal, his hair just as dark. His face was thin and ancient; a network of wrinkles and lines that spoke of long years, perhaps even centuries, walking the land and working his magic. A solitary black stone was wedged deep into the skin between his eyebrows, so small and well placed that it looked almost like a birthmark, or a very tiny third eye.

Despite the thin clothes he wore the biting cold had no noticeable effect on him. A cold heart perhaps needs no warmth to keep it healthy.

He looked down at the bodies for a long while and felt his stomach rumble. The smallest child was plucked from the frost and warmed in his hands. He whispered his words and the infant gasped, cried out and struggled in his grip. When the boy drew in a deep breath for a second wail of protest, he bit down and tore the throat of the child away. The blood was sweet enough and the meat tender. It would suffice.

He finished his meal and took the second toddler's body with him placing it inside a leather pouch. When he had procured his meal for later, he settled down and contemplated the dead people in front of him.

Some of the People called the invaders "White Men," and others preferred to think of them as "Round Eyes." Neither term satisfied the Skinwalker. He preferred to think of them as what they were, victors in a war that was not yet finished.

The future was written in the blood and semen that littered the ground around him. The women's screams of degradation still rattled through the air, carried by the frigid winds.

He was not vengeful, exactly. He could hardly seek revenge against those who treated the People the same way that he did. No, not vengeful. He was curious. He had seen no fear in the faces of the conquerors. Nor had he sensed mercy was a part of their nature. Instead, he felt only their anger and lust. They knew what they wanted and took as they pleased.

He could understand their motives.

And he sensed...another. They bore with them something precious that they did not comprehend. He wanted to know what would happen with their unusual burden.

He gave long contemplation to the corpses around him and finally summoned the dead woman closest to him. She rose obediently and lowered herself to the snow in front of him, her dead eyes looking at him and seeing what he was behind the flesh he wore. The dead could still fear, and so she trembled.

"You and yours have been murdered."

"Yes," her reply was a hiss, her anger overwhelming her fear for a moment.

"Would you have revenge?"

"Yes!" Her answer was what he'd expected. The woman had watched her man murdered and his body desecrated even as she'd been raped. Of course, she wanted revenge, if not for herself then for her man and the child she'd been carrying. He did not need to see a swollen belly to sense the second life that was extinguished when her life was taken.

"You and your sisters must come with me." He touched her face and felt her fear. It made him smile. She was right to fear him. His plans for her were nowhere near complete. "Your men will have your revenge. They will kill your murderers and find you the justice you demand."

"What will become of me? Of my sisters?"

"I am a man. I have needs that you will satisfy." She shivered, though the cold could no longer touch her. The Skinwalker smiled again.

The women folk rose from their frozen graves and he gathered them around him like saplings to a mighty tree. When he was satisfied with his prizes, he granted the favor of revenge to the dead around him. One by one he stood over the men and then leaned in close enough to kiss them if he had the desire. Instead of a peck on the lips, he drew the small pebbles from the necklace he wore, rolling each of the tiny stones in his fingers and feeling the markings meticulously carved into them. He worked each small pebble between his fingers until the stones were glowing hot and then shoved them into the half-frozen flesh of each man's face. The skin hissed and split where the stones touched—directly between their eyes— and then the wounds healed themselves, leaving a mark unsettlingly like the one he bore on his own face. With a word the dead men rose, no longer still or at peace.

Their bodies warmed, and they moved with simple grace. The mate of his first new wife spit a stream of frozen piss from his mouth and throat and, when he was done, screeched his rage into the skies.

"What of our women?" The dead man looked at him with rheumy eyes.

"They are mine now."

"What of our weapons?"

"Find new ones."

"What of the ones who killed us?"

"They are yours to find and to kill."

The dead men looked from one to another for a time and finally nodded. "That is enough."

He'd already known that. In the long run, vengeance was almost always enough.

CHAPTER THREE
WHEN THE DUST CLEARS

Dan Kaufmann

Kaufmann's Saloon was busy. These days it was always busy, not that he planned to complain. In the last three weeks the only time it hadn't been booming in the place was when Kaufmann ushered everyone out and locked his doors.

The floors were smooth wooden planks brought over from the mill in Denver. The wood was properly finished and a layer of sawdust was deliberately laid down to soak up spilled liquor. Daniel Kaufmann was nothing if not meticulous about the details. No one drank for free, no one with a brain got into a fight and damned few of the locals would consider drawing a weapon in the place. Sadly, there weren't that many locals left since the prospector found his gold and staked his claim.

Dan Kaufmann was a very large man, both in height and in girth. He was not in excellent health, but neither was he a heart attack waiting to happen. His face was usually clean shaven and his head had lost most of its hair when he was a much younger man. On the off chance that his physical size did not properly intimidate others, he also kept a Winchester repeating rifle and a Remington shotgun on the premises and within easy reach. They were the main reasons that not many people got too jumpy in the saloon. That, and Dan was good at judging who would get meaner as they got more inebriated and notorious for cutting off the people he considered high risk.

Some days all the care in the world didn't stop things from going poorly. The weather was bitter, and the fireplaces were loaded with wood and blazing with warmth. That by itself was enough to guarantee warm bodies. But it was also the sort of situation that didn't mean the bodies in question wanted to spend money. Dan did not look at his saloon as a charitable business. If a few people didn't start ordering libations he was going to remove them by force.

Three of the sorriest looking bastards he'd ever seen were a perfect example. They'd staggered in as soon as he opened the doors and had settled in near the stove in the far corner, like he wouldn't be able to see them all of fifteen feet away. Each of them had deep bruises on their faces, and not one of them carried so much as a buck knife. The most pathetic of the lot nursed a deeply bruised jaw and whimpered endlessly. Like as not he couldn't have sipped a beer if it had been offered for free.

Perhaps he'd have felt more pity for them, but he knew them too well. He'd seen them looking over the different patrons and finding the ones who appeared to be carrying the most valuables. He'd also heard stories of the three and how they worked together to separate those people from their wealth. He wasn't the law, not outside of his bar, but he also didn't approve of criminal activities.

It seemed like they'd fallen on hard times, the three. They were beaten and shivering when they came into the building and wearing far too little protection from the weather besides. So, for a while he let them sit and warm themselves but now the businessman that ran the bar was thinking the time had passed for kindness.

He ambled over to where the men sat and stared down from his imposing height. "I believe you men have warmed yourselves enough. Time to pay for a few drinks or be on your way."

"Come on now, Dan. You know us. We're good for it." Morris Biggs was a whiny man if ever he'd met one. Most times when Dan was ready to close up, the bastard was trying to convince him to stay open for two more drinks and maybe a free bed besides. He stared at the man for several moments. A lot of times in the past he'd let the man slide because he carried a set of Peacemakers that looked perfectly capable of blowing even a man the size of himself completely out of his boots. The weapons were missing.

"This ain't a church, Morris. It's a business. You stink and you're ugly. Go get a bath and come back with money."

"You sound like one of your whores." Morris stood up as he spoke. He'd never been the brightest man and he seemed determined to prove exactly how foolish he could be.

"Now, see, I was being nice to you earlier when I decided to let you warm your bodies, but you've just lost that privilege. Next time you come here, I'll treat you like one of my whores would. You come in waving money or you'll not so much as sit down at a table." Dan leaned his balled fists down on the edge of the oak round top in front of Morris and every man at the table heard the wood creak in protest.

Before Morris could bury himself any deeper, a silver dollar landed on the wood between Dan's hands.

"That should set them up for a drink and a meal, shouldn't it?" The voice was soft, almost scholarly, and came from the left, back toward the doors of the saloon. Dan looked in that direction and saw a slender man standing there, spectacles on his long face, and a thin, enigmatic smirk plastered on his features. The eyes behind the lenses were brown and intelligent.

"That'll do just fine, I believe." Dan picked up the coin while the three men in front of him stared at the stranger. "Three whiskeys and three bowls of mutton stew." He stared at the men. "I believe you owe your new friend thanks for letting you sit a bit longer, gentlemen."

"The hell you say." That was Rodney Cambridge, who was, hard though it was to believe sometimes, even thicker than Morris.

The stranger smiled as the three men rose from their seats.

"What sort of thanks is that to give a man?" Dan felt a sudden flutter of doubt as he spoke. The men in front of him could be dangerous, just like any man could be if pushed too far. He'd let himself forget that fact.

"Man took my weapons and my hat. I don't much feel like thanking the bastard that robbed me." Morris's voice was low, bordering on a growl, and he stepped past the table with a sneer of rage marring his already unpleasant face.

The stranger's smile grew bigger instead of fading as the three came toward him. Dan stepped out of their way, giving contemplation to how best to reach his shotgun. Normally he didn't have to fire it, just cock it once.

"You fellas want to settle a dispute, take it outside of my establishment." He eyed the stranger and saw that he was, indeed, wearing not only Morris's weapons, but also Rodney's heavy coat. Small wonder the men looked so wretched.

The stranger looked toward him and nodded briefly. "Don't you fret. This won't take long." He stepped back toward the doors of the saloon and opened them. "Come along boys, let's settle this a second time."

The men were not as willing to wait as the smiling man. They charged toward him like a pack, and he stepped back into the bitter cold instead of standing his ground.

In his long years Dan had seen a few sights he'd not likely forget. The first time he saw a Coolie he'd stared at the strange features on man's face until the man stared him down. That was a strange sight indeed, as the man had a long braid of jet-black hair that was almost as long as he was tall, and he wore the oddest clothes Dan had ever seen. He had also had the dubious pleasure of watching the man beat down a white man who tried to take his hat from him. The white man had been trying to impress his friends with his wild antics. Instead, he wound up with his face in the dirt and two of his fingers bent into new shapes.

The next day he also had the unpleasant experience of watching the Coolie getting lynched for his efforts to defend himself.

There was a reason he'd left Arizona.

Now he walked toward the doors of his bar and stared out the heavy glass of the window to watch what should have been a massacre and wondered if the stranger was part Chinese himself.

Rodney charged at the man and the stranger stepped to the side, dodging the full bulk of his attacker with ease. As Rodney staggered past, trying to regain his balance, the man struck a savage blow to the back of his neck that felled Rodney like an axe. The snow was the only cushion that stopped Rodney's face from getting broken by the impact.

The third man, Dan still didn't know his name, just knew he liked to stare at everyone and licked his lips too much, came forward like a boxer, holding his hands up and weaving slowly around the stranger. Judging by the knot on the side of his head, he'd learned his lesson when it came to expecting an easy fight.

The stranger slid toward him—it looked like his feet never even moved from the ground—and struck him in the jaw hard enough to rock his entire head. He hit the man two more times before letting him fall to the ground.

Morris stared at the fight with a look that surely mirrored the one Dan was wearing. No one should move that fast. It was damned near unnatural.

The stranger looked hard at Morris, who promptly held up both hands to show he wanted no part of the beating. One finger on Morris's hand was swollen and purplish. Dan hadn't even noticed it before.

Without another word, the stranger touched the brim of his hat—well, Morris's hat, arguably—and started for the door again.

And while his back was turned, Morris reached with his good hand for the derringer at his belt. The worried expression vanished, replaced by a cold, murderous hatred. He took aim as the man reached for the door, and at that moment, the stranger looked toward Dan.

Dan's eyes flicked from the stranger to Morris and back again.

The stranger turned fast and threw himself sideways as the derringer fired both shots.

Two explosions rocked the door on its hinges and blew chunks of wood halfway across the room. Dan yelped and so did a few others.

The thunder that answered the gunshots seemed too loud, seemed to shake the very foundations of the building. Dan looked outside again just as Morris fell forward, screaming like a teakettle boiling over. Most of his left hand was gone, leaving a bleeding stump.

The stranger walked back into the bar, not bothering to look back at his handiwork. He nodded his thanks toward Dan and settled down at the table where his attackers had been sitting before.

While he made himself comfortable, a half dozen people ran out into the cold to either look at his work or just possibly to render aid.

Dan was not among them. He had a business to run.

The stranger had mutton stew and half a loaf of bread while he waited for the sheriff to show himself.

He didn't have long to wait.

Anson Meade

Anson and Pace walked into Kaufmann's and took the time to stare long and hard at the patrons. Most of them were busy trying to look elsewhere.

Meade had already torn through his new deputy for over an hour the previous day and now the man seemed to understand that his employment could be ended without much thought or effort on the sheriff's part. He was acting like a proper deputy. At least for now. Meade doubted it would last long. Pace was the sort that didn't seem likely to remember any lessons a week after he received them.

In the meantime, he'd enjoy the company.

Kaufmann, the owner of the place, nodded amiably enough. There were bloodstains outside in the snow. As he understood it the man whose blood was painting the side of the closest building would probably live through the experience. He'd be crippled forever, which meant he probably wouldn't be trying to shoot anyone else.

The room was full of strangers. Most of the people in town might know him, but he hadn't been in Carson's Point long enough to know much of anyone except the town officials and the woman he was paying to keep his house in order. As it stood, he still couldn't remember the woman's name half the time. Myrna or Mildred or something that started with an M.

The point being that he had no idea if anyone around him was acting suspiciously. The only certainty was that one man sitting near the wall didn't much seem to care if he was there or not. He was too busy eating to notice much of anything.

He spoke to Kaufmann first. "Understand you had a problem out front. Did you see anything?"

"I saw three no accounts try to beat a man down and saw them lose."

That was hardly the answer he'd expected.

"And to whom did these no accounts fall victim?"

Kaufmann pointed with his chin toward the man eating. There were a few people in the establishment with plates of food, but most had been forgotten. The one he'd noticed originally was the only one who seemed to have any appetite.

When next he spoke, it was to the eating machine. The man only looked up after he'd finished cleaning his plate with the crust of bread that he'd saved for that purpose.

"I understand there was a dispute earlier."

The stranger looked up at him and smiled politely. "Well, I suppose you could call it that."

"And what would you call it?" He crossed his burly arms over his chest.

The smile grew broader, and the new sheriff felt his stomach flutter. "Schooling."

"I don't follow."

"Three men who needed to be taught manners learned them. I call that schooling."

"And are you a schoolmarm, then?"

The stranger smiled and leaned back in his seat, finally seeming to notice Meade for the first time. "You have an interesting sense of humor, Sheriff."

"No sir. I have a town to keep the peace in."

"Well, so far I'd say you're doing a barely sufficient job." He reached for his glass and took a small sip of whiskey.

He bit his tongue and glared at Pace, who snickered at the comment before catching himself. The deputy's time as an employee of the town lowered substantially at that moment.

"Happily, I am only recently appointed and I don't believe I need to worry about a replacement just yet."

"Was there something else I could help you with, Sheriff?"

"The witnesses I already spoke with outside claims you were the one getting attacked. None of them knew your name."

"Jonathan Crowley."

"Well, Jonathan Crowley, I don't much take to brawlers. I take even less to the sort of men who settle arguments with guns. I have enough on my plate without having to deal with this sort of mischief."

"Then I suggest you talk to would-be thieves and ruffians about choosing a different town. I am neither. I only defended myself."

There was a strong desire to reach out and slap the cocky from Crowley's face. He resisted it.

"Stay well away from any more troubles, Mr. Crowley. Should we meet under similar circumstances again I might have to hold you until the closest judge can decide your fate."

Crowley stared at him silently until he decided it was time to leave. The man could make as many challenges as he wanted. Unless he was foolish about it, Meade would leave him in peace.

He nodded to Kaufmann and ushered Pace out of the building before the spirits could find their way to the deputy's lips.

As they walked back into the cold Pace spoke up. "You think he's going to be trouble?"

"Probably. If I were a betting man I'd surely wager your job on it."

"My job?"

"Oh yes, my friend. Because the next time I catch you laughing at my expense you won't have one. So the current value of your job is within the affordable range."

Pace had the good sense to keep his mouth shut as they moved back toward the offices.

Marcus Darby

"What's bothering you, Marcus?" Silas was his second, a good man who was too fast to notice when he was having troubles. He looked over at the man and sometimes had trouble understanding how it was his friend managed to stay around. Even in the cold of winter with no one to see them, the man insisted on staying well-groomed and as clean as possible.

Silas wore a long coat he'd taken for himself from a Texas Ranger, and even kept the buttons polished. His blond hair was kept short and his lean face clean-shaven. He looked every part of what a proper gentleman should, despite the fact that he was currently associating with a pack of mad dogs, and Marcus considered himself one of those curs.

"We've been here before. That's what's bothering me."

Silas looked around carefully before answering. "The Irish folk. We took them here."

"Exactly right. But look around. Do you see any bodies?"

Silas frowned. His eyes squinted as he thought about the scene, perhaps replaying it in his head. Silas didn't participate in the women often. He didn't much care to take a woman by force. A few people thought that made him weak. Darby knew better. The man had his own code of honor and it didn't permit the violation of a woman. Not when he had a wife waiting for him.

"No. Nor any sign of animals." He took off his hat and adjusted the hair he kept short despite the cold. "But there are hoof prints over to the right and there're tracks from a sled."

Darby sighed and rubbed at the thick, itchy stubble on his jawline. "Well, maybe they'll get proper burials after all."

Silas grunted. It was a point of contention between them. His right hand preferred to bury the ones they killed, and he'd allowed the man his eccentricity a few times, but not since they'd crossed into Utah a few weeks earlier. The ground was too hard, too cold, and they hadn't the time to waste.

"Nothing wrong with wanting to see to a decent burial." Silas's voice was as bitter as the weather around them. "We aren't savages. Or at least we aren't supposed to be."

"I told you. We want this to fall to someone else, and that means we make it look like the Indians have been having their way. Soon enough we'll change our tactics."

"How much have we gathered since we started into Colorado?"

"Not enough."

There were three different treasures the men sought. First was money. Second was worldly possessions and finally there was the small collection in the satchel.

He didn't begin to understand why any man would want to collect the objects, but he also knew the price offered for it by the man who'd hired them was enough to let them buy their way out of the troubles they'd gotten into when they fled from their battalion. That alone made the hunt worth the trouble.

So far they'd collected less than a tenth of what they needed before they'd be rewarded for their diligence. His fingers moved to the small satchel around his neck and felt the beads within the sack, small pellets, hardly worth noticing, and valueless to most people. But when he held them they shone with a strange light, and when he placed them just so in his palm they seemed to fit together comfortably, like they belonged that way.

They'd been searching since Texas and had almost nothing to show for their efforts. Hell, they'd already moved past the area south of them by a day or two where armies of men were carving the land apart and laying track for the railroad to move up to Denver and beyond. But soon, he knew, they'd find what they were looking for. The man had told him most of their treasure rested in one spot. It was a precious prize they sought and they would find it between Texas and Colorado.

That had to be enough. They'd already risked too much on the quest for what little they had. To be sure it would be an easier task if they'd leave the locals alone, but the boys got restless and a few of them were just, well, degenerates.

When they'd come across the camp of Swedes almost a month ago, they'd come in hard and fast and killed the men before they could gather their wits about them. Four men versus eighteen wasn't much of a conflict. Before that point they'd killed and then left, regretting only the need to kill so many in their search.

That had been the first time the men got it into their heads to have more than food and supplies. Lawrence, a natural fighter if ever there had been one, climbed from his horse and grabbed one of the womenfolk, pinning her down and forcing himself on her while everyone watched, the gang and the other women alike. Then almost like he needed to prove he was more violent, Hotchkins grabbed a girl no more than eight and had her, biting and twisting her flesh like an animal the entire time. When he was done he looked down on the girl and put a bullet through the back of her sobbing head.

He'd asked Hotchkins about that later, called him to the side as they rode slowly down the trail and demanded to know what the hell the man was thinking, because he couldn't make himself lose the sight or sound of that child crying and screaming her throat raw.

Hotchkins looked at him long and hard, his face half buried under a thick growth of beard, his eyes squinted against the wind and the glare, and spoke softly. "She reminded me of my girl back home."

Hotchkins had three daughters. It took an effort not to kill the man right there. The thought that anyone would do that sort of thing to his own flesh was beyond unsettling.

And yet, not even a full month had passed and he found himself joining in on the rapes. Had anyone asked him even after he'd first deserted if he would ever violate a woman—not including the occasional slave bitch or Indian squaw of course—he would likely have taken his saber to their heads for even mentioning the idea.

"We should move on." His fingers worked the small leather bag tucked under his shirt. "I think we're getting close to the next one."

Silas nodded his head. "Good. The sooner we're done, the happier I'll be."

"That would be all of us, old son."

He felt the soft tug of the pieces, like a string pulling gently against the medicine bag, drawing him on. Not urgent, but insistent.

Silas stared at him for a long moment without speaking and then whispered low enough to guarantee no one else heard him. "I'm not so sure about that. I think a few of the boys have come to like this too much."

"Well then, they'll only be our concern a little longer. We need to get our business here settled."

"Storm's gonna slow us down."

"The storm already happened, last I checked."

His second looked off toward the west and pointed at the dark smudge of the nearby mountaintops. "Keep your eyes on those hills and look for a black cloud. One thing I know is weather. What we've dealt with so far is just the scout. There's a damned mean blizzard heading this way, Marcus. We need to be in a proper shelter before it finds us. A couple of Indian lean-tos and a cave aren't going to save us a second time."

"There's settlements to the south of us a bit. I seem to recall seeing a few homes we could use."

"There's a town not far from here. Might be a better choice."

"Why do you say that?" Silas sounded too nervous. Worried men tended to do foolish things. He'd have to keep an eye on the man and make sure he didn't get too twitchy.

"Those settlements to the south of us belong to freed slaves and I believe I saw a Union flag flying."

"You thinking buffalo soldiers?"

"I'd say there was an unpleasant likelihood."

"Can't be but a few of them. Not enough houses, not even but a small barn." He frowned as he tried to remember the details.

"Might be true, but did your necklace tell you to head into an area where a cannon might be waiting for us?"

Cannons or worse were a real possibility. A couple of men with good range rifles could pick them off before they got very far.

"So we'll head to town."

"Might be wisest." Silas tapped his heels into his mare's flanks and sent her forward. Marcus watched him go and nodded his head, to himself if to no one else.

He'd wanted the town anyway. What they sought might be there. And if not, maybe it would be closer at least.

They rode on, moving as quickly as they could in the hopes of missing the storm coming their way. They would have ridden faster still if they'd sensed what was coming toward them just ahead of the storm. They'd have ridden as if the Devil himself were on their tails.

And they'd have had every good reason.

Moses Blake

There were four houses in the settlement, each well built and fortified with thick walls and narrow windows.

Moses Blake was not a foolish man and he understood the need for good protection. The territories did not take to slavery, but that did not mean his kind were easily welcomed.

They'd fought hard to be free men, and every one of them had papers to prove it. Of course, half the white men he'd met couldn't read better than most of the ex-slaves around him, so that didn't exactly help his situation.

There were four families to go with the four homes and the pens had been built to hold their cattle. They had the money, they'd earned it the hard way, and they had the desire. Now they just had to get the herd and move them.

Easy enough, he supposed, once they finished with the fortifications.

Moses stared out at the western sky and frowned as he looked toward the mountains. A damned fearsome gathering of clouds had overtaken the mountaintops and he suspected the storm would be a vicious one.

"See here, Loretta, this is why I wanted everything built first." His voice was a low, pleasant rumble.

His wife moved closer to him and he put an arm around her slender waist. "Why's that?"

He looked at her. Her eyes were wide and sincere and so very curious, and he loved that about her. Her mind was as sharp as a knife.

"Those clouds look like they'll take most of the fields and bury them in snow. That's all well and good as long as we've got a place to keep the cows when a storm like that comes."

"More snow?" her smile was infectious. She'd lived her whole life in southern Georgia and never seen the stuff until they moved.

"Oh yes. More. You'll be sick of it soon enough."

"I could never grow tired of this, Moses."

He knew what she meant. Not just the snow, but the notion of working for themselves to make a better world of their own. Not working for an overseer and a man who could refer to them as property. Loretta was a fine-looking woman. She'd suffered more than most would ever know at the hands of the overseer.

Thinking about that made Moses want to find the man and kill him. That was foolishness of course. He'd killed the man when the war started. That seemed so long ago.

Out in the darkness of the mountains he caught a glint of light and tracked where he had seen it. Several men were heading toward the house, walking at a slow and steady pace. None of them carried weapons or rode horses. Just the same, he reached for his rifle and aimed through the scope until he could see them as they came closer.

Indians. Like as not they were running from the storm, looking for shelter.

"Loretta, you need to go gather the men for me." His voice was stern, though not deliberately so, and she ran all the faster for it.

And while she ran he looked at the men coming toward him and felt the first twinges of dread.

They were pale for Indians.

They moved stiffly, and their faces held no expression.

The glint he'd seen had come from their eyes, which burned with a fire of their own, and there was nothing pure or natural about that fire.

He'd been schooled in the ways of the Lord and could read the Good Book.

He had no doubt that the things coming toward his house were not the sort of things that would much like the word of God, and so he reached for the Holy Bible and touched the soft leather cover for strength.

Death was coming toward his home, his family, and he had doubts that he could stop it from reaching all of them.

CHAPTER FOUR
COLD FRONTS

Pace Peabody

Pace stared nervously at the trapper. He'd seen the man more than once and though he'd never seen Miles in a fight, he feared him just the same. There was something to him, to his eyes, that promised pain to anyone crossing him. Pace had a decided fear of pain. He found his life was simpler without it.

And yet, that bastard Meade wanted him to find out if the trapper had been jabbering away about the bodies he's brought into town.

He found the man at the Piedmont, eating a breakfast of ham and eggs with fresh bread.

"'Scuse me, Mr. Miles."

The trapper looked up from the ham steak he was cutting and raised one eyebrow. Pace's stomach grumbled at the lack of food and fluttered at the look the man shot him.

"I'm not much for conversation when I'm eating, Deputy. What can I do for you?"

Pace looked around the dining room, saw that no one was at any of the nearby tables and spoke his mind. "Sheriff wants to know if you've been talking to anyone about the bodies that you brought into town."

The man stared at him long enough to make Pace shuffle nervously from one foot to the other and finally answered. "Do I strike you as the sort of man that needs to tell other people about his business?"

"No sir. But I was told to ask you just the same."

"I've told no one."

"Well somebody has been spreading stories."

"Did I just tell you I was minding my own concerns?" The voice dropped a bit.

"You did. I'm just telling you why I have to ask."

"Well you've done your duty. Feel free to run along now."

Pace stared, torn between outrage at being dismissed and relief at the very same. Still, it irked him, being treated like he didn't matter.

"You should maybe learn a little civility, sir." His voice was low as he spoke, and his heart was hammering along at a frightening pace.

The trapper set down his fork and knife and looked down at the table for a moment before pushing himself back. "You'll forgive my lack of manners. I've been trying to eat my breakfast in peace, you see, and some damned fool is running around and accusing me of talking out of turn while I set to do that task. Being accused of anything other than minding my own business is the sort of nonsense that I find offensive." He stood up, and Pace was reminded of exactly how large a man the trapper was. "It's the sort of nonsense that makes me want to lose my patience and my good sense. Do you understand me?"

The deputy stepped back. When he'd started at the job Carson's Point had been a speck on the map. There hadn't been trouble in town and finding it took effort. These days the risks and the angry people seemed to be moving in along with the prospectors.

"Now see here. You have your duties to perform as a trapper. I have mine to perform as a deputy. If the sheriff tells me to find out who's talking out of turn about dead bodies and whether or not the women among them were done improperly by savages, then, by God, man, I do it." He settled his hand on the butt of his revolver. "You have a problem with it, you can feel free to discuss it with my employer or you can feel free to get the hell out of town."

The man laughed. "Fair enough, boy. Just make sure you wait until I'm done with my meal the next time."

Pace watched the man sit back down and then nodded his head once before walking out of the Piedmont. His knees shook, but he carried himself with squared shoulders. The feelings in his gut had changed enough that he wanted to scream instead of puke his guts out. Instead, he kept walking and took deep gulps of the cold air to soothe his ruined nerves.

Damned if he'd let every rat bastard that came into the town walk on him. He had a job to do and he'd do it, even if he wanted to wet himself instead.

———

Anson Meade

Slate stared at the sheriff and shook his head. "I've never felt a reason to tell anyone what happens in this establishment, Sheriff Meade. Nor would I presume to spread rumors about Indians and what they might have done to the poor women who are regrettably brought to me."

The man's indignation was not faked. Meade was certain of it.

"Then would you have any idea who might be spreading rumors? All I can tell you is that I have had no less than four different people come to my offices in the last day worried that Indians might be coming to take their women." And that was the absolute truth. To make matters worse, the men in question were demanding to know what he intended to do about the situation.

"I've no notion. I don't believe Mr. Miles is the sort to tell tales out of turn. I have no reason for spreading malicious rumors, and to my knowledge no one else was aware of the delivery." He paused for a moment and then, "I certainly don't mean to cast aspersions, of course, but young Pace Peabody has been known to speak of matters that he felt would garner him a free drink." That he didn't want to say the words was obvious.

"I've already had a conversation with my deputy and explained how poorly I'd take any unprofessional behavior, but I'll check with him again to be safe."

Slate moved to one of the bodies that he'd been preparing and carefully examined the work he'd done. They were all clothed now, though both men had seen the frozen corpses when that hadn't been the case. The sheriff had done his best not to stare at the frozen women, but he'd had no doubt that they had been violated. Their state had made it clear enough.

"I had no luck finding a tenth body."

"I'm sorry?" The undertaker seemed surprised by the comment.

"A tenth body, the one you believed was missing. I never did find any signs of what might have happened."

Slate shook his head and looked over. Meade made himself look back, despite the man's unsettling eyes. "I must have been too tired for my own good. I can't recall a tenth body."

"Fair enough," he sighed. "I reckon that's one less reason for me to stay busy." It wasn't worth yelling at the man. He hadn't invested a great deal of time in the investigation and so far no one had found a spare corpse lying around.

"I must apologize if I caused you any inconvenience, Sheriff." The faint southern drawl made his words seem even softer, more regretful.

He waved it off and looked away, no longer feeling the need to be polite. "Don't think a thing of it."

"For what it's worth, I have no doubt you've been doing your best in a bad time."

"Much obliged, but what makes you think this is a bad time?"

"You haven't been here long, and I suspect you've seen far worse in other areas, but this town is going sour, Sheriff." Slate shook his head and the long fine hair moved in a soft sway around his shoulders. "There are too many changes happening too quickly and none of them for the better. You might do well to consider a few more deputies, before matters get too far out of hand."

"I'll take that into consideration."

The albino looked at him. "I say that as a man who benefits when times are bad, Sheriff. I should rather not get wealthy on the misfortunes of good people."

The sheriff nodded and moved toward the stairs to the world beyond the pale white man and his half-frozen corpses. He was not easily bothered by death, but the man's statements left him unsettled. They confirmed what he'd already decided for himself. Carson's Point seemed a troubled town.

To make matters worse, the latest news he was hearing, though it was unconfirmed, was that Summit Town, a small place not all that far to the north and west, had burned to the ground, with few survivors. He felt in the pit of his stomach that the blaze was an omen and an ill one at that.

Much as he tried to convince himself that he was not a superstitious man, he believed that disasters often came in threes. So far there were the slayings in the woods between the burned town and Carson's Point, there was the slaughter of Summit Town itself, and that left one more to deal with as far as he knew.

He kept that thought close to his heart as he walked back toward his office. The morning hadn't even grown old yet and noon seemed a long time off. He hoped it came soon just the same. Food always helped him settle his nerves.

Miles

The trapper sat in his room and closed his eyes. The deputy had irked him. He disliked the weaselly man and liked him even less when he was interrupting a perfectly good meal.

He'd managed to get a pot of coffee from the kitchen—it helped to know the owners—and now he was reading a dime novel about a man named Luckless Murphy and savoring the bitter taste in the privacy of his room.

Word was spreading that there had been a fire in Summit Town. Word was there were almost no survivors. He sighed at the notion. The woman who had married his father would likely be among the dead. That was a pity as she was a lovely lass.

His father? He set down the book for a moment and rubbed his fingers along the bridge of his nose. Could he be lucky enough that his very own father would be dead in the blaze?

"Not likely. I'd have felt his soul being dragged down to Hell."

He thought back on the days when he was young enough to live with the man and shook his head. They had gone to church every Sunday, had said their prayers and visited with other families, first in New England and later in other parts of the country as he was growing up. His father had seen to it that they never stayed in any place for too long, but always long enough to leave a good memory or two.

And when the locals were not looking, his father had done dark things in the places where no one would look.

At fifteen he'd left home and swore that he would never go back. By seventeen he'd accepted that his father was not a good man. By nineteen he'd gone back just the same. His father was not a good man, true, but he had always been good to the trapper. He had treated him as family, as a son, and had loved him in his own way.

When the man had remarried, he'd moved toward the territories, and while the trapper couldn't have proven it, he thought the old man had come into the territories to be near him. Well, at least that was one of the reasons.

Whatever else he had sought out in the woods near that dreadful Lake Overtree, it seemed to have finally brought the old man his ruination and much as the idea saddened the trapper, it also brought him an undeniable sense of relief.

The world was better off without his father around to cause more mischief and mayhem. That was all there was to it.

News had not come in yet as to who, if anyone, survived the fires that destroyed Summit Town. There was the chance that the man had managed to escape whatever fate befell the rest of the people in the area.

The trapper hoped against it.

Much as he hated himself for the thoughts, he felt the man who'd sired him was too dangerous to be left alone.

Albert Miles was a monster, pure and simple. His own son thought it and knew it in his heart. It was hardly a testimony to the man's good nature.

Jonathan Crowley

The woods to the west of town were almost silent. Crowley intended to remedy that situation. The Peacemakers were settled on his hips, and the trees he'd chosen as targets were marked with the whitewash he'd purchased for just that purpose.

Bullets cost money and most of the revolvers he'd seen were as different from each other as snowflakes. Rifles were more reliable and he had no intentions of using the guns on his hips until he knew how they fired and where they liked to aim themselves.

He took his time and sighted down the barrel of the left revolver. The first bullet missed the central mark by almost half a foot at twenty paces.

He tried three more times and got the same results. The barrel had a decided bend to it. He holstered it and pulled the other weapon. It was closer to a true mark and he easily compensated for the slight angle of the weapon. Still, he'd fix them both.

A few muttered words and he watched the metal heat up, steaming in the cold air until he had to squint his eyes against the blazing white heat. He didn't have to touch the barrel, but he had to concentrate fiercely. When he was done, he set the weapon down on the stone he'd cleared of snow and reached for the troublesome Peacemaker on his other side. On careful observation he could see the bend of the barrel. Like as not some damned fool had used the weapon as a hammer and bent it out of shape. Hell, he could have done the damage himself on the fools who tried to rob him, but despite the force he'd used when employing the weapon for that very purpose on a few skulls, he doubted that his use had caused the warping. He was always amazed by how foolish people were when given half a chance.

The same spell worked on the second weapon, but took considerably more effort and required that he force the metal by hand.

Anyone looking would have simply seen him holding a white-hot piece of metal and not burning his hands at all. There was more to it, of course, like maintaining the cooler surface of the rest of the weapon so that the cylinder didn't get deformed and the bullets didn't fire off spontaneously. It would hardly do to work the weapons into shape and put a bullet through his fool head simultaneously. It would have been easier for him to remove the bullets and eliminate the risks, but now and then he liked a challenge.

The next few rounds confirmed that he'd made the adjustments he needed to. The guns would fire true.

He hated the guns. They weren't noble things, the destructive forces that men used to kill other men. There was no grace to the firearms, no artistry to their use. They were simply designed to kill whatever you pointed them at.

Swords were elegant. They required finesse and the use of muscles that few people ever thought about. The bow could be graceful, as with the archers he'd seen in Nippon, phenomenal horse riders who could pluck the pit from a peach at three hundred paces while riding at a full run. Most of the people he'd seen in the New World had little skill aside from knowing how to point and shoot, and in a few cases draw quickly.

The notion was rather depressing.

He carefully reloaded the weapons. He needed to be ready. There were already people in town who were looking at him strangely simply because he'd stopped a few imbeciles from taking back what he'd gladly taken from them in the first place.

There was something wrong with the people around him. Half of them seemed sane, the others like they needed to prove something to the world. If you could draw a weapon with decent speed, they wanted to prove they could do it faster.

He holstered the weapons and closed his eyes, listening to the woods and the animals around him, hearing the wind as it played among the half-frozen branches and hissed past the slowly melting ice.

He could still hear the girl screaming and sobbing as the men raped her. His mouth curled down into a sneer. He could still taste piss in his mouth. Animals marked their territories. Only humans marked their kills.

The silence of the world was a wonderful thing, a rarity that he savored when he could. Now the death of a family of near strangers was marring his blissful silence and the stench and noise of a town was permeating his world like a stain. He couldn't go back to his research until he took care of certain matters.

He couldn't take care of those pressing matters until he either found the culprits or was asked to help. It was possible in many places that he could have asked a few questions and tracked the killers. But he didn't know exactly how long he'd been

Dead! I was frozen to the ground! Dead! Again!

incapacitated. The animals could have made it all the way to California and he'd be no wiser, especially since even after his years in the world he hadn't figured out how to track a target through the snow. Not a normal, human target at any rate.

Crowley opened his eyes and felt his lips pull toward a smile. He'd find them. He'd kill them. He owed that to Molly and her family. They had been decent people and as he'd told more than one person over the years, decency was a rare commodity and one that was growing rarer all the time.

The wind shifted and for a moment the stench of Carson's Point was replaced with a distant taint of wood smoke. He looked toward the odor and saw a faint drift of haze against the mountaintops. Whatever was burning was a good way off.

It was time to get back to town. He'd wasted enough bullets and he needed to prepare himself for whatever was going to happen.

Moses Blake

Moses Blake was not dead, though he felt certain he should have been. The air howled around him, a cold scream of mourning for the corpses around him. Loretta's wretched remains lay not far away, still smoldering and spitting an occasional flame.

He coughed and pushed himself from the ground, his muscles protesting, his head throbbing with every beat of his heart.

He'd been raised with pain. Born into it, forced to live with it and work through it for his entire life. Slaves did not question their masters, and he had been a prized slave for a long time before he became a free man.

Moses stood in the biting cold and looked at all that was left of his family, his friends, his wife, his world.

The tears wanted to come, the screams nearly demanded release, but he refused them their due. Later, he promised, he would let his tears fall and his cries be heard by the Lord Almighty and anyone else who wanted to hear them. For now, he had killing to take care of.

The Indians had not spoken, had barely even looked at him as they came closer. He'd called to the others, each of them a seasoned soldier and a man willing to fight for freedom and kill for it, and they had come. Six soldiers and five women with three infants and children, they'd hardly been a formidable force, but they'd been armed and they'd been ready to handle whatever came their way.

Up until the Indians showed them that weapons aren't always enough to handle a problem.

The first of the braves had looked down at the snow even as he came closer, and when Moses had called for him to stop, he simply shook his head and charged.

Willy Henderson was the leader of the ex-slaves. He was a tall man and hard muscled from his years. He was also one of the finest shooters Moses had ever seen. The man raised his rifle and didn't bother calling out to the Indian again. Instead, he fired directly into the charging man's chest and blew a wedge of flesh away. The weapon he used was designed for killing bison. The shot was true and would have taken down one of the massive animals. He had no doubt of that.

The brave was blown backward by the shot and lifted into the air as easily as if he were thrown from a horse. He hit the snow and lay still for a moment, a halo of blood spritzing around his body.

The other interlopers stopped where they were and looked at their fallen brother, staring as if they'd never in their lives seen a fallen body.

Moses stared, too. There had been a few people to come by their small settlement and consider causing troubles, but all it had taken was a look at the men and their weapons to stop any difficulties. These men did not seem to feel the same way and the end result was an unwanted death.

They wanted a new life, not more blood on their hands.

The Indian got back up.

Moses near pissed himself when it happened. The man was dead or at least dying. His breaths had stopped, leaving an absence of the warm steam that came with every exhalation. His chest did not move. Moses had looked at him for a long moment and seen the blood spill out from beneath him, had seen the lack of movement.

He wasn't alone. Every man and woman from the settlement let out a panicked noise as the dead Indian sat up and then stood.

Willie took aim a second time, but he did not fire.

"You and yours need to leave this property. We'll defend what is ours." His voice shook, but his aim was true. Willie was a battle-hardened soldier, and he did not let panic take that from him.

The Indian looked at him with dark eyes and opened his mouth to speak. The sound that came from him was not meant for human ears. Moses heard the noise and stepped back, his skin drawn tight and his manhood shriveled and hiding. That noise, it was like a train's whistle, but higher, louder, and filled with odd syllables.

And while he was trying to understand how the dead man could make such a noise, the Indian attacked in earnest, leaping across nearly fifty feet of snow to pounce on Willie. It was a day for the impossible. Willie looked up at the brave dropping toward him and tried to take aim, but he never really had a chance. The dead man struck him feet first and landed with all the force of a dropping anvil. Moses heard the bones in his friend's body breaking. Willie's body was half buried in the snow in an instant, and the thing that had been an Indian once stood over his broken body and hissed toward Moses and the remaining landholders.

Hissed! Like an oversized snake! And damned if the thing didn't have teeth as big as a rattler's in its mouth. Big, fat fangs that rolled out from behind the other teeth and dripped with some thick, pasty fluid.

Moses shot it four times, fast as he could aim and fire. The bullets hit their targets, cut holes in the body of the dead thing in front of him and sent it falling again and again.

And it kept getting back up.

And while he worked at killing something that would not die, the men with him opened fire as well, listening when he told them to take care of the other red men instead of the one he was busy killing himself.

The clouds had threatened a storm and he and his men provided the thunder. Moses aimed a fifth time, prepared to kill his enemy as many times as he could until one of them fell, but he never fired a fifth shot. Something hit him from behind instead and knocked him into a fitful sleep.

And now he was waking up and wishing he could claim the nightmare he was seeing was merely a bad dream and not what his world had become. Dear Lord above, how he prayed for that mercy. Unfortunately, the Lord did not heed his requests.

Loretta was barely recognizable. He spotted the shoes she'd been wearing and recognized her only from that. The rest of her was lost to fire and ashes. She had burned in the flames of what had been his fireplace, if he had to guess. The rest of the house was lost, ruined in the blaze.

The others were dead as well, all except one tiny child. The little boy shivered and cried weakly in the cold, his eyes nearly frozen shut with his tears.

Moses picked up the boy and carried him through the cold until he made it to Willie's house. The door was closed and the fire still had enough spirit to it to keep the cold at bay. He closed the door and locked it, then settled the boy on the bed in the corner of the main room.

He searched the house until he found what he needed, weapons. Willie liked his guns.

Moses settled on a shotgun, and two more exotic hand-held weapons that were cleaned and well cared for, even if they were nearly never used. He found shells for all of them and he gathered what little food he could find.

There was a storm moving in fast and if he waited it out, he'd lose the tracks from the horses the Indians had stolen.

That wasn't going to happen.

The problem was simple enough: he needed to kill a few men and he needed to get to them before he could do that.

The weapons were gathered, including a few extras he'd known were somewhere in Willie's house. The boy was warm enough, but to make sure he wrapped the child in three thick blankets when he returned from the stables.

No horses were left. The Indians had taken them. Moses was forced to use the oxen and a wagon to carry the supplies. They would be slower than the horses, but they were also all he had.

He left only a short ways ahead of the weather, knowing he'd likely be caught by it before he could find his targets.

The winds screamed again as he rode away. The infant cried in its bundle, scared and cold.

He understood the feelings of the child and the elements alike.

The Dead Men

They did not speak. They did not need to.

The men understood that whatever the Skinwalker had done to them had remade their flesh.

More than that, it had changed their spirits. That was not a part of what they had agreed to, but they had not forbidden the transformation. They would do whatever it took to get their revenge.

They no longer had names, not that they could remember. Names were power and the Skinwalker had stolen that from them. Instead, they merely understood each other, without the need for words or names.

The first of them had been destroyed by weapons fire and should have been dead. Instead, he was recovering, and his changes took place all the faster as a result. He was the least human of them now, the farthest from what he had been before death.

He looked to his brethren and they in turn let him see himself with the changes that were taking place. His skin was scaly, a thin, gentle layer of scales, more lizard than snake. His face was almost unchanged, but his jaw hung differently, accommodating the deadly weapons his teeth had become. Pressure in his jaw and below his sinuses told him that glands had come in to generate deadly poisons.

Those were just the obvious changes. There were more going in below the surface, transformations that were continuing even as they moved.

The greatest changes were still happening, still to be discovered. They knew this, as surely as they knew where the men they sought were heading.

The town of Carson's Point was known to them. They had been there before, to trade in some cases and to sell in others. There was little they needed from the round eyes, but weapons were a necessity.

His hand touched the rifle at his side in an unconscious gesture. Even now he felt reassured by the presence of the firearm, fully loaded and ready for use.

The horse beneath him was scared but obeyed his commands just the same. He willed it to continue onward, despite the fear, the desperate desire to escape from a predator, and the animal obeyed.

He was changing.

The men with him were changing, too. He could see it in each of them, even if the alterations were not as obvious. The Skinwalker had gifted them with great powers and taken from them the weaknesses of human flesh and the human mind.

He was grateful, and he hated the demon-shaman.

The stone resting between his eyes moved and twisted inside his skull, taking root in his mind and his body alike, a warm stream of mercurial energies that grew and pulsed, taking the place of the heartbeat he no longer felt.

The storm was almost upon them.

They were almost to Carson's Point.

Death rode with them, a welcome companion.

CHAPTER FIVE
COLD TEETH

Lucas Slate

The storm swept into town just after sunset. Before that happened, however, a goodly number of people desperate for real shelter from the hellish blizzard arrived in Carson's Point.

The newcomers who had already settled themselves as best they could in wagons or tents or even lean-tos, did the best they could to brace themselves for the brutal weather. Wood was stocked up, small openings were patched or sealed, and extra layers of clothing were pulled out of storage and slipped on hastily.

The storm hit with a fury that reminded everyone of exactly how small human lives were in comparison to the fury of nature when properly enraged. Ice quickly formed on tree branches and roofs alike, pressing down and threatening to break everything under the weight. More than one tent collapsed early on, and quite a few of the would-be miners learned a hard lesson in shoring up the structures they had created.

The hotels in town had been close to full previously and that stayed mostly the same. Wanting a room is not the same as having the money for a room. Several arguments started as a result of families desperate for shelter seeking a room without the funds to afford them.

At the Piedmont, the tracker sat in his room and sipped at a bottle of whiskey he'd purchased with his monetary gains. The dead could not thank him for his decency, but they could, by God, afford him a few shots to stay warmer.

A couple in the next room prayed fervently, asking not only for safety from the storm, but for good fortune in their quest for a solid gold strike.

He listened to them and shook his head. Some people were simply fools. He could have told them there was no gold to be had in the area. Could have, but chose not to. That knowledge was his alone to have and he intended to keep it that way.

A little trick of his father's. The man had laid the claim out and then gone back to Summit Town after flashing his gold. Why he did so was one of many mysteries his father had never bothered to share.

Just down the street at Kaufmann's Saloon the proprietor watched over the crowds that swarmed into his place, desperate for warmth and booze alike. Anything to stay away from the elements. He let them stay, for a while at least.

At the undertaker's place, Lucas Slate finished his work, driving the final nails into the eighth coffin. Nine bodies, nine coffins, and half of his lumber used. He'd have to order more soon. There would always be a need for more coffins. It was one of the few things about his job that he liked.

The cold outside barely reached him. The wood burning stoves he'd had placed in various locations kept the rest of the house warm and took care of the basement work area as well. He was not a fool and he knew that cold could bring more than frost with it.

The ninth coffin held the body of a lovely young woman. He'd done his best to keep her beauty, knowing full well it would not last in the ground. Still, the world could be a very ugly place and he preferred to find beauty where he could.

Her hair was red, her skin pale and her facial features delicate. She'd have been a true beauty in life.

He'd found clothes for the violated women. The mercantile had a small collection of out-of-fashion outfits from a foolish investment a few months back and he managed to purchase them at a reasonable price. Better to bury them with a bit of dignity; it made up for a few of the sins done to them in life, or at least he liked to think so.

His father had believed very firmly that the dead rested comfortably until the Rapture. His mother had told him once, when Father was away, that she did not agree. The dead, she believed, lingered around their loved ones to watch over them in some cases, or haunted the ones who had brought them to death in others.

Lucas had never seen a ghost. That did not mean he didn't believe in them. He had a certain reverence for the dead, and he made sure to treat the bodies with as much respect as he could in order to let them know it.

There had been another man who worked as an apprentice with him back at the Lewis funeral home in Savannah. Rodney Crompton. Rodney had been an odd bird to begin with. He was opinionated, convinced that any physical deformity was a sign of sin carried on to the child from the parent—and while he could not say what the sin had been, he made sure to notice Lucas's albinism with his eyes when he made his comments— and from a family of lawyers and doctors alike. That he chose to work as an undertaker instead should have been a sign, but perhaps he was simply the family embarrassment.

The third time Rodney was left to take care of a corpse on his own, Lewis had waited fifteen minutes with Lucas at his side, and then carefully moved back to the preparation room as quietly as he could. Lucas had come with him, because he insisted on a witness.

They found Crompton having sexual relations with the cadaver of a married woman who had been his neighbor. The vile man had been biting at the dead breast and rutting with savage glee when they walked into the room.

Crompton was dismissed from his apprenticeship. A letter was hand delivered by Mr. Lewis explaining why. Not long after that, Crompton committed suicide.

Lucas took his time when he prepared the man's body, and he resisted the strong urge to either spit on the dead man's face or carve away his genitalia and feed them to the neighborhood dog.

He carefully examined the dead woman's body one final time and then lifted the wooden lid to the casket in place.

As he did so, her eyes opened wide.

He was not a skittish man, but the undertaker took a step back and barely repressed a scream. He examined her again, cautiously, and placed a hand on her delicate neck to see if he could feel a heartbeat. When that failed he reached for the mirror he kept for exactly that reason and placed it to her mouth, her nose, looking for any sign that breath still came from her body.

Nothing. She did not breathe and her heart did not beat.

"You gave me quite the scare, my dear." He spoke softly, to himself, really.

He placed his hand over her eyes and closed them.

"Rest in peace. Tomorrow or the day after, we'll see you with a proper burial."

The corpse did not respond, and her eyes stayed closed as he slipped the lid in place and reached for his hammer and his nails.

Outside the wind screamed and threw icy shot against the side of the funeral home and, inside the warm room, Lucas Slate shivered briefly and told himself it was only the cold that caused it.

Jonathan Crowley

Her lips kissed the back of his neck, and Jonathan Crowley stirred, smiled as she wrapped her arms around his waist. She'd settled on the bed behind him, and he could feel her breasts pressed to his back, her legs playfully moving along his.

His body reacted and he turned, drawing her into his arms, kissing her neck in return before their lips fused together.

She felt so right, so perfect, exactly as she should. Her body pressed in closer and the only thing that stopped them from coupling was the blanket between them. He pulled the blanket aside hastily, so eager to be in her, to be with her.

Molly looked into his eyes and her pretty face grew serious. "You can't do this, Jonathan. I'm dead."

"What?"

"Dead. Me and William and our little Billy. We're all dead, remember? You saw them killing me, tried to stop them."

Jonathan Crowley awoke with a small noise and stared at the wall of his room. Outside the storm screamed.

Marcus Darby

"We need rooms." Marcus Darby spoke slowly, carefully, his hand eager to reach for the pistol at his side.

"I can't help you. Every room is taken." The stout man looked at him with apologetic eyes. "I've already got people sleeping in the hallways, sir. There's no room left."

His fist smashed down on the counter between the two men. "Find a room!"

"Sir, I can't give you what I don't have." He was still polite, but there was an edge creeping into the hotel owner's voice.

"Well then, where do you recommend I go?" There was no attempt to be polite. Marcus was not in the mood put up with any guff.

"There are five other hotels in Carson's Point. I don't know that any of them have rooms, but the Piedmont is completely full."

He stared at the man and ground his teeth together. On the trail he'd have already killed the bastard, but he was in a town now, and had to at least pretend toward civility.

More importantly, he could sense that the artifacts he looked for were nearby. The tugging sensation near his chest was stronger than ever before and he could very nearly taste the money he'd been promised. Enough to start a new life almost anywhere he could imagine.

So he couldn't just shoot the damned fool and take a few rooms for the boys.

Silas put a hand on the counter and stared at the hotel's owner. "May we stay in the stables?" His voice was calm and reasonable, and Marcus envied him that ability.

"The stables? They're hardly the best place for a man to rest." The man frowned, doubtful.

Silas smiled in return, his voice soft and his demeanor nothing but pleasant. "They were good enough for Jesus Christ when he was born, they're good enough for us."

"You'll have to deal with the horses already there, of course. We can't send them out into the storm…." His frown increased as he contemplated everything.

Silas smiled. "We just need a place free of the wind to keep us warm."

"Well then, by all means."

"Much obliged." Silas looked at Marcus pointedly and headed for the barn. Despite his desire for a warm bed, Marcus followed.

"You don't think I could have talked him into rooms for us?"

"I think you could have called more attention than you want to us. I think we have enough challenges in front of us without getting the local sheriff looking too closely at who we are and what we're carrying." Silas's voice was calm and steady and made Marcus grind his teeth. Every word the man said made perfect sense, but that didn't mean he wanted to listen.

The same problem then. He'd hope it was the wilderness that made him impatient, and maybe it was, but that Silas had to remind him to act civilly was not a good thing. He was the one in charge, the one who was supposed to urge caution from others.

"A good argument. Still, I could do with a proper bath and a real bed."

Silas nodded. "Then we'll stay for a few extra days. You said what we want is in the area. The blizzard comes in, the blizzard goes away. When it's gone the prospectors will go back to looking for their gold and we'll have our pick of beds."

He hated Silas sometimes. Mostly because the man was usually right.

"The boys are likely not going to be happy."

Silas turned fast and shoved a finger into Marcus's chest. Most men would have died for the presumption, but he needed the man to keep him level.

"The boys are acting worse than the savages. You'd do well to put them on a leash while we're here." His voice was a low hiss, and Silas's eyes blazed with repressed fury. "We're in a place that has heard of God and Jesus and the sins they've been performing, that you have committed, are the sorts that will get us strung up or burned at the damned stake."

Marcus took a step back, the venom in his second's voice taking him by surprise.

"Silas, I-"

"I'll not hear a justification, Marcus. There is none. Keep them in check, because I'll kill any of them that look to get us caught and you'd be wise to do the same."

The man turned and walked away, not bothering to look back. Every step that his second took was carefully measured and balanced by the stiff back and slow menace that seemed to come from him in waves. It was best not to underestimate the man. He was a killer, even when he was acting particularly self-righteous. Marcus watched him go, and he nodded to himself slowly. Silas was right. He still hated him for that, but he was wise enough to know when he should listen.

The stables were large enough to accommodate twenty horses or more with ease. There were seven horses total and one, a massive black stallion, that looked large enough to fight off a bear without too much trouble. Otherwise, the place was empty.

Fine. It would do for the night.

The Dead Men

The snows did not come gently. They brought with them a wind that howled and roared between the trees and shook them hard enough to break branches. Ice formed on every surface the wind touched, and that included the clothes of the dead who rode toward Carson's Point.

They did not reach the town before the full fury of the weather came to them. The horses huddled together and continued to move, more afraid of the things that rode them than of the icy winds that cut at their hides.

Despite the changes moving through their bodies, the dead men knew they needed to find shelter and so they looked carefully as they rode through the hellish storm.

And looking, they found what they needed.

Four wagons had been set together as a barrier against the worst of the storm and the people in those wagons had used hides and extra canvas to place a makeshift tent over the wagons themselves to keep their animals safe.

They moved carefully around the wagons, unconcerned with the cold, though the wind cut at them. They were dead, or at least they had been. The elements held little to unsettle them. After their examination they agreed that the camp would work well enough.

As one they slipped down from their horses. The animals did not flee, or panic, much as they might have wanted. The braves, nameless in their new incarnations, continued to change, and one of them merely spoke to the animals' minds and told them to stay where they were. Against their nature and instincts, the horses did as they were told.

Anna Harris

Anna Harris looked at her parents and shivered in the cold. The winds shook the wagons but did not quite reach to where her family huddled together for warmth. They couldn't light a fire, not beyond the small flames in the two lanterns that gave light and warmth in meager doses. The wagons carried too many flammables. One flame in the wrong place and everything they owned would be destroyed.

She'd almost drifted to sleep when she heard the sounds from outside change. The harsh winds rattled and shifted when it should have been impossible, and her father looked up from where he'd been resting, his hand immediately reaching for his rifle. The last few months had taught them to be careful, to be vigilant against the dangers outside of civilized places.

"Stay here." He spoke softly, just loud enough to be heard over the wind, and then he moved toward the back of the wagon and the center of the area they'd formed as a community.

Anna listened as best she could, but her curiosity insisted that she at least see what her father was doing. She peeled back the canvas flap that served as a window in the wagon and looked into the twilight atmosphere of the center of the wagon train. Ten horses took up most of the area, all of them nervously shifting, none of them quite worried enough to try running. That was good as there was nowhere for them to go, but they could do a sight of damage if they tried to get somewhere anyway.

Her father stood and stretched his back, looking toward Mr. Chambers from the lead wagon. The man had arranged for everything, had convinced the families to head west together for protection, and had been wise enough to come prepared for the elements. According to her father, they would have all been in much worse shape without Mr. Chambers to lead the way. All she knew about him was that he was pleasant enough and never talked down to her merely because she was young.

The two men spoke, but the words were lost to her, stolen by the wind and the nervous whinnies of the horses.

The two men moved quickly, going to the other wagons and knocking at wood or fabric, whichever was available, calling out to the others. A moment later Mr. Smith climbed from his wagon, adjusting his pants and scowling worriedly. He was a very large man, overweight despite the lean times upon all of them, and he carried with him a shotgun that looked big enough to kill a horse with ease. Unlike Mr. Chambers, the man did not make Anna comfortable. He scared her, instead. There was something untrustworthy about him as far as she was concerned, though she would never say as much to anyone else.

Billy Barker and his father both came from the last wagon, ready with rifles and looking deadly serious.

She strained to hear what the men spoke about, but the horses were acting up, throwing fits and dancing about like they were trying to avoid a dozen snakes.

The sounds got worse. One of the horses made a sound she'd have thought impossible. The animal shrieked, a very human noise, and a second later fell down, flailing limbs and thrashing body all she could see until the blood fountained into the air where the horse had been a moment before.

Anna flinched. She loved the horses, thought them among the most elegant animals in existence. The thought of them being hurt, being killed, was horrid.

The men outside looked toward the dead or dying animal and moved carefully, avoiding the panicked dances of the other horses.

Mr. Chambers was the first to die.

Anna was looking at him, watching the way he carried his rifle, admiring the economy of motions the ex-soldier used, when something came at him from between two of the horses and wrapped itself around him with the speed of a striking snake. Before he could do more than let out a grunt, he was down and out of her view.

"Mr. Chambers! Daddy!" She could think of nothing else to say.

Her mother looked toward her and reached out with one strong hand. "Anna! Get back here and away from the horses. They could kick if they panic."

Her mother didn't understand, hadn't seen what she had just seen. From the corner of her eye she caught the oversized form of Mr. Smith. He was staggering backward, his hands clutching at the shotgun and he let out a bleating scream that was dwarfed by the explosion of his shotgun firing into the air. The sound was thunderous and the result immediate. The horses that had managed to remain calm despite the odds gave up the pretense of behaving themselves and tried to bolt, running and rearing up, wild-eyed and panicked.

Her father was too close to one of the stallions. Anna let out a gasp as she saw the horse knock him backward. "Daddy!"

"Anna! Get back!" Her mother's hand pulled her away from the window before she could see more.

"Daddy's been hurt!" She screamed, pulling her hand free from her mother. Before she could reach the window a second time her mother was pulling her back forcefully.

"This isn't the time or the place. You stay back from there! Your father wants you safe." As she spoke, her mother reached into a steamer trunk and pulled out a revolver. Anna's eyes flew wide. Her mother's hands shook, but only a little, as she checked the chamber and clicked the cylinder into place.

"Momma, what are you doing?"

"I've been shown by your father. I'll keep us safe." Her voice was surprisingly calm.

From outside the commotion grew louder. Horses shrieked and men did too. Anna covered her ears, wishing desperately for silence. She was not granted her desire.

The sounds grew worse and the smell of blood permeated the air.

And then the silence came and brought even worse feelings. Her father was a loud man, boisterous. That he made no sound was terrifying in the implications. Worse still was the silence of the horses.

Anna looked to her mother, who looked back at her with wide, frightened eyes and pointed the revolver toward the canvas door of the wagon. In the dim light of the lanterns her mother's face was a pale, dim moon.

The hands came from the wrong side of the tent, punching through the fabric from the outside and letting in the cold and the hideous winds. Anna had only just opened her mouth to scream when the hands reached through and caught her mother's hair and scalp in long, powerful fingers.

The nails on those hands were thick and jagged and curved, more like claws than anything that belonged to a human hand.

Her mother pulled the trigger, and an explosive noise overwhelmed the howl of the wind and even the sound of her mother screaming for a moment. Anna shrieked as she reached for her only remaining parent, but far too late to help her. The hands pulled and her mother's wide face twisted into a second yowl of pain, but no sound could be heard this time, and the canvas bucked and stretched before it tore. Her mother reached for her as she was pulled away, drawn through the canvas and into the storm.

Anna screamed and scrambled for the hole where her mother had been, her voice worn ragged.

Anna was still screaming when the figure climbed through the hole and stared at her with glittering red eyes.

What looked at her was the color of the raging snows and utterly impossible. She was still trying to understand all the things that were wrong with the creature when it lurched forward and sank thick teeth into her neck and shoulder.

Anna stopped screaming.

And not long after the silence was complete, save for the wind and the snow.

The Skinwalker

The Skinwalker stared at the wall around Carson's Point and squinted his eyes against the roaring arctic winds. Wendigo was being a vicious bitch.

He smiled at the notion and gripped the clay amulet around his neck. The seeds pulsed against his hand and he could feel similar, smaller pulses from within the town's limits.

There was little for him in the town, save for curiosity. Somewhere within the place the men who had raped and killed his new pets sought shelter from the elements. He had no doubt of that, for he could feel the power that they were collecting. It was a power he could understand and that he was moderately interested in examining.

For that reason alone he carefully worked one of the seeds from his clay necklace and worked it in his fingers until it grew warm and then hot.

The seed steamed in the bitter cold and he reached into the pouch he carried over one shoulder, feeling among the various oddities he'd collected until he found what he sought. The worm's body was stiff and frozen, but with a little work he thawed it enough for his purposes. He worked the seed into the flesh of the fat worm and then dug into the bag again until he found the snake body he'd come across almost a week earlier and several hundred miles to the south.

His fingers plucked the eyes from the snake and he sucked them into his mouth, relishing the flavor. Instead of consuming the snake as he'd intended originally—it was a rattler and the venom had a taste he found quite savory—he pried open the mouth and forced the worm into the skull, pressing the struggling form into the brain cavity.

The snake hissed and twitched and then thrashed violently in his hands as it took on a mockery of life.

He smiled, baring black gums and yellowed teeth.

"See. Live. Breathe." The snake listened, and as he stared at it the writhing shape grew new dark eyes and gulped in bitter air. The snake had been cold-blooded, but the creature in his hands grew hotter, steamed in the cold and grew hotter still.

He dropped his prize and listened as it hissed through the falling snow and started burrowing into the icy ground.

"Go to the town. Eat the horses. I want them here. All of them. There are games we can play." He spoke though there was no need. The beast would understand what he wanted without the words. They were simply a distraction from the winds of the storm.

The Skinwalker shook his head and the ice that had formed in his hair shattered and fell aside.

The wind roared between the trees and threw plumes of white snow toward the ground with a violence that the demon admired.

Beneath his feet the snake shuddered and burrowed deeper, breaking through the frozen soil and growing larger with each convulsive twitch of its body.

The roar that came from beneath him rivaled the winds and the Skinwalker smiled, content to let the game play out as it would for now.

The air shivered and shook and the ground echoed with the roars of the thing that burrowed its way toward Carson's Point.

CHAPTER SIX
WHITE

Anson Meade

The world was cold and frozen. The fortunate ones had solid structures and fires to keep the worst of the cold at bay, but there were more who were not as lucky.

Throughout Carson's Point tents had collapsed under the weight of the storm's fury, buried under ice and snow.

Sheriff Meade walked along the interior wall of the town's meager defense and helped pull people from the disasters that had befallen them. He was not alone. The man he'd met a few days earlier, Crowley, was there as well and already well ahead of him in helping out. The two of them did not speak, but they acknowledged each other's existence.

Most of the people who had tried to sleep in fallen tents had the good sense to do what they could to prop up the protection they had, but a few were foolish and simply went to sleep. Those were the ones who wound up in trouble. The weight of the ice and snow was crushing, and the heat of their bodies under the canvas or furs was enough to melt the closest layers. By trying to stay warm without space, they'd pinned themselves.

The foolish were saved by the handful that took the time to find them and pull them free.

Daniel Kaufmann did not go out into the bitter cold and work to save the foolhardy and desperate, but he did begrudgingly allow them to come to his saloon and get warm. Hearty beef soup and bread waited for them, but any whiskey they wanted they had to pay for.

Several families were occupying the inside of the place, sitting at tables and huddling into whatever blankets or cover they could find as they shook off the cold.

A few weren't quite as fortunate. Two men and four children died as a result of the storm and poor decisions. By noon the sheriff had no choice but to approach Lucas Slate.

It was easy to find the man. He was standing outside in the cold, wrapped in his thickest coat and supervising several men in their duties. Starting at sunrise the undertaker had pulled back the canvas he'd set over a large piece of land in the local cemetery. While the men worked at clearing the space, he dealt with the problem of thawing the ground as best he could, using hot coals from inside his building and a layer of wood chips he'd procured the last time he was in Denver and picking up supplies. The snow kept the dangers low, and the heat from the blaze did a good enough job of thawing the ground that it was possible to dig graves. By the time the sheriff arrived along with his deputy and the six new bodies, the men Slate had hired had hacked and scraped nine deep holes in the ground for the bodies he had already prepared.

The air was smoky and cold and every man out there stood in the glare and squinted against the sting of the smoke's irritants. From time to time pine sap crackled and popped in the remaining fires.

Slate watched him coming closer and nodded a greeting. Not far behind him, the laborers prepared to lower a body into a grave while a heavyset priest spoke to God on behalf of the deceased.

"I have more bodies for you, Mr. Slate." Meade stood tall, doing his best not to shake violently in the cold.

"Your timing is impeccable, Sheriff. As luck would have it, I still have able-bodied men who wish to earn money available to me."

He beckoned with one hand and one of the laborers came over in a hurry. The undertaker spoke quietly and pointed to a spot where the fires still burned. "How many bodies are we dealing with, Sheriff?"

"Six more, Mr. Slate."

The albino nodded his head and made a *tsking* noise. "We shall make the arrangements. Do we have names and families in this case?"

"We do in three cases. For the others, unfortunately, no."

The man nodded his head. "Just the same, we'll do our best for them." He spoke softly to his man again and the hired helper bobbed his head a few times before walking stiffly toward the others.

The men—every one of them lean and hungry and cold—stood around and then nodded or grumbled as they saw fit when they received the news. Money was money and the times were beyond lean. They'd stay and work for the earnings they could get.

"Please have the deceased brought to my work area, Sheriff. I believe you know the way."

Meade looked toward the wall surrounding the town and saw a stranger coming through the open gates. The man rode on a wagon drawn by two oxen. The wagon, the oxen and the man were all covered in a thick layer of ice. The beasts wore blankets over their bodies and the man was covered with a thick buffalo hide that draped over his shoulders. The tall hat he wore, and the hide alike, were crusted with the remains of the last night's storm.

The driver was a black man, unusual in the area, but not unheard of, and the thick beard he sported was as heavy with ice as the hide he wore. His dark eyes looked from one man to the next until he spotted the star on Meade's coat.

"You'd be the sheriff?" His voice was raspy and deep.

"Yes indeed. How can I help you?" He eyed the man warily. Not because of his skin color—he'd always believed that color meant little though he still held his uneasy bias against Slate—but because the man looked both dangerous and desperate. He looked like he'd have little trouble killing anyone who crossed him the wrong way.

"My name is Moses Blake. Indians killed my kin and left me for dead. They looked to be heading in this direction, but it's hard to say for sure. The blizzard took away my sense of direction."

Meade frowned. "My condolences for your loss, sir."

"Much obliged, but that ain't why I'm here. I need you to be warned. These aren't normal men. They're dangerous and I think they might mean to do harm to anyone they meet that ain't red."

Slate stared at the man for a moment and then looked away. He was from a place that didn't much think fondly of freed Negroes. Still, he managed to keep anything he might have wanted to say to himself.

Meade watched the two men staring at each other and interrupted before the silence could grow tense. "How long ago did they leave your lands?"

"Might be two days ago. Might be they stopped somewhere to escape the storm. I rode straight through."

"You took a big chance."

"Got an infant with me." He opened the front of the thick hide around his shoulders and revealed the tiny child inside. "Need to find a woman who can feed him until he's big enough to eat solid foods."

The sheriff nodded. "I'm afraid that might be difficult here, Mister Blake. There aren't that many women with children that I know of."

Slate cleared his throat and spoke up. "There's a whorehouse at the edge of this road, three intersections up. That particular location has a woman due to give birth in a few weeks. I'd lay fair odds she would take care of the boy's appetite in exchange for a few coins."

Blake looked at the ghostly white undertaker and nodded his head slowly. "Thank you for that."

Slate's pale blue eyes stared at the black man for a moment and Meade acknowledged how many differences there were between the two. Slate was lean, clean-shaven and neatly dressed. Blake was heavier, shaggier and dressed in furs to stay warm.

Slate spoke again, his voice soft. "I should rather not have to bury any more children, Mister Blake." His accent was more pronounced, and Meade wondered if that was a result of dealing with an ex-slave or merely his imagination. "I should very much prefer to see the little one live through all of this."

"Sheriff Meade!" Pace Peabody's voice called out, sounding remarkably like a squealing piglet in the cold air.

He turned to face his deputy and made himself stay neutral. The man was a pain in his side that would not go away. True, he was doing better, but he was still not overly impressive as deputies went.

"How can I help you, Pace?"

The deputy stared at the man on the wagon and licked his lips nervously. Moses Blake stared back, his eyes half-lowered and his breaths blowing softly from his flared nostrils. Meade had little doubt in his mind that the wrong words from the deputy would see him dead before he could respond.

"Speak up, Pace!" His voice was sharper than he wanted it to be.

The deputy looked back at him with a start. "Um. We had an incident at the Piedmont."

"What sort of incident?"

"Someone stole all the horses from the stables."

"Excuse me?"

"The horses, Sheriff. Somebody took all of them. Well, all except the really big one that belongs to Mr. Miles." Pace's head bobbed on his shoulders, as if he was practicing a proper cringe so he could duck if Meade took a swing at him.

"And did you talk to anyone down there to see if they knew what was going on?"

"I did. I talked to Curtis Hunnicutt. The stable boy. He said the horses were all there last night before the blizzard hit."

Meade nodded his head and sighed. "I'll have the bodies brought around, Mr. Slate."

"Thank you, kindly, Sheriff Meade."

The black man nodded briefly and used the reins to get his oxen moving again.

He'd only gone a few feet before Meade walked over to where the wagon struggled through the thick ice and snow. "Mister Blake?"

"Yes sir?" The man looked hard at him, inconvenienced by being made to stop.

"First, thank you for the warning. Second, what else brings you to town?"

The man studied him, dark eyes unflinching, unblinking for long enough to make Meade uncomfortable. Finally he answered. "You're welcome. And I came here because those Indians will be coming here. I intend to kill them. Each and every one. And then I can see about my homestead and my life afterward."

Meade nodded his head and stepped back allowing the man to move again. What could he do? What could he say? If the man's tales were true, the savages were coming here. If that were the case, he'd want all the help he could get.

"What about the horses, Sheriff?" Pace's voice cut through his thoughts and he turned to the man with a scowl.

"Go find out what happened to them, Deputy Peabody."

"Me?"

"Earn your damned pay!" He snapped the words out and took two steps toward the man. "Before I change my mind about keeping you on."

Pace stared at him for several seconds, his eyes searching Meade's face for God alone knew what, and then nodded and turned away, heading for the Piedmont.

Meade watched him leave and said nothing.

So Slate spoke up. "There was a time, and not all that long ago, when the work I have done by the men I'm paying would have been handled by slaves in my father's stable."

"Slavery is frowned upon these days, Mister Slate."

"That it is, and the world's a better place for the lack as far as I'm concerned."

That caught Meade's attention. "Really?"

"Oh, yes. I don't believe anyone should own another man, or a woman for that matter. We are all God's children and I don't believe He wants us answering to any master but Himself." He shrugged. "My point here, is that even the lowliest and least effective slave that my father owned knew they would be treated with a modicum of decency and given three meals a day."

Meade crossed his arms over his chest. "Is that so?" Slate nodded. "And why was that?"

Slate's nearly colorless eyes stared into his for a long moment before he answered. "Because if you whip a cur often enough, it'll fight to defend itself and like as not it will remember every slight. If you treat the animal with kindness, it has no reason to bite."

Meade looked at him and finally nodded. "You think I'm too harsh on Pace?"

"It's not my place to say, Sheriff Meade, but I know the look of an angry man when I see one, and your deputy is looking deeply angered." The man looked away to where the men he'd hired were doing hard work without complaint.

"You're a very perceptive man, Mr. Slate."

"One does not live long with my conditions if he can't tell the gentlemen from the troublemakers around him, Sheriff."

"What happened to your family after the slaves were freed?"

"My father continued to employ the same men who'd worked for him before. He offered them a roof over their heads, food in their bellies and a few pennies besides."

"Did they stay?"

"All but one of them. That one, he wouldn't have stayed if my father had offered to adopt him as a son."

"Why not?"

"He found the south inhospitable and the people not to his liking."

"Did he go north?"

"No. No he did not. He rode west, looking for a new home."

"I wonder how far he went."

"Not very far, I'm afraid. The first white man that found him away from his proper place strung him up as a reminder to other slaves to keep their tongues and their place in society."

Meade had no answer to that. Instead he made his goodbyes and headed for the gates to Carson's Point. Indians. If he'd had any sense he'd have gotten details from Blake regarding the possible attack.

There was a whorehouse he needed to visit if he wanted to find the man.

Jonathan Crowley

Crowley walked along the perimeter of the town, keeping company with himself as he most often did. There was no reason to deal with others. They only got in the way of his studies.

Somewhere out beyond the town there was a steamer trunk full of his notes. He needed to get back to his research as soon as he could, if only to get him away from the town.

Away from the people and all their troubles.

Away from the death. There had been quite enough of that in his life, thank you kindly.

He didn't think he wanted to handle any more death. Not now, not ever.

Molly had made that clear enough for him, and to a lesser extent William and Billy. He regretted their deaths, knowing full and well that he should not have. In two days' time the woman had insinuated herself into his life and his mind, and as proof of that he had to look no further than the fact that he hadn't forced her spirit to rest.

That was his duty, his calling. He hunted and destroyed the things that haunted humanity. He had done so for as long as he could remember, at least until he decided not to.

How long had he been wandering the continent? Not long enough. He still remembered everything. But, oh, how wonderful to forget, if only for a short while, to hunt for the monstrous and demonic.

Common sense demanded that he put Molly down. If he didn't, she'd haunt him again until he got revenge for her and her family.

He was wise enough to know that the dream he'd had of her during the storm was no normal entertainment from his mind, but rather a visit from her spirit. He just hadn't been his expecting her to come to him in that sense. He knew what she wanted. She wanted the revenge he'd already been planning. She wished to get justice in one form or another for her life and those of her family. Crowley wanted the same thing, but for his reasons, not for hers.

A man had killed him—or close enough—and that same man had pissed on him. That sort of insult couldn't be forgiven. Was it petty? Probably, but he had to let himself have a few small satisfactions, didn't he? That or go mad. So he would hunt down the people that murdered Molly. He would do that. But he wanted to believe it was only because of what they had done to him.

It was best to avoid attachments. He'd learned that lesson a hundred times at least.

Pity the lessons never seemed to stick.

Molly showed up as he rounded the last corner of the perimeter. He'd felt her presence for a while, known she was going to show herself, just hadn't known exactly when.

She looked pristine, innocent, nearly perfect. Beautiful, really. For a ghost.

"They're here, Jonathan. The ones who killed us."

"Are they?" He glanced at her for only a moment and then started walking again.

"Will you avenge us? Avenge me?" Spectral hands touched his shoulders, caressed imploringly.

Crowley sighed. "If I say yes, will you go away?"

"I-Jonathan?" her voice was hurt.

"I mean it, Molly. I don't want to see you again. If I see you, I'll have to do things I'm trying to avoid."

Her hands faded from him, and much as he hated it, a part of him longed to call her back. She was the closest thing he'd had to a lover in a very long time. *I should buy a whore and be done with it.*

He looked back, hating himself for the weakness, and saw her again, a wounded expression on her face.

"Molly…I don't want to hurt you. I don't…I don't want you to suffer. That's all I can offer you. I want you to be at peace. So yes, I'll get revenge for you. I'll see the whole lot of them dead within the week."

She came closer, her hands once again touching, a faint, ephemeral feeling.

"You are a dear, dear man, Jonathan Crowley."

"Never let anyone hear you say that." He smiled despite himself. And then he stopped and listened. Up ahead there were noises, the sounds of men laughing. He had heard that laughter before, not so very long ago.

Molly made no answer. She had vanished from sight, though he could still feel her.

Twelve paces through the snow, and he could see them. Not the whole group, not by any stretch, but several of the filthy bastards who had killed a family, raped a fine woman and then watched her bleed to death.

The one that pissed on him wasn't there. Pity. That would have to wait then.

There were five of them all told, huddled together and talking in the frigid air. They held mugs in their hands, and every cup steamed with heat.

Crowley's lips peeled back in a smile.

Sometimes life could give the most delicious surprises.

Silas

Silas listened to the men talking. They had slept in a decent shelter for the first time in over a week, and they seemed more themselves than they had for a long while. Was it the fresh breakfast that still filled their bellies? Was it the calming effects of civilization? He didn't know, but he was grateful for it just the same.

Henderson was telling a story about his life on the farm, and Silas listened raptly. The story wasn't the thing here. It was simply that Henderson was so sullen of late that hearing him laugh, seeing him smile, was a wondrous surprise. It almost made up for the sins the man had committed of late.

He worried about their souls. All of them. They'd done horrible things in the war, which was why they had fled in the first place really, but now? Now the sins they committed were not done for any sane reason. Now the marks against them would be theirs alone come the Day of Judgment. He dreaded that thought.

The man who came toward them from the left walked with purpose. He strode across the thick snow, knocking layers of the ice aside with each step. And he smiled, oh, how he smiled, a dark and savage expression that spoke not of kindness or joy but instead of blood and pain. The expression seemed one that the plain man's face was accustomed to, and that notion unsettled Silas deeply.

"Charles," he interrupted Henderson's story and nudged the man with his hand. "Charles, does that man seem familiar to you?"

Henderson looked first at him and then at the stranger and as he stared his face grew pale and his mouth hung open with shock.

"God above…." His voice was faint and the mug he'd been holding in both hands fell free and sank into the snow soundlessly.

"Gentlemen," The voice was clear and loud and oh, so very cheerful. "I believe we have unfinished business."

Only Henderson reacted so strongly. The rest, Silas among them, might have seen something familiar in the face, but not enough to set off alarms.

"And what would that be, sir?" Silas kept his voice calm and made sure he was heard. Not far away several other people who had been minding their own affairs turned at the exchange and studied the players.

The stranger came closer, his eyes flickering from one man to another as he approached. He stopped a solid thirty feet away.

"Why, that would have to do with murder, sir. Murder and the soiling of an innocent woman and her family."

There was no consideration of guilt or innocence after that bold statement. While Silas might well have wanted to deny the accusations, Smith and Hotchkins drew their revolvers and aimed at the man.

"You'll be wanting to stop right there, you son of a whore." Hotchkins growled the words and took the time to aim carefully.

That maddening grin grew wider on the stranger's face and a second later Hotchkins let out a scream as his gun hand exploded.

Smith fired once. He was just exactly fast enough for that. The snow behind the stranger jumped, a plume of white that settled quickly. By the time the snow had fallen back down Smith was dead, his neck and throat blown away.

Silas didn't think beyond that point. A good soldier doesn't need to think. Instead, he acts. His hands flew down and caught the revolvers at his sides. The Colt Paterson revolvers had served him well, and he prayed to God that they would continue to serve him as he drew and fired.

The weapons fired true, and two more explosions of snow struck behind where the stranger had been. Unfortunately, he was moving, and a damned sight faster than he should have.

Hotchkins screamed again, and dropped to his knees, desperate to find his handgun. He held his bloodied hand off the ground and whimpered in his throat, the wound jetting a thick streamer of red across the snow.

Silas noticed that as he fired again and stepped to the side. A moving target is harder to strike. He needed to not be killed just then. He had things he needed to do before he could let himself die.

Hotchins's head snapped back twice, and at the same moment, his skull exploded backward, throwing red blossoms into the air and across the whitewashed ground.

The stranger dropped low to the ground and then dove to the right as Owens opened fire, snapping the trigger as fast as he could, and fanning the hammer with his free hand to keep the cylinder spinning hard.

A thin line of red seeped from the gunslinger's shoulder. A grazing wound at best.

Owens stopped firing when the bullets hammered his chest into a new, fatal shape.

Before he hit the ground the smiling maniac moved closer, firing at Walters, and that was all Silas saw before he turned and ran, his legs pumping furiously. Around him the people who had been watching the start of the exchange now stood frozen with shock or crawled for cover, all pretense of civility removed by the imminent fear of death.

Behind him the stranger called out. "You tell your friends I'm coming. You hear me, coward? I'm coming for all of you! Every last one of you miserable bastards! There will be a reckoning!"

Silas didn't answer. He was too busy praying to a God he dearly believed in, and whom he hoped, still believed in him.

CHAPTER SEVEN
THE NAMELESS ONES

The Dead Men

They had no names. They did not need them. The Skinwalker had given them gifts that stretched beyond mere names. The reborn rode toward the town at a slow, steady pace, unworried by the weather, or the blood that they had shed.

The sun was bright in the sky and they wore hats, every one of them, to hide their eyes from the worst of the glare.

From a distance the lot of them looked fine. Most would have taken for granted that they were not only men, but white men at that. The clothes they wore belonged to white men, after all. A good disguise for approaching a white settlement.

Carson's Point was silent but bustled with activity. The people were pulling themselves from the cold, recovering from the storm that had buried a good number of them.

When they'd risen from their shelter for the night, the Nameless had pushed past the thick snowdrifts that had almost completely swallowed the wagon train. Had they still felt the cold, they'd have suffered from the chill. Their victims could not feel anything. The dead seldom did.

There were exceptions. The Nameless was among them.

A family had gathered together and wailed out their misery for the world around them. Two of their kin were dead, killed by the vicious storm and the relentless cold. They barely even noticed the Nameless. The creatures returned the favor.

Anson Meade

"And did anyone at all happen to see who was doing the killing?" Meade looked at Pace and tried to keep his voice pleasant. His deputy still didn't make that easy. The man had come to him screaming like a damned fool about a shootout. Not a consideration for the fact that everyone for a hundred yards could hear every word he said. He had not a bit of a worry over how tongues loved to wag when they found a new flavor to sample.

"Well, no." Pace had to think about it. Meade could see the strain that thinking hard caused the damned fool. "Not that I ran across. A lot of folks saying they were there, but no one could tell me who was firing at who."

He sighed.

"Let's go look at the bodies, shall we?"

"Mr. Slate is already heading in that direction. But he knows not to touch until someone says he can."

Meade nodded. The undertaker was unsettling to look at, but hardly dense.

"And no one knew the man doing the killing?"

Peabody looked at him for a long moment. "I did say that already, didn't I?"

"Yes, you did. I just want to make sure I'm hearing you right."

The deputy kept staring. "I'm not a fool, Sheriff."

He nodded. He had this coming, and now, if he was to listen to the albino, he had to accept the consequences of his actions.

Meade gritted his teeth for a moment and made himself speak calmly as he stared hard at his deputy. "I'll grant you that most of the time, Pace. And I owe you an apology for my attitude earlier, and I'll gladly give it, but I need to point out that running down the street and screaming that there's been a shootout doesn't do much to prove to me that you're a wise man."

The deputy blushed a bit and nodded. "Fair enough."

"I'm not a patient man, Pace. I don't take to thieves and I don't care much for troublemakers. That's why I do what I do. And I was wrong to yell at you earlier, but I also can't abide loud people who cry out about any possible danger, Pace, and you can be very loud."

"Okay. I had that coming."

He pointed a thick finger at the deputy. "You also spent my first night in town getting so deep into a bottle that I had to handle your business. So while I can understand your issues with me, Pace Peabody, you need to understand my problems with you as well."

Pace was already looking distracted, so he shut his mouth. You have to know your limits.

A crowd had gathered at the sight of the shootout. One of the men, a heavyset fellow with a leather apron and a meat cleaver in his hand, was pacing in front of the bodies and stopping a few children from getting better looks at the dead. Kids, as far as Meade was concerned, were too curious for their own good.

He stepped closer to the scene and looked at Leather Apron. The man nodded his head, his lips pressed together and his brows knitted above dark blue eyes.

"Sheriff Meade." He tapped the star on his jacket, just in case the man missed it. "You know if anyone saw anything?"

"I did." The man pointed with his cleaver—an unsettling sight as the blade was still bloodied—and aimed the business end toward Jonathan Crowley.

Crowley looked at the man for a moment and then looked to Meade and nodded.

"It seems you like to be in the thick of things. Mr. Crowley." Meade walked over to where the man stood, both Peacemakers on his hips, easily reached but not on display.

Crowley didn't quite smile, but the look on his face showed it was an effort for him not to. "I find it hard to avoid from time to time, Sheriff, but I've never been one to seek out conflict."

He looked at the man long and hard. The same plain features, the same brown hair and brown eyes. He could have been designed to blend into a crowd. His expression was a study in indifference, but a smile was lurking around his mouth, and his eyes, behind their spectacles, looked too alert to match his attitude.

"Care to explain to me?" He nodded toward the closest corpse.

"There were a few men who took it upon themselves to shoot at me on my way into town. They also shot and killed a family that was with me on the trail. I saw a few of them and decided to take care of the problem."

"There's a sheriff in town, Mr. Crowley. It's my job to avoid this sort of thing. People could have been killed in the crossfire."

"People were killed, Sheriff. But no one I didn't want to see dead."

"And if they'd fired at you and missed?"

"Then they'd have fired into the snow behind me, which is exactly what happened." The smile peeked out for a second and faded. The bastard was cocky. He had too much confidence in his abilities.

"I don't much take to people who commit murder in my town." He kept his voice low, and stared hard at the man, who, in turn, was looking properly bored with the conversation.

Just like that Crowley was looking at him and stepping in closer. Not quite close enough for the gesture to be a sign of aggression, but close enough to be surprising. Most people didn't tend to get aggressive with the men who could have them locked up.

"I didn't much take to being shot at, dragged behind a horse, or pissed on, Sheriff. I liked even less watching a woman get savaged by a herd of pigs who walked like men." The rage behind his glasses was nearly a physical thing, and Meade took an involuntary step back, while Pace stared at the both of them with a wide-open mouth.

"I'm a patient man, Mr. Crowley. But I have limits. Back away from me before I decide to take offense." He kept his calm, but it wasn't easy. There were few men who stood up to him in the first place and this one was deliberately insulting and aggressive.

"Take offense as you see fit. I confronted the men who committed a crime against me, and when they drew on me, I fired and defended myself."

Pace Peabody reached out and grabbed Crowley's jacket, his face set into a snarl. "You need to show some respect, mister! The Sheriff is here to decide whether or not to set you behind bars!"

Pace had been speaking even as he reached. His fingers caught the man's jacket and started to pull him toward himself. A moment later, Pace was staggering backward, clutching at his face and cursing under his breath.

Crowley had turned and driven his fist into the deputy's face. Then, as the man was staggering back, he'd turned to face the sheriff again as if any possible problem was already handled. His eyes flicked over to Pace. "You'd do well to keep your filthy hands to yourself."

"You'd do well not to strike my deputy, Mr. Crowley."

"Seems to me your deputy was asking for a whuppin'." That from Leather Apron, who crossed his beefy arms over his chest and scowled. Meade was beginning to think it was the only expression the man was capable of.

The undertaker chose that moment to show up. He climbed down from the horse-drawn sled he rode on and walked toward them, a virtual ghost in the snow-laden landscape. He was dressed in his formal finery, and he looked from one man to the next until he reached Crowley. The albino stared at the object of his attention with wide, unsettled eyes and if it had been possible, Meade would have said he grew a shade or two paler.

"I believe there's been an incident that requires my attention, gentlemen?" He ignored the expressions of the people around him. Not everyone knew him, or expected an albino, but Meade guessed the poor bastard was familiar with the looks of shock and revulsion that accompanied him wherever he went.

Meade nodded and turned his attention to the man. "There are several bodies, Mr. Slate. They should be attended to as quickly and discretely as possible, please."

He turned back to face Crowley and blinked in surprise. The man was gone. He looked down, just to make sure there were at least footprints, and there were. Then looked around.

Crowley was gone.

Fifteen people around and the man had vanished.

Meade shook his head. He liked the stranger less by the minute.

Dan Kaufmann

Dan Kaufmann stared at the crowd and scowled. He was uneasy, to be kind.

There were a goodly number of people in the saloon and most of them were still soaking wet and desperate to stay warm.

Not a good day for profits. Not at all.

Dan frowned and shook his head. "Hardly a good way to stay in business."

"There's the business of the merchant and the business of the Good Samaritan to consider." The words came from the mouth of a preacher. They were hardly a surprise. That the preacher was one of the people taking advantage of Dan's charitable mood did nothing to strengthen his argument.

Dan looked at the other man. The preacher was short, lean and kindly of face. He was getting on in his years and most of his hair had gone gray, but he was hardly ancient. Currently he was wrapped in a blanket and sitting near one of the woodburning stoves, and a bowl from his free meal was still near his left arm.

"All due respect, Padre, but being a nice person doesn't pay my bills."

"There are the bills we pay on earth and those we pay on Judgment Day."

He shook his head. The man would spout more of his self-righteous drivel every time Dan spoke and it was best to know when you were going to lose an argument.

Dan turned fast to his right and stared at a man who had just pocketed a spoon. "You can put that cutlery back or I can break your fool hand." The man tried to play innocent for a moment and then looked down as he put the spoon on the table rather sullenly. "Good choice. Now get the hell out of my saloon, before I beat your fool head in."

The preacher opened his mouth. "Well, now…"

"No." Dan looked his way and sneered. "Let God take care of his sorry ass and yours too if you say one more word about how charitable I need to be."

The preacher got a look on his face. Either he had a bad case of the burps or he intended to get all righteous. Dan didn't care either way.

"I just said no. I meant it." He pointed to the door. "Get out of here. Don't bother coming back in when your old butt gets cold, either. Just go."

He helped the spoon thief out of his chair when the man took too long. One hand opened the door, the other tossed the man out into the snow. The cold outside was harsh, but Dan didn't let that stop him.

One more withering look at the preacher had him leaving the premises under his own power.

"Folks, I've let you warm yourselves and eat my food. Now, unless you intend to pay me for drinking, it's time to leave." He made sure his voice carried. A few people looked hurt by his attitude, but most got the hint the first time around. Damned near everyone in the saloon stood up and gathered their belongings. As the exodus for the door started, Dan looked outside and saw the men coming his way. They were unusual simply because they were dressed well. The air outside was hideously cold, he knew that and regretted that he had to send people out into it. The men coming toward his saloon were coming out of that cold, but something about them set off warning bells in his head.

Dan looked at them, stared hard while he tried to understand what was wrong.

They climbed down from their horses and the animals danced nervously in the snow. Every last one of the equines looked ready to bolt. He thought about warning the men, but decided against it when he saw their faces. Each of them had slack features, their heads lowered toward the ground. They moved with a steady gait but did not swing their arms. Everyone he knew moved their arms when they walked but not the six men coming toward him.

He kept looking, almost catching whatever it was that puzzled him so much about them. It wasn't just the way they moved. No, there was something else.

A group of people left his saloon, shivering in the cold and gasping at the sudden change in temperatures. He saw their breaths plume out from mouths and noses, captured quickly by the bitter, cold wind.

Their breaths.

Dan felt a shiver that had nothing to do with the cold from outside. He looked at the men coming his way again and tried hard to swallow the dust that was suddenly covering his throat.

The men coming toward the bar did not expel a thick cloud of moisture.

Either they were already as cold as the weather outside, or they did not breathe.

Dan stepped away from the door. His ears were ringing. He wanted so much to move forward and close the doors, to lock them and then to hide away in the upstairs rooms, maybe even grab Eleanor—hands down the finest looking whore he'd ever met—to keep him company. He wanted that so badly that in his mind he was already halfway up the stairs.

Unfortunately, his body did not respond to his desires. Instead, he stood perfectly still and watched the men moving past the threshold, pushing through the tide of people still leaving the establishment and ignoring the looks and occasional comments of the people they brushed aside.

As they came closer, he saw them more clearly. They were pale, the whole lot of them. Their features were broad and flat, the faces of Indians, or even a few of the Mexicans he'd met. But the skin color was wrong, too white, almost as pale as that undertaker that always left him with goosebumps.

The one at the front of the group looked up at him and Dan felt his knees threaten to buckle.

Oh, Lord his eyes! What in the name of God is wrong with his eyes!

They were completely black, as dark as a snake's and the skin around them was scaly to boot.

The man smiled at him, but the expression was wrong, like the muscles didn't quite know how to move the way he wanted them to. His teeth were wrong, too small and flat, misshapen. Except for the canines. They were long enough to stand out and looked about as sharp as a good carving blade.

"I-That is, umm…How can I help you gentlemen?" He wanted so very much to tell them to leave, but the words refused him.

The one with the rattler's smile nodded his head loosely and sat down at the bar. "Whiskey. Six glasses. Leave the bottle." The accent was pure Navajo. Worse, even though the man was making a pleasant enough order, he reached for the Colt at his hip, making sure the handle was clear. His hand—so white that the dirt ingrained in the palm stood out—rested on that weapon.

Dan nodded his head and moved to the bottles behind the bar. Six glasses slid across the wood and he positioned them in front of each man as they settled in at the bar, doing his best not to stare.

Christ above. Every last one of them is so cold I can feel it coming off them.

His hand tried to shake as he started pouring from the bottle of Old Patron. He forced it to stay steady and licked his dry lips with each glass he filled.

Snake Eyes looked his way and nodded when he finished pouring. The rest of the men barely acknowledged his existence.

Three men were heading for the saloon. He could see them walking with the sort of strides that marked them as either confident soldiers or cocky gunslingers.

He prayed desperately that they would be soldiers.

As the men came closer, the six sitting at the bar stiffened, their heads cocking as if they were listening carefully to sounds that Dan could not hear. They could have been puppets on one set of strings their movements were so well coordinated.

Intuition is a wonderful thing. Dan listened to the instincts that told him to get the hell away from the six men. He walked to the other end of the large bar and made himself busy with wiping glasses. His knee rested against the shotgun he kept there, and he took some small comfort from the weapon's proximity.

The men coming toward the saloon were of grim disposition. They spoke little and looked at the streets around them like men who were expecting a conflict.

The ones inside the saloon, sitting only a dozen feet away, stayed frozen, waiting, their chests unmoving, no breaths causing a rise or fall where they should have.

Dan watched the men reaching for the saloon door and dropped down to the ground, holding his arms over his head and cringing.

The men at the bar turned and moved as one.

Hell was unleashed on the three strangers heading into the place.

Marcus Darbys' Gang

The plan was to get together the whole gang and discuss what had happened earlier. Marcus Darby was furious, and no one in his or her right mind planned on adding to his anger.

They'd agreed to meet at a spot away from where they were staying. The idea was simple enough to understand: According to Silas—and while most of the men thought of him as an odd bird, none considered him a fool—somebody who should have been dead was gunning for them. Unlikely as it seemed, they'd let a witness live. That would be bad news if they were found out.

The trio walked past a dispersing crowd of people and skirted the area where several horses were shifting nervously in the street. Seemed like everyone was in a nasty mood, most likely brought on by the storm the night before.

Broaddus and Dunlap were in foul enough moods, but the news that they could find themselves on the wrong end of a noose had only made them worse. Terwillier was stuck in the middle of them and trying to keep them calm enough to see the mess through to the other side.

It was Terwillier who opened the door to the saloon. He pushed in while looking toward Broaddus. "You need to calm your fool-self down before we get into worse trouble. Just wait until we hear from Marcus. He hasn't done us wrong so far."

Dunlap shook his head. "He said we were gonna be rich men, but so far all we've done is look for some trinkets. I'm tired of this. I have a family waiting for me back home."

"We all have families, you damned fool." Broaddus spat the words.

Terwillier stepped into the saloon just in time to watch the fat man behind the bar drop toward the ground.

His eyes moved naturally toward the commotion, and just as naturally toward the six men turning and rising from their seats.

Had they still been the same creatures they'd been before encountering the gang, Terwillier would not have recognized the men. He made it a point not to remember the faces of the people he murdered. He slept better when he didn't recall the details of their deaths, or their screams.

His lack of recognition made no difference to the Nameless. He was one of the men they sought and that was enough.

Six bullets smashed through muscle, organs and bones, blasting Terwillier into so much meat. His body was lifted clear of the threshold and thrown back by the impacts. To Broaddus and Dunlap it looked like a mule had kicked their comrade backward.

They weren't foolish enough to miss the signs. Six men stood and fired. Terwillier died. The math was easy. The two men had not entered the building and they intended to keep it that way. They ran in opposite directions, Broaddus to the right, in front of the large window, and Dunlap to the left, along the wooden wall of the saloon.

Broaddus dropped low, duck walking and letting out a few squawks of panic in the process. The window exploded above him, sending thick blades of glass flying through the air. The man dropped to all fours and scrambled as quickly as he could while Dunlap pulled his revolver and took aim at the door.

They were combat-hardened. They had seen more violence in the last few years than most people would know in their entire lives, and their recent stint as pillagers had not made them any softer. By the time the first of the men from inside came through the door, Dunlap was ready and Broaddus was standing again, his face bloodied by glass shards.

The pale man cleared the door and looked first toward the horses outside, then toward Dunlap. He turned just in time for Dunlap to fire a slug into his chest. The gun he'd been carrying dropped to the ground and the man staggered toward Broaddus, making no sound as he fell. The blood that spilled from his body was thick and black.

Broaddus took his time, aimed, and blew the bastard's head off.

The second one never even cleared the window. Broaddus took him down as he tried getting out through the broken panes of glass. Two bullets punched a hole in his stomach and shattered his left thigh. Dead or not, he fell to the ground.

After that, there was silence from inside. No one moved, no one spoke.

The horses outside finally lost their nerve and bolted, knocking aside two people who'd moved in their direction at the sound of the gunfire. A young man who was caught by a moving animal was knocked to the ground. His arm broke on impact and the horse that came down on his ribs did nothing to help the matter. He was the lucky one. He lived.

The man standing with him, a preacher by trade, was caught first by the horses and sent staggering, and then caught by the bullets that came from inside the saloon. None of the shots were fatal in and of themselves, but the perforations in his abdomen bled slowly and dragged the poisons from his bowels into the rest of his body.

While the preacher crawled across the ground and tried to hold in his entrails, the remaining men inside the bar stepped out in unison.

The two on the left moved together and fired their weapons at Dunlap. He backpedaled as quickly as he safely could, pressing his backside to the wall and praying hard for an opening to fall back into. He got what he wanted in the form of an alleyway. Snow half-blocked the passage but he managed to fight his way through the drifts and get himself a little breathing room.

He wanted to check on Broaddus—despite their constant gripes with each other, he considered the man his best friend—but there was no time. Two men were planning to kill him. That took precedence.

He checked his weapon quickly. Five bullets left. He had no idea how many people were after him aside from the two, so he knew he had to make each shell count.

The first of the strangers came forward, his face expressionless, and Dunlap took aim.

And froze in his tracks as he recognized the face of a man he'd already shot dead once. Unlike Terwillier, Dunlap remembered every face. He never forgot a kill. It was more than a resemblance. The skin color was wrong, the eyes had changed, but the dead man facing him had a thick scar across one eyebrow, a cleft that was hard to forget.

Dunlap kept staring as the man pulled the trigger and fired. And then fired again. Again. The bullets took pieces of him with them and he fell back into the snowbank that he'd been forcing out of his way. His bladder let go and his bowels voided themselves as he watched the dead man coming closer to him. Fires were burning in his chest and stomach but he couldn't move, couldn't put them out.

He coughed out a wad of bloody phlegm and tried to lift his hands to ward off what was coming next, but his hands were useless, twitching things that refused his requests.

The two men moved closer until they were looking down at him. Dunlap tried to speak, but the blood that spilled from his mouth got in the way of words.

The pale men both took aim and fired.

Dunlap's eyes blew out along with the back of his head.

Broaddus fared a bit better. The two who came for him were looking at the height of a man's face when they climbed from the window, but he'd already made a change in altitude. Broaddus sat on his ass in the snow and took careful aim. By the time the first of them came for him it was already too late. He fired a bullet through the man's chest that took out his heart and a piece of his spine. The pale man fell back hard and fast, dropping his revolver in the process.

The second one came for him and he fired again, cursing as the bullet missed.

He fired a second time and the bullet slapped across the man's hat and took the cover with it, but did no other harm.

Broaddus fired again and heard the empty noise of a hammer striking a spent shell. He could have wept.

The shotgun blast that struck the stranger cut him in half, or close enough that no one would have seen the difference. The shot tore muscle and bone apart and scattered the ruin across the snow. The pale man flopped across the ground, his body shuddering and twitching, his legs dancing a mad tattoo even as thick black blood soaked the snow.

The man who ran the saloon stepped through the window and looked down at his victim. His face was red with fury as he cocked the pump and then fired again, the blast ripping the pale face apart.

"Done with this! You hear me? I'm done with this! No more killing!" His voice was nothing in comparison to the sound of the shotgun blasts.

Broaddus stared up at the innkeeper and started to say his thanks for having his life saved.

The first man he'd killed reached into the snow, picked up his weapon, and fired a bullet through Broaddus's throat.

The man who'd come to his aid stepped back, his eyes as round as saucers in his head, looking at the dead man that slowly dragged himself to his hands and his knees, the smoking gun still aimed at Broaddus.

The last thing Broaddus saw was the barrel the dead man aimed at his face.

CHAPTER EIGHT
DEALING WITH THE DEAD

Lucas Slate

Lucas Slate stared at the sheriff and shook his head. "All due respect, Sheriff, but I do not have the time to gather more bodies. They'll have to be brought to me."

"That's decidedly inconvenient." Meade's voice was lower than usual, and a touch louder. "I've got six more bodies, and they need to be off the streets."

"I haven't finished with the men you had me pick up earlier. I can only be in one place at a time, and with the business I'm getting just at the moment, I need to handle the bodies carefully to avoid troubles."

"They're dead. What sort of troubles are they going to cause?" The man's voice was irritated.

Slate put down the hammer he'd been using to build another coffin. "There are diseases the dead can spread. There are coffins that I have to build. I simply do not have the time to keep up with the bodies that are showing up here."

"Well what do you recommend I do then?"

"Hire someone to bring the bodies to me."

"Maybe I should hire a different undertaker."

Slate allowed himself a thin smile. "I understand Wilkes and Son are quite good. But I don't know that they'll come here clear from Denver. And if he survived, there's a fine gentleman in Summit Town who's a bit pricey but would probably make the journey. Name's Sanderson."

The sheriff scowled deeper and shook his head. "I'll have them here as soon as I can."

"If you should happen to run across some spare lumber, you might want that collected as well. I'll be using the last of my supplies to handle the bodies I'm already dealing with."

"Are you completely mad?"

"No, Sheriff Meade, just busier than I've been in the last four months. Nine bodies, then six more, then a shootout that brought in four, and now you say there are five more bodies to consider." Lucas reached for the hammer he'd set down and then looked at the man again. "Currently, I'm supposed to handle twenty-four bodies with enough supplies to accommodate twenty if I scrimp a bit."

"What is this all about?"

Those unsettling blue eyes stared at him for a long moment, and then a thin smile—humorless at that—creased the man's white face. "It would seem that's your purview, my good man. You are the law in these parts now."

He could almost see the man's heart beat harder.

The sheriff left a moment later.

When Lucas was working on the third coffin for the victims of the storm, the sheriff, Pace and four rugged men began bringing down the fresh kills.

They worked diligently at hauling corpses while he closed the third casket and began nailing the lid in place. Each of the bodies had a name, and he made sure to write them on the lids.

Ten minutes later the bodies had been brought down and the burly men came back down the loading steps carrying a collection of scrap wood. Most of it was barely acceptable for charity work. None of it would suffice for the paying customers.

"That's the best I can do." Meade's voice was gruff.

"It's quite sufficient, Sheriff, and thank you for your efforts." The man was angry and, in hindsight, Lucas realized he'd probably overstepped his boundaries earlier. He was not an equal. Not in the eyes of most men. He was a freak. He was just a slightly fortunate freak in that he was needed for the present time.

The Yankee seemed mollified by his answer and calmed down noticeably.

Within five minutes the men had left him alone again. Remarkably few people wanted to deal with the dead, a fact that he had long since accepted.

The bodies were in hideous shape. Much like the last batch he had gathered. Like most of the bodies he'd recently come across. Violence is an ugly thing and it stains what it touches. The marks were impossible to ignore.

Lucas looked over the new bodies carefully, and as he always did, he meticulously examined and collected the valuables to set into drawers and later into the safe he kept for just such reasons.

He stopped when he found the albino. The corpse was as pale as he was, but with hair that was dark as midnight. He looked at the ruined face on the man and shook his head, unsettled. Even with the blood pooling in their bodies, few corpses managed to look as pale as he did.

The features were Indian. He could distinguish that much. And as he studied the ruin near the eyes, he saw a small bead wedged into the flesh. It wasn't an accidental thing. He could tell that much. He looked at the stone for several seconds, noticing the intricate swirls and convolutions along the surface of the thing.

With delicate grace he peeled the flesh away from the wound that held the pebble. The stone was revealed easily but did not fall free as he might have expected. Lucas leaned in closer, eyeing the oddity, and then nudged the stone with his index finger. The object did not move. It may as well have been nailed into the bone of the skull. He pressed harder, until the skin of his fingertip ached from the pressure.

"Odd." He frowned as he contemplated the situation.

In the long run, he decided he couldn't bother with the stone. It was a trinket at best, and not something he could waste time to retrieve. Besides which, there was little chance that the man's family would be coming for his valuables, or that they'd have an address he could ship the items to.

Lucas left the stone alone.

And in the process he saved his own life.

Anson Meade

The sheriff rubbed at his jawline and waited for the man sitting in front of him to answer his question. Sadly, the small wooden carving he was working on seemed far more important than Anson Meade.

"No, Sheriff, I wasn't at Kaufmann's. I rather wish I were, but not this time." Crowley looked at him over his glasses, his eyes sharp, and Meade had no doubt the man was taking his measure.

Sadly, he was fairly sure the man wasn't impressed with what he saw. That wasn't a notion that sat well with him.

"So it's just a coincidence that the men who were shot down happened to be associates of the fellas you claimed shot at you?"

"Maybe they're just not nice people." Crowley's fingers deftly scraped away thin layers of wood with a knife that seemed unwieldy for the task.

"This has to do with your claims that they were killing people when they shot at you."

"It does indeed."

"I don't know where you're from, Mr. Crowley, but I don't take to vigilante justice."

"I've told you who shot at me. I shot back. I was a better shot."

"According to Silas McPherson, who was with the men you killed, you threatened to kill him and every man with him."

"I didn't threaten anything. I gave fair warning." The blade moved faster, and the shavings fairly fell like the snow from the night before.

"You see, that's my problem here, Crowley. You need to not threaten people. You need to not give them fair warning. I've had enough deaths in Carson's Point. I don't need any more."

"No one ever needs more death. Some people just want it."

Meade's hand slid to his revolver. "You seem to want to be argumentative. Let's just take this the easy way. Let's you and I walk down to my office."

"Are you planning to arrest me?" Crowley set the carving down. It was a startlingly good bust of Pace Peabody's face, complete with a dazed expression that was fairly common on the man.

"I want you to come with me and stay as my guest until I get to the bottom of this matter. I don't want any more deaths in town."

"If you want to avoid deaths, you should consider arresting Silas McPherson and any of the filthy pigs he's associating with." Crowley made no effort to rise from his seat.

"Come with me, Crowley." He lowered his voice and scowled.

"Not without a good reason." Crowley put away his whittling knife.

Meade felt his headache growing worse. He was trying to be very patient. "I've already told you I don't intend to have any more deaths in town."

If Crowley was the least worried about him he hid it well. The man flashed a small, smarmy grin. "Ever? That could require some serious sorceries...."

"Now you listen to me, Crowley! I'm about done with this nonsense."

"I've been listening all along." The man's expression did not change in the least despite the volume of Meade's bellows. "I have a room at a hotel here in town. I don't feel a particular need to be your 'guest' at the local jail."

The man was infuriating! Rather than reaching out and throttling him, Meade reached for his weapon, fully intending to hold Crowley at gunpoint until he could get him to the jail.

He had the grip in his hand and had pulled the revolver halfway from its holster when Crowley aimed both Peacemakers at his face.

Despite the desire to piss all over himself, Meade managed to keep his pants dry. His hand held the half-drawn weapon and slowed down its ascent.

"You plan on finishing this, Sheriff?" Crowley's voice was as cold as the wind outside. "The smart choice would be to put that back where it belongs and back away before I decide I don't like you."

"Mr. Crowley-"

The man drew back the hammers on both guns.

"I look like I'm in the mood to discuss this?"

Meade pushed the weapon back into its holster, trying hard not to shake.

"Listen well, my good man. Never, ever draw on me unless you intend to kill me. I'm rather fond of a good debate. Like as not I'd have gone with you and stayed as your guest in a jail cell, but as it stands right now, I don't see that as much of an option."

He looked at the man carefully and saw the quiet challenge in Crowley's eyes. "Fair enough." He nodded his head and took a step back. Crowley slid his Peacemakers back into their holsters and noticeably relaxed.

"Now then, Sheriff, I don't intend to do anything but defend myself. Before I got to this town, the men I shot and their associates killed several people and did their best to make the attacks look like they were done by Indians. They killed one man, one young boy and one woman. They violated her first." Crowley's eyes stayed on his the entire time he spoke. "I don't think they much liked me finding out what they were doing, because they almost killed me, too."

"And how long ago did this happen?"

"Three days, maybe four."

"You'll understand my hesitation, Mr. Crowley. I'm not seeing any wounds on you."

"I heal fast. Also, they tried to strangle me to death."

"And you let them?"

"I am one man and at the time I was unarmed. I didn't have much choice."

"But you lived through it?"

"I'm stronger than I look."

Meade sighed. He could probably push the matter. He would if any more deaths occurred, but he had doubts. Crowley was faster at drawing a gun than any man he'd ever seen. It was exactly that simple. He didn't much feel like getting himself killed in the line of duty. He'd have to be better prepared than he was.

"Fine. You're free to go. But stay well away from Silas McPherson and the men he's with. If you go after them, I'll have no choice but to lock you away."

He paused for a moment and then leaned in again, staring hard. "You may not feel I'm worth your trouble, Crowley, but whether or not you're worried about me, you'd do well to avoid getting into a jail cell. The judge in these parts is Alan Keene, and he's got a decided love of hanging men who break the law in his territory."

Crowley said nothing. He simply kept looking at Meade and reached for his carving again.

Meade left a moment later, his knees shaking only a little, and held his breath until he was well away from the man.

Marcus Darby

Marcus shook his head. "What the hell is going on in this town, boys?" His voice was trying to be cheerful and failing.

Silas stood behind him, pacing furiously. He knew that meant the man was thinking about possibilities, ways to handle their troubles without losing any more men.

The rest of the gang sat or stood as they pleased in the stables that had become their temporary home.

"Why don't we just get the hell out of town, Marcus?" Eliot Whittaker was normally one of the quietest men in the group, but he was also one of the most damaged. He hadn't been the same since the shootout at Fort Sumpter and that had been almost a year ago. He was not a coward, but he whimpered every night while he was sleeping. "There's been nothing but trouble since we got here and the storm's over."

Silas looked over. "Because at least one man in this town knows who we are." His voice was low and calm, but his eyes glittered with anger. "He's killed three of our men and he damn near killed me. We leave him alive and word gets out about what we've been doing, and I'd wager we'll be hanging from gallows by the time summer comes around again, Eliot."

Marcus shook his head. "Wouldn't have been a problem if you hadn't gone to the sheriff to report the shootings, now would it?"

"Four-to-one odds, Marcus!" Silas spun on him fast. "He killed three men and never got a bullet and I was shooting at him. He's fast and he's a mite annoyed about us trying to kill him. He also doesn't strike me as the sort to let bygones be bygones."

Marcus lifted his hands in surrender. "That was uncalled for on my part and I'll own up to it." He sighed. "We've lost six men, fellas. We can't afford to lose any more. Not if we want to get out of this with the riches we were promised." He fingered the bag around his neck unconsciously. "I can feel them, boys. I can feel the treasures we're looking for. They're either in this town or very, very close. We need to get this finished so we can all go home again."

Damned near every man in the room listened to him raptly, with the fervor of the faithful listening to a thunderous sermon.

The only exception was Silas, who simply nodded his head in agreement. There'd be arguments later, but. with few exceptions. he never disagreed with Marcus in front of the men. He wouldn't have a moment earlier, but Marcus had been foolish and called him in front of everyone. He was lucky Silas hadn't shot him dead on the spot. Silas was a good second, but a decidedly bad man to make an enemy.

He needed to remember that. Of all the men he ran with, the last one he needed to offend was Silas.

"So tell me about this man, the one who did the killings. Do you know his name?"

Silas nodded his head. "I heard someone call him Crowley. He dresses like a dandy. He stands like a man of breeding, but he shoots like the devil himself."

"Crowley?" Marcus shook his head. "Never heard the name before."

"He said we soiled a woman and killed her family."

"That hardly limits the people we've dealt with." Marcus kept his voice low and dry as he responded.

"A woman." Silas stared hard. "Only one. Most of the recent…indiscretions…have involved more than one woman or girl." Oh, the quiet anger as he spoke. Marcus felt a quick flare of shame before he forced the guilt below the surface again.

"The redheaded one. She had a family. After we were done with them, we had the man who interrupted…." Whittaker spoke again, his eyes wide.

"That's not possible." Marcus waved his hand in dismissal.

"How so?" Silas looked his way. Silas, who had been looking through the wagon and then managed to be elsewhere when the rape took place.

"Because I killed him myself. He wasn't breathing when I pissed in his face. Well, not the second time at least."

Silas shook his head. "This one was breathing. And smiling like a madman."

At that last comment, Marcus shivered. The man he'd hauled behind his horse had screamed and cursed and bled. He'd tried hard to hold onto the ropes that bound him and he'd grinned furiously as he was dragged.

Impossible. Simply impossible. The dead did not rise.

Lucas Slate would have disagreed.

Pace Peabody

Pace Peabody looked around the undertaker's work area and tried not to panic. He hated dead bodies.

"You wanted to see me, Mr. Slate?"

"You or the sheriff, Mr. Peabody."

"Call me Pace. Everyone does."

"Then call me Lucas." His thin lips flashed a quick, tentative smile, before he grew somber. "Pace, somebody has stolen corpses from me."

"Beg pardon?"

"Somebody has come into my shop and taken two bodies, for whatever reasons they might have."

Pace bit his lower lip as the world tried to gray out on him. The very notion made him feel sick. "Why in God's name?"

"I assure you, I have no answer to that, Deputy."

"I-Did you have names for the bodies?"

"No. They were from the second shootout. Both of the bodies in question were as pale as me."

Pace nodded. His face felt wrong on his head. "What, uh, what do you want me to do about it?"

"I've absolutely no idea. I felt I should report the incident."

Pace scratched the back of his neck and looked around the room. There were dead bodies to spare. He couldn't find a comfortable spot to stare at.

"I suppose I can tell the sheriff, but I don't know what he's going to want to do, either."

"That should be sufficient." Lucas reached over one of the corpses and adjusted the flaps of skin at the neck. Pace felt his stomach do a slow roll.

"I'll, I'll get right on it."

"There's one other thing, Pace."

"Yeah?"

"There are footprints."

"Footprints?" He frowned.

"Oh yes." Lucas pointed to the ground. He looked and saw the bloodied trails that headed for the loading doors off to the side of the room.

"Did they drag them? The bodies?"

Lucas looked at him with pale eyes and that whimsical almost smile on his face again. "Well, I rather doubt they got up and walked away."

Pace looked at trails. He could clearly see bare footmarks in the red streaks.

"I hope you're right about that."

The Dead Men

They gathered together in the cold beyond the town's limits. There were still six of them, but the changes were happening faster. The decomposition was showing on the two who'd been shot down, and there were shapes sliding under their slack, pasty skin.

The changes were not painful. They were very inconvenient.

The one who had developed scaly skin looked at his hands, at the odd shapes of his fingers, and scowled.

An hour earlier he had summoned his brethren to his side without speaking a word. Then he had called to the one who raised them, unaware if the thing would respond.

As the sun began to set behind the trees and the fires began to show more easily at campsites, the Skinwalker appeared, walking over the snow as easily as a man walks on solid ground.

He looked at the six of them and nodded his head with satisfaction.

"You are growing well, ripening." He spoke their native tongue.

"What is happening to us?"

"You are becoming what you are meant to be."

"We are men."

"No. You are other now."

"We only want revenge, but the weather slows us and there are too many men." He looked closely at the Skinwalker and wondered if what the creature in front of him was had anything to do with what they would become. He suspected the answer was a yes.

"I will help you one more time. After that, I will watch and judge whether or not to help you again."

"We need better weather. We need more warriors."

The Skinwalker smiled, his thin lips peeling back from dried, blackened gums and yellowed teeth.

"The weather I can fix. I will show you how to gain new warriors."

He kept his word. Had the sorceries he showed the Nameless been offered to them when they were alive, they'd have fled in fear. Some powers are too dark for human beings to accept.

They were the Nameless. They were no longer human. They learned the sorceries eagerly.

When he had shown them the spells they needed, the Skinwalker started walking away, and stopped as if suddenly remembering something he had let slip his mind.

The Skinwalker danced, a writhing, serpentine movement that should have been impossible for any human form to make. He called and howled and spat vile sounds into the air as he thrashed and threw his body through violent contortions. Within four minutes he had finished. His body did not sweat, but his skin was flushed enough to almost resemble a living thing.

"Your weather will be better when the sun rises." Without another word the Skinwalker stepped away, heading back to the women he had taken as payment.

They were no longer wounded by the taking of their women. They could barely remember the mates they'd had in their previous lives. The Nameless were creatures of passions that had nothing to do with love.

CHAPTER NINE
BAD WEATHER

Pace Peabody

Pace Peabody looked out his front door and shook his head. The weather was not at all what he'd expected. First, there was the mud. When the sun set it had done so on a field of snow that covered everything, even half of the buildings. Now there was no sign of ice or snow and instead there was a muck-covered world of mud and filth.

The road was half washed away, lost in a stream of water that had softened the oiled dirt roads to the point where the hardpack had been obliterated.

He stared, trying to absorb that simple change and to accept that the temperature of the air was completely wrong. There wasn't even a bit of cold left. The breeze he felt belonged to summer, not winter.

"What do you make of that?" No one answered his question. There was no one to answer it. He checked his pocket watch and winced. He'd surely be late for work if he changed all his clothes. So instead he simply shucked the overcoat and set it to the side. He'd hang it later. There was little reason to worry about what others might think. He lived alone.

The closest thing he had to an ongoing relationship was the money he spent on Eleanor Hardy now and again when his urges outdid his common sense. He contemplated the fine-looking whore as he slogged toward the jail and his duties. The mud was thick and sticky and left a layer of itself on his shoes despite his best efforts.

The stable boy from the Waite Inn was standing outside the closed door of the sheriff's office when he arrived, looking anxious as he nearly hopped from one foot to the other. Lewis Winthrop was a slightly slow man who'd been hired because he was good with horses and worked for remarkably little.

"What seems to be the trouble, Lewis?" He nodded a greeting as he spoke to the younger man.

The man shook his head and waved his arms. His lower lip was red from being chewed on. "Every horse in the stables is gone."

Pace shook his head. He'd heard about the same sort of problem from the Piedmont yesterday, and while he'd done what he could there wasn't all that much to be done. No one saw anyone taking horses away and there weren't any tracks.

"Did you tell the sheriff about this already?"

"No sir. I ain't seen no one but you." His eyes shone with unshed tears and Pace understood why. The loss of the horses meant the simpleton would lose his job if they weren't recovered immediately.

"You see anyone last night? Or see any tracks?"

"I don't know. I don't know what I saw."

Pace rolled his eyes. "Come on then, Lewis. Let's go take a look around."

It shouldn't have been possible for this to be a problem. Somewhere around thirty horses had been taken in the last day, and finding them should be easy enough, because, really, there was nowhere to take the animals.

Nowhere at all.

Jonathan Crowley

Jonathan Crowley sat down for a meal, ready to eat after a hard night of gambling. A few men who didn't mind being parted from their money had set up a game of poker and he'd joined them. He didn't win every hand, but he won enough. After many, many years, he'd fairly well mastered the art of the bluff and cards held few secrets for him.

Wealthier by almost three hundred dollars, he ordered his breakfast and then ate in solitude—his preference—while listening to the other people at the hotel. The Piedmont was apparently the closest thing to a luxury spot in Carson's Point. That was one of the reasons he'd chosen the place.

The folks around him were mostly calm, but a few were outraged by the disappearance of their horses, despite the promises of management that they would be found. He could understand that. Horses cost a small fortune, and they were the only way most of the people around him had of getting around.

He didn't much worry about that. His ride was always nearby if he needed it. His hand slid down and touched the side of his hip where his weapons should have been sitting. They were always nearby, too. He had taken care of that after his confrontation with the sheriff.

It wouldn't do to be caught without his firearms in a town where several people were likely already aiming to see him dead, the sheriff quite likely among them. Very few men took well to having strangers threaten them with death. Funny how that worked.

The people around him were worried mostly about their horses, and though they didn't dare speak it out loud, he could tell a few of them were worried about his disposition. Less than a day after he came to town, he'd already developed a reputation as a gunslinger and now he'd been in two fights.

His plan for the day was to go to his room and sleep.

He had no intention of dealing with the unnatural weather, or the horse thieves or the grave robberies that were being whispered about. None of it mattered to him.

He could think of better things to do with his time than help foolish people take care of their problems.

Molly's specter settled in the chair across from him, not speaking at first but looking at him with lost, frightened eyes.

"Jonathan, they took my body from the ground."

He looked around the room to make sure that no one was listening in on his conversation. There were enough people nervous about him. He didn't need to give them any more reasons.

"I heard something about that." He did his best to look nonplussed.

"Help me, Jonathan."

"No. I'm already helping you. It's a body."

"It's *my* body." Her face was half lost in shadows that didn't exist. The light fell on her skin in a position that had nothing to do with the sunlight in the room, a sign that she was getting further and further away from the influences of life. Maybe that meant she'd be moving on soon and that the haunting would stop. He couldn't quite bring himself to cast her away. Not yet. She hadn't annoyed him enough yet.

"It's meat rotting in the ground."

"No, Jonathan. They took me. They took all of us."

"Who took you?" He leaned in closer, his eyes narrowed, his voice little more than a whisper. "Who stole your body, Molly? Was it the men who took your life?" If so, he'd finish the matter all the sooner. If not, he'd ignore the problem and get his sleep.

"No. They were something else. I don't think they were even human."

Crowley swallowed the dryness that filled his throat. That explained a lot. More than he wanted to think about. Those few souls who knew him would have understood why. Little could kill Jonathan Crowley, but many things could hurt him. However, he healed quickly in the presence of the unnatural.

He could heal from almost anything, even being dragged behind a horse and left for dead. Even being frozen to the ground.

He shook his head. "I can't help you."

"You must!" her voice was a loud, desperate plea that no one in the room could hear but him. Her face twisted, a mask of anger and sorrow. "No one else can help me, Jonathan Crowley. No one else knows I'm even here! I'm nothing! A ghost!"

She sobbed and he slid back his seat, no longer the least bit hungry for the food in front of him.

"You're dead, Molly. The only thing that can hurt you now is your memories." A lie. There was so much more than that, but none of it was his problem, his domain.

A quick look told him that several people were now deliberately not noticing him. They'd heard his one-sided conversation. They didn't understand it, but they heard it.

"Jonathan, please!" Her voice broke and echoed through the room and he turned away, refusing to look at her lovely, wretched face.

The silence around him was as loud an accusation as any he'd ever heard. He ignored it as he walked slowly to his room.

No one living had asked for his help.

He intended to keep it that way.

The Dead Men

The Nameless stayed outside of Carson's Point. They sat on the horses that had now been tainted with their touch for long enough to no longer be afraid, and they watched the opened gates of the town.

One of them, a thin man who had always believed in peace while he was alive, reached out and ripped a small oak sapling from the ground. With no idea as to why he was doing it, his hands began running over the wood, easily peeling away the bark and running hard-tipped fingers over the surface in smooth, steady strokes. In very short order the wood had been stripped and smoothed, and still the group sat outside and waited.

Somewhere inside the wall around the place, the men who had killed them continued to breathe and that was not acceptable. That simple fact had to change and soon.

They could feel the pull of the men they sought. Not in any way that would have made sense to them when they were alive, but the stones in their skulls sang to them, called to the winds and listened to a song sung only for them by the men they wanted dead.

They could have gone in on their horses and taken what they wanted, but at the moment they were too tired and the people in the town were too many. Like an anthill that had become overrun, the tents and wagons around the town carried more of the white men and a few who were darker. They all hovered around the bloated town and picked at whatever they could find to continue living their miserable lives.

The Skinwalker had shown them new, wondrous magic and they had used them while the storm raged. Their voices had called out to the universe and made requests, which had been answered favorably.

It was best not to think about what, exactly, had answered them. Even the dead can be driven insane.

After almost an hour of silence, save for the light scrape of hard fingers on wood, the thin man lifted his newly formed spear above his head and then brought it down hard, striking the ground with a blow that called forth thunder, but no lightning. The sound pealed across the landscape and echoed from the distant mountaintops.

And moments later, the dead clawed their way from their graves. Cold flesh pushed and strained against wooden caskets and defied the weight of fresh soil and waterlogged mud until they broke free from their wooden prisons. They rose and walked with unsteady motions, refamiliarizing themselves with gravity and motion. The bodies of the dead were not meant to walk, but they did, and they changed in the process, rebuilding the systems they needed to achieve the impossible. Their hearts did not beat, their lungs did not breathe, but their senses worked well enough to tell them what surrounded them and who they had to obey.

They did not reason. They merely served.

In the woods not far from Carson's Point the dead stood and waited, unmoving, unblinking, for the command that would send them after the living.

They had specific targets.

They were prepared and they were patient.

Sooner or later the sun would set and then they would move.

At least that was the plan. Everything changed when the first bullet hit one of the Nameless in the heart.

Moses Blake

Moses Blake took careful aim, checked the wind, and when he was satisfied, pulled the trigger on his buffalo rifle.

The shot was true and caught the monster that had killed his wife in the chest. The impact knocked the rider from his horse and sent him into the mud and dung behind the animal.

He aimed again and shot the second of the riders. The results were exactly the same.

By the time he started aiming for the third, the riders were in motion, charging toward Carson's Point and the wooden wall of the gate where he was standing.

The walls had been built to withstand Indian attacks and to hold soldiers. Despite the missing pieces of wood that had been stolen away by the desperate or the lazy, there were still plenty of places where a man could stand several feet off the ground and take aim at would-be attackers outside of the town.

Had he had a wall like this around the homestead, his family and friends would still be alive. Or at least he liked to think so.

The baby squealed and thrashed against his back. He did his best to ignore it completely as he sighted on the third rider.

The thing was pale and as expressionless as he remembered from when it leaped at him and cleared the distance that should have kept him safe. He had no intention of letting it get that close a second time. The bullet caught the Indian in his shoulder and knocked him off the horse. A glance told him the left arm of the thing was barely intact, but there was no expression of pain or loss as it climbed to its feet and looked in his direction.

The other three demons rode hard, heading toward him and reaching for their weapons. He tried to aim, but they were moving too fast and the ground beneath them was uneven. Their bodies shivered and jumped too much for him to properly sight on them.

The baby screamed, thrashed against his back from the makeshift papoose. He shook his head to clear away the irritating sound and set down the buffalo rifle. The shotgun was better for what he needed now.

"Hey! Hey, mister! You can't be shooting at people!" Somebody was yelling at him. He didn't have the time to look into the situation.

The riders were still coming fast and hard and the one closest to him was aiming. They were still out of range of his shotgun, but that didn't mean he was out of range for their revolvers. Different weapons had different purposes.

Moses ducked down and felt the impact of bullets striking the wooden barrier like hammer blows. He heard gunfire after the fact and stayed where he was, sidestepping further from the gate's entranceway as he prayed to avoid getting his fool head blown off. The baby screamed even louder and he continued to ignore it.

"I'm going to get the sheriff you damned fool! The war's over you can't just shoot whatever you want!" The voice was indignant and nervous.

Moses almost turned and shot at the man. He decided to look over the wall instead.

The riders were closer, close enough now for him to return fire. He aimed—not all that carefully, as the weapon was loaded with shot—and fired. The pellets slashed at dead white skin and blasted away meat and gristle the color of manure. The rider didn't so much as flinch, but instead took aim and shot. Moses ducked again, hoping he could avoid the bullet.

He did. The baby did not. The screaming stopped around the same time Moses felt the blood of the infant running down his back.

"Ah, Jesus! Help me Lord!" He fought back the angry tears that wanted to fall. He should have left the baby with the whores, but they wanted little to do with a black child or any other extra mouths to feed.

He lunged back up and fired again, aiming almost straight down as the rider thundered through the gate. This time the shot struck the man across his skull, his shoulders and the horse as well.

Pump. Aim. Fire. The shot struck again and finally the pasty bastard fell from the horse, which shrieked as it fell to the ground mortally wounded.

Pump. Aim. Fire. The next rider's leg exploded. The shot hadn't been clean but it did massive damage. By luck or otherwise, the horse was not injured.

Pump. Aim. The bullet slammed into his arm and shattered the bones at his elbow. Moses howled and fell backward, stumbling off the walkway and grunting as he hit the ground.

The riders drove past, momentum carrying them away. Moses watched them and felt his world grow cold. Shock was trying to steal him away already, when he wasn't prepared to call his job done.

The pale men did not come back but kept riding into the town proper. Moses could not rise, though he struggled to.

Failed again. Lost to a group of monsters. The blood of the dead infant sank into his clothes, his skin and Moses felt the tears in his eyes as the darkness swept him away

---

Albert Miles

The trapper fell onto his bed only moments after having finally dressed. He was cold despite his feverish skin and the sweat that stippled his brow.

He closed his eyes and saw his father's face within his mind and shivered all the harder. His father was not a good man, nor was he kind, though he often played the part for those around him.

He seldom bothered trying to appear kind for his son when they lived in the same house.

Albert Miles had never been a kind soul, not as far as his son could tell.

They'd last seen each other over fifteen years earlier and that suited the trapper just fine. If he never saw the man again his life would not be made less pleasant for the loss.

His father's voice echoed through his skull. *I need you boy.*

He shook his head. "Go to hell, I'll not help you."

His father's laughter was a cold thing.

The pain that caught him came on so suddenly that he never had a chance to scream. Instead, he bucked and thrashed and rolled himself off the bed, smashing into the hardwood floor and bruising himself.

The trapper died a moment later, lost in a maelstrom of pain.

Albert Miles opened his eyes as his son died and smiled. He looked down at his body, strong and young and fresh. So much better than the form he had worn for the last few centuries. The trapper was big and strapping and strong. Just the way he'd wanted his son to be.

"Boy, what made you think there was a choice in the matter? I only allowed you to live so I could have a proper replacement."

He rose from the ground and stared around his hotel room. The sweat cooled quickly now that he had settled himself in the new form.

Off in the woods near Summit Town his old body rotted into the soil, decades of time quickly catching up with the flesh that had defied the years so cleverly.

He listened to the wind blowing past the hotel and got accustomed to the body he'd stolen from his whining, useless pup of a son. The boy would have never amounted to anything of value, he knew that. He'd known it all along.

In the last week Albert Miles had lost his wife, his home and his son. His plans had gone horribly wrong and the decade he'd spent preparing for the rituals he'd committed in Summit Town had proved little more than wasted time.

Still, he smiled.

There were other plans and other possibilities.

He closed his eyes and focused on the ether, the world beyond common senses. He heard the song of the Skinwalker, felt the dead rising from the ground, noticed the stones that hummed in response to the Skinwalker's whims and he also felt something entirely different. Something-

Albert Miles recoiled as if burned. He stumbled back and caught himself before he would surely have fallen on his rump.

"Is that even possible?" His voice was weak and trembled as he thought about the implications. "Did I just feel the Hunter?"

Everything changed at that moment. His plans had been to take what he needed and leave the area immediately, but that wasn't possible if the Hunter was present. He'd heard vague rumors, of course. He'd even questioned a few of the nightmares he'd summoned from Hell about the existence of the Hunter and had never been able to decide if the claims the demons made were true or merely more attempts to confuse him, for demons were nothing if not clever creatures and capable of deluding anyone who grew careless.

"The Hunter." A smile played around his mouth for a moment and then faded away.

He looked to the mirror on the wall near the washbasin and studied his face. He'd planned on shaving away the beard his son had grown but quickly changed his mind. Better to avoid being easily spotted by the Hunter. Better still to avoid being easily recognized if he did get noticed. The beard would work as a disguise for now.

"The Hunter…." His voice trailed off, lost for a moment with a sense of wonder he thought he'd surely grown past by now. "Imagine the possibilities." He allowed himself a smile as he washed his face, and headed out of his room. There was a new game to play, and he would have to be very careful indeed.

Lucas Slate

Lucas stood in the unexpected warmth and shivered anyway. The water in the holes had lowered, revealing the ruined, emptied caskets.

Meade stood next to him and removed his hat, lowering his head in prayer.

"What sort of swine takes the dead from their graves, Sheriff Meade?" His head ached; his eyes seemed too large for his head and, despite his best efforts, his hands kept clenching into fists.

"Try to calm down, Mr. Slate." The sheriff's voice was hardly any calmer. "I'll find out who's responsible. I swear it."

Lucas shook his head. "Every last one of them, Sheriff. All of them. Even the ones I hadn't marked yet."

"You sure it wasn't animals?"

"Oh, it was animals. Just not the sort that live in the woods."

"How can you be sure?"

"There's easier prey for animals than a body buried six feet down." He looked at the sheriff. "You saw the holes. They were deep enough and then some."

The man nodded his head. His brow was drawn down like a thundercloud and his lips were pressed into an angry sneer.

"Somebody had to see this. There are too many bodies gone for no one to see."

Lucas shook his head and sighed. "It's dark here. There's no need for lights. No lamps or torches and it was raining. I doubt we'll get lucky enough to find someone who was watching."

"I surely hope you're wrong." The sheriff shook his head and looked around, his eyes scanning for anyone or anything that might be helpful. There was nothing to see.

A barrage of gunshots echoed from the west, toward the main entrance into the town. Meade looked up quickly, his eyes sharp, and took two steps, automatically moving to protect Lucas.

He opened his mouth to speak, but the sheriff was faster. "You'll want to step back, Mr. Slate. I see men coming our way."

He didn't listen. There wasn't time. The riders came in fast, their horses pounding into the mud and sending thick sprays of muck into the air with each movement of their horses' hooves.

The undertaker stared and felt his eyes fly wide. He recognized one of them. The one on the left, riding just as hard as the others, had been brought to him just the day before. He'd been dead at the time.

Lucas stepped back and gasped. He'd reported the corpse missing to Pace Peabody when the body vanished. Now the dead man that he had seen on his table less than fifteen hours previous was riding toward him, just as white as he had been before.

"Dear God have mercy on my soul...." His hands clutched at his chest. Lucas had accepted many things in his life, but the dead rising was not among them. And there was no doubt at all for him that the man was the exact same one he'd seen and reported stolen. The wounds on the body were the same, though they did not bleed as he'd have expected.

The riders stormed past, never bothering to look toward the sheriff or the undertaker. Lucas was grateful for that.

"What the hell!" The sheriff spoke sharply, his voice breaking like a young man in the throes of puberty, and Lucas understood. He too had recognized the man.

Meade's hand reached for his revolver again, and Lucas reached just as quickly to stop him. "No."

Meade looked his way with a nearly murderous expression.

"They've not drawn on you, Sheriff. And at least one of them should be dead already. You are outnumbered." He spoke steadily, despite the tremor running down his arm. "I don't believe either of us would benefit from you taking aim at those things."

Meade nodded his head and relaxed, his face easing back from anger into a stunned expression.

"That man is dead." Meade's statement was direct and to the point.

"Yes, I know. I believe they all are."

As they spoke, three more horses charged past with riders. Two of the animals were bloodied and moving as if the injuries caused them no pain.

Lucas stared long and hard, focusing on the wounds that should have killed the animals. They did not bleed. He could see muscles in motion, bared to the air, could see bones when the torn muscles shifted the right way, and still the animals stormed along at a mad pace.

The two men kept staring after the riders. Neither spoke nor moved for several moments, and when they finally did, they moved after the charging animals and their riders against all common sense.

Sometimes, the need to know outweighs the need to survive.

Silas

Silas saw them coming first. They rode at an insane pace, the sort of speed that almost guaranteed the horses would slip and fall in the treacherous mud, and yet as he thought that very thing, three additional horses joined the first group.

The way they rode, the way they stared, was enough to send off alarm bells in his head. They did not look around but came directly for the stables without hesitation. There was no doubt in his mind what the men wanted.

"Marcus! We've got trouble!" He bellowed the words and drew his weapons, ready to do what he had to in order to survive another day.

Marcus came quickly and brought the rest of the men with him. The riders were clearly visible, the light nearly making their pale skin glow, and showing their dead faces all too well.

Marcus strode from the stables and cursed as he looked at the men. He recognized them. He couldn't help it. They'd only been killed a few days before.

Silas recognized them too, and while he was not a cowardly man, he was frozen in that moment. The dead did not rise. It could not happen.

Marcus grabbed him by the collar and hauled him back as the riders closed the gap. Silas felt the ground move under his heels and staggered, moving at last to keep from falling on his backside in the street.

With one hand pushing Silas, Marcus used the other to draw and fire. He wasn't alone. Two of the men who'd answered the call also took aim.

The bullet Marcus fired struck the closest rider in his chest and Silas saw the damage the missile caused as it spun through flesh and exited the back of the rider's torso. The pale thing shuddered as the wound blew out in its back, but did not fall.

The riders stopped.

They'd been coming hard and fast, and, if he'd been asked, Silas would have sworn they meant to kill every man in front of them. Instead, they drew up short and came to a halt, all six of the creatures—Silas could not consider them men, for they were too wrong to be men—staring hard at Marcus.

No. Not at his face at least.

Their eyes were not right. Their faces were dead, expressionless and bloated. Their bodies did not seem quite right, though Silas couldn't have expressed why to save himself.

They stared, the whole lot of them, not looking at anything or anyone except for Marcus. And Marcus, in his turn, stared back, just as frozen, with a strange expression on his face. His eyes were narrowed in concentration, his hand steady as he kept the revolver aimed at the closest rider.

The men stood frozen on both sides, lost in their own worlds of contemplation. All Silas could do was focus on the impossible and whisper prayers to Jesus and God alike.

They might have stayed there until they took root, for all he knew, but strangers came from behind him and from behind the riders.

A heavyset man came from the Piedmont and moved in their direction, his eyes first on Silas and Marcus and then on the riders. He had a thick beard and mustache and a wild mane of hair. He was dressed in his pants and a shirt that was collarless and half unbuttoned, and his expression belonged on a bear rudely awakened from hibernation.

There was something about the man that drew Silas's eye; that called to him, though he could not have said exactly what that something was.

The man looked at the riders and turned his head slightly, studying them as intently as they stared at Marcus.

And then the sheriff came up with another pale freak. This latest one was on foot and while he was surely as white as the riders, he was obviously not one of them.

Meade looked at the whole tableau, his expression as puzzled as Silas felt, and then he pointed at the riders. "You! All of you!" As one the riders turned toward him. "Get off those goddamned horses!"

The bear of a man smiled a tight little grimace. "Damned indeed."

The closest rider spoke, his voice low and unsettlingly cold. He spoke with no inflection, not even an accent that should have been present from damned near any red man who'd learned to speak English. "This isn't your concern. Leave now, before we begin."

"Hell if I will. I'm the sheriff here, and you'd do well to get out of this town before I lock up the whole sorry lot of you." He was doing his best to stare the rider down, but his luck was poor. The dead man—and the longer Silas looked at the riders the more certain he was that they were in fact deceased—did not intimidate.

"What the hell do you want?" That was Marcus. His patience was at an end, and Silas could tell it from his tone alone.

This time it was only the one who talked that turned his head. "Revenge." The word was spoken with the same lack of concern or emotion. The hand that drew a bead on Marcus was completely steady. The sheriff reached for his piece and the remaining riders did the same. By the time he was ready to fire, five dead things had weapons aimed at him.

The wounded horse let out a belch and vomited a stream of black blood. Otherwise, everything was silent for several seconds.

Marcus cocked the hammer on his pepperbox, the four barrels unwavering.

And everyone with a weapon opened fire.

Meade's aim was true. His bullet struck the rider in the chest and sent the man and his ride staggering to maintain their balance.

The riders fired true as well and blew away any chance Meade had of bragging about his marksmanship. The bullets tore him into shreds. Sheriff Anson Meade died on the spot.

The spokesman for the riders shot Marcus in the chest. The bullet struck him directly over his heart, but instead of killing him, it hit the bag he sported around his neck. The satchel burst open and the impact sent the man sprawling. He didn't take the time to assess his damage, but instead started standing immediately, even with the barrage happening around him.

And behind him the albino let out a scream and backed away as a spray of blood and gristle slapped across his torso. He was a smart man. He turned and ran from the volley of bullets. What was left of Anson Meade was on the ground and on the poor fellow who staggered away, shaking his head and clutching at his left arm.

Silas looked toward the riders and reached for his guns. They were already changing their targets and one of them was aiming for him.

The shaggy man from the hotel nodded his head and spoke softly as he stepped back. Whatever the situation, it did not seem to involve him.

Marcus fired a second time and the other two joined in, all of them concentrating on the same rider, firing again and again to make up for their earlier failure to kill the pale man.

The patrons of the Piedmont ran for cover, those few who had been on the street, and Silas couldn't blame them. Madness had taken over and there was no reason for a sane person to stand still and watch it.

A bullet caught him across his left thigh, a grazing wound, thankfully, and he yelped as a line of fire carved itself across his leg. And as he hollered, he shot at the rider, and missed.

Garrett, one of the two men who'd come to help, screamed as a bullet took him in the hand and continued in through the meat of his chest. He dropped his gun and reached for it just in time to catch another bullet, this on in the side of his head. He continued reaching for the revolver and wound up on the ground, slumped and dead.

The man standing beside him was a good soldier, one of the few who had resisted the urge to treat the people they met as lower than animals. He died next, four of the riders doing to him what they had already done to the sheriff. Lars Johnson never made a sound before the bullets took him down.

Silas didn't have time to watch anything else. Marcus grabbed his shoulder and pushed him hard, running already and trying to get away himself. The dead men moved, spurring their unnatural steeds onward, toward the men who ran. One of the horses stomped down on Lars's chest and another ran over what was left of the sheriff as they continued onward.

Silas didn't wait to be told. He ran, his long coat flapping behind him as he took long strides back toward the stables. The other men were there. They'd help.

The noise came from behind him was worse than the loudest peal of thunder. The air shook and his teeth rattled in their sockets. His eyes bulged as the pressure changed around them and, a second later, he was lifted from the ground and thrown forward. There was no elegance to his ascent. He rolled through the air screaming out his shock. The world roiled and shifted madly around him until he was landing in the muddy lawn of the hotel.

Before he could recover another explosion blew through the air, sending him sliding through mud that slipped past his lips and into his nose.

A third, final explosion rocked the ground under him and Silas curled into a ball and held his breath, waiting for the end of the world to finish with him. When it didn't, he finally risked opening his eyes.

The landscape had gone through several changes. The riders were lying scattered across the ground, some intact and others literally blown into pieces. Their horses were ruins, broken or blasted apart, though one of the poor things continued to scream its pain out into the air.

Silas stood up shakily, balancing himself against the way the world still wanted to tilt.

Marcus crawled through the mud next to him and slowly rose, his broad face a stunned, filthy mess.

Nearby the bearded man from the hotel stared at what was left of the riders and turned back toward the Piedmont. "Gentlemen, kindly take care of your own messes in the future."

Without another word the man walked away.

Marcus coughed violently, spitting mud and water from his mouth in the process.

"Get the boys. Get them now. We're done with this." Marcus's voice was shaken.

"What the hell did he do?" Silas stared after the burly man. "How did he do that?"

"Don't much care. Let's get out of this town, now."

Their plans made, they prepared to get out of Carson's Point. Unfortunately, it wasn't meant to be. The world that had gone mad when Silas wasn't looking was not yet finished with them.

CHAPTER TEN
COMPLICATIONS

Pace Peabody

The death of Sheriff Anson Meade did not go unnoticed.

Pace Peabody looked around at the office and shook his head. Until another man could be appointed—assuming there was any interest in doing so—he was now in charge of the peace in Carson's Point, and that thought scared him enough that he wanted to reach for the bottle of rye he kept in his bedroom.

Sadly, his arms weren't quite long enough for the task.

He didn't have time to get comfortable before he was on the move again. There were bodies to clear up, and he was now the man in charge of making sure it happened.

"Gotta get a hold of Slate. He'll handle the bodies." He smiled, pleased with himself at the notion. He was not, in his defense, at all aware of what had happened at the cemetery and did not make the connection to the workroom of the undertaker.

The bodies of the dead had been gathered together. Meade's corpse was handled with deference. He was new in town, yes, but had been working hard to keep the town safe. The two men from the Piedmont were lying in the road, covered by sheets that had been commandeered from the hotel by Pace himself. Better to owe for a few sheets than to let the dead sit in the street.

He stared long and hard at the bodies and tried to wrap his brain around the idea of handling the mess. It wasn't going well.

The gunslinger came out of the hotel, wearing his odd collection of clothes, his eyeglasses glittering in the sunlight. Nearly everyone who had walked past had stopped to stare at the bundles on the ground, but the man completely ignored them, save to avoid actively stepping on the corpses.

He wasn't wearing his weapons, not that Pace could see, and that made him breathe a little easier. He had no desire to get himself shot.

Then Jonathan Crowley offered a quick flash of a smile—unpleasant enough to make Pace want to back away—and kept walking.

Pace turned away from the man, ready to head back for his offices or maybe to the undertaker's home, anywhere, really, that didn't involve looking at the bodies in the street. He did not like dead things.

Miles, the trapper, came out of the hotel now, looking around with an odd expression on his face. His broad nose was wrinkled and his lips were turned down in an expression that could have been a small sneer or a stuck sneeze as far as Pace could tell. All he knew for certain was that he had never run across that sort of expression on the man's face before.

"Morning, Miles."

The man looked his way and forced a quick smile. His eyes just as quickly flicked away again, locking on the back of the gunslinger.

"Morning, Sheriff Peabody."

"Heard about that, did you?" He shook his head. The thought was still too intimidating.

"Not really, no. But it makes sense, doesn't it?"

Pace nodded his head. There really weren't many other choices available.

"Tell me about that man, Sheriff. Tell me what you know about him." The trapper pointed at Crowley's distant form. The gunslinger kept walking, heading for the gate into Carson's Point.

"Name's Crowley. Jonathan Crowley. I hear he's a scary fast draw."

"Odd he isn't wearing any guns...." Miles' eyes stayed on the distant figure until he was completely out of view. Only then did he look at Pace again. "Still, it's been a day for oddities."

"Did you see what went down here, Miles?"

"Yes. The end of it, at least. The men in the stable seemed to be minding their own affairs when the riders came on them."

"I heard there were explosions...."

"Not that I heard. Then again, it wasn't my fight to be around, so I chose to be elsewhere." He wore a tight smile that never reached his eyes.

The man reached down and plucked a stone from the mud. He examined it for a second and then wiped it off and pocketed it. Pace shook his head. Maybe the man thought there was gold in the pebble.

"Can't say as I blame you, Miles." He looked down at the bodies again and shivered. "At least it's over."

"Is it?" The trapper looked his way again. "Are you sure about that?" He squatted again and grabbed another lump from the mud.

Pace didn't have a good answer to that, but he answered anyway. "I hope so. I really do."

Jonathan Crowley

The shootout hadn't gone unnoticed. Jonathan Crowley had seen the entire thing and resisted every urge to head down and help the dead things that had been shooting at the living filth responsible for trying to kill him and far, far worse.

He could have gone to help. He did not.

Any way he looked at it, the situation required that he not be seen or heard in the middle of it.

The last few years had been mostly peaceful, and he wanted to keep it that way.

He walked through the woods not far from Carson's Point, heading unerringly for his steamer chest. He wanted his notes. He wanted to start working out the details of the manuscript he would write, a scientific examination of flora and fauna of a new world, unseen by scholarly eyes.

The ground was soft beneath his feet, but he trod carefully, barely disturbing the leaves and patches of snow that had survived the violent rains.

Unnatural rains. He wasn't a fool. He knew all too well that the pleasant weather was a sign of sorceries. Worse, of magic with which he was unfamiliar, and that was a rarity in any age. He pondered that fact as he kept moving toward his prize.

Molly walked with him. He didn't see her, but he could feel her presence. He heard her when she spoke to him. "You could have killed them, Jonathan."

"I told you before, Molly, I can't kill them for you."

Her anger came to him like waves of heat.

"I have to do other things. I can't settle into answering your requests. If I did, I'd be breaking the rules."

"What rules?"

"You wouldn't understand." He was explaining himself to a dead woman. The very notion made him shake his head. He didn't deal with the dead. He didn't offer them comfort or vengeance or anything. That was the way it had always been. His life was chaotic enough without offering solace to the dead.

"You can't leave me like this, Jonathan."

"How am I supposed to help you, Molly? You're dead!" He forced anger he did not feel into his voice to make a point. "Your husband let you get raped and killed, not me." A flash of guilt. The words were too harsh, deliberately savage in an effort to drive her away. He knew they would fail.

"He was protecting Billy." Her voice was hurt. The anger was still there, but a deeper, bitter sorrow moved with it.

"Damn it, Molly, let me see you." He didn't want to expend the power to see her. Something was out here that had a power of its own and he wanted to avoid being noticed.

She showed herself as she was last seen by a living man, nude and bruised, her long hair loose and wild. She was once again lit by a different light than the one that affected him, and she was heavily shadowed. More unsettling, the shadows showed clearly the background behind her. He made himself look at the shadows. Looking elsewhere was distracting. She had been a lovely woman.

"I could still offer you pleasures, Jonathan." Her voice was soft, desperate but quiet. She'd tried seducing him once when he was asleep and now offered what pleasures she could to him while he was awake.

He shook his head. "At my worst, I wouldn't take advantage of a woman that way, especially not after what you've already been through."

"I'm offering, you're not taking."

"And were you raised to be a whore, Molly?" He let the edge back into his voice. Anything to make her stop this insanity.

She vanished instantly and stayed quiet, but he knew she was there, lingering, waiting for him to make his move and finish what he had started.

He'd made it most of the way to his steamer trunk when she spoke again. "Jonathan, no one else will punish them."

"Something else is already punishing them, Molly. You don't need me to kill them when something else is already doing it."

"I want them killed for me, Jonathan! For William and Billy and me." Her voice broke. He took the risk and looked for her and found her nearby, hugging herself against a cold that only she felt. "Where are they, Jonathan? Where are my boy and my man? Why aren't they here with me?"

"Maybe they're at peace, Molly. Maybe they moved on and maybe you should as well."

When she looked at him again the hatred and anger burned inside of her, made her as brilliant as the sun to him though no one else around them would have noticed. "I cannot rest until they're dead!"

"And I can't kill them for you, Molly. It's forbidden."

He grabbed his trunk, which lay exactly where he had left it, undisturbed. The trunk carried most of his life within its confines: volumes of papers and his scant collection of clothes. It weighed close to three hundred pounds. There was no one around, so he hoisted it onto his shoulder and started walking. When he was closer to town he'd set it down and drag it. For now, he wanted to get back to the hotel and away from the woods that reminded him too much of his defeat and Molly's violation.

"Kill them for me anyway, Jonathan. Please. Avenge me."

He didn't answer her. He didn't dare.

He was close to agreeing, even with full knowledge of the consequences.

"You know what my problem is, Molly?" He spoke mostly to hear himself. Molly had already gone away to wherever she went when she wasn't haunting him. "I'm too nice. It'll come back to haunt me."

He moved quickly, forcing himself back toward Carson's Point. The warm weather wouldn't last much longer. He could feel that as easily as he could feel the sun on his skin.

When the cold returned it would do so with a vengeance and he intended to be back in his room and safely locked away before that happened.

There was no reason for him to take care of the situation as far as he was concerned. Jonathan Crowley didn't want to hunt down the dead things. He didn't even much want to kill the men who had done him wrong.

He just wanted to be left alone.

We seldom get what we want in this world. That much was true of Crowley as well.

Albert Miles

There were dead men in the road beneath his window, and there were other things, stranger things, laying with them in the mud.

Albert Miles looked at the bundles below and watched them carefully. Six of them were moving.

He looked away and frowned to himself, his eyes found the man walking back toward the hotel from wherever he had gone. Crowley pulled a steamer behind him, taking his time to ensure that the trunk was not damaged by friction. Not that he had to worry. Miles could see the complex spells that had been woven onto and into the luggage even from a distance. Most would not have seen them, but he had been alive for a long while and had gotten very good at seeing what should have remained invisible.

"What are you, Mister Crowley?" He kept his voice very low, the better to make sure the thing walking toward the hotel did not notice him. Some entities hide among humans to hunt, others merely to stay hidden. Some were there for different reasons, and whatever the case with Jonathan Crowley, he wanted to make sure the thing did not decide to pay him any attention.

Was that creature the legendary Hunter he had heard of? He didn't know but the possibility fascinated him.

He had plans of his own for the world and they had nothing to do with the stranger coming toward him and dragging a trunk that could have carried anything at all.

Marcus Darby

The dead Indians stood up at the same moment. Each and every one of them. There were no warning bells, no sudden alarms to let the people around them know that the dead were not willing to rest peacefully. Instead, they simply stood and started walking toward the edge of town.

There were several people present when it happened. One woman and one man, both fainted dead away at the sight. Even in times of war no one expects the dead to stand up and head off on their own. That they were dead was obvious. They had open wounds on their bodies and dried blood crusting their flesh and their clothes alike.

One of the dead things—it was later agreed by the witnesses that this one had scaly skin and the most unholy eyes they had ever seen—called out in one of the Red Man's vile tongues and stopped long enough to watch the reaction. The two white men they had murdered stood up as well, moving with jerky, spastic steps and twitching almost constantly. Anson Meade stood as well, swaying, his eyes still closed, and then followed.

By the time Meade was walking for the gate of Carson's Point the word of the obscene migration was spreading through town. Some people laughed the notion off. Others did not.

At the Piedmont, the men who were planning to leave Carson's Point for greener pastures had a change of heart. There were two deciding factors.

First among those reasons was simply that dead men had risen and walked away from town. Silas watched it happen and fell to his knees, praying for forgiveness, begging the Lord for mercy. There was no immediate response, but at least the dead things went the other way instead of coming for him.

Marcus watched too. He stood stock still and felt at the spot where he'd earlier had a small leather pouch full of treasures. Three of the stones were missing. The others were now in his shirt pocket, except for the one Silas didn't pull out of his skin.

The bullet that should have killed him had struck the pouch and sent its contents driving into Marcus's chest like a hammer. The small stones were hard enough to survive the impacts, and all but the three that had vanished, wound up stuck in his skin, stinging and aching like mad. Silas carved them out carefully when they finally had a chance to rest in the stables again, but that single piece he didn't retrieve was too deep into meat. He'd tried carving it free, but only managed to worry it in deeper. Without surgery the stone would stay where it was.

At least it was safe.

The wound was small and it itched as if he'd rolled himself in poison oak, but it was survivable and no blood was seeping through the bandages.

Silas was a good field medic, even if it seemed he was becoming a bit of a coward.

He'd proved that twice in the last few days. Marcus would have never believed it, but there had been two shootouts where the man ran rather than fight. He couldn't blame the man overly much. He could even understand the fear to a certain extent, but his second's willingness to flee wasn't helping him trust the man.

He kept that to himself. Best not to worry the others too much.

Silas looked over at him, his skin pale and sweating, and shook his head.

"What do we do now, Marcus? Those things are out there, waiting on us."

He stayed quiet for a long while and thought about that. When he finally answered, his voice was deceptively calm. "We stay right here. No one can sneak up on us, and we've got numbers. Even with seven of us dead, we're doing all right."

Silas licked his lips and nodded, listening raptly.

"When they come back, we'll be ready for them."

"There's another problem." Silas spoke softly, his eyes averted.

"What?"

"The gunslinger. The one who shot at me yesterday. He's in the Piedmont."

Marcus considered that for a few seconds again and finally nodded his head.

"So go kill him."

"What?"

"Take three of the boys with you. Find out what room is his and go kill him." His voice was calm and deadly serious. "He killed some of ours, Silas. I don't know why, and I don't much care. Any way you figure it he's a threat to us and needs to die."

"The sheriff-" Silas started.

"Is dead. His deputy looks about as dumb as a mule. Go handle this, Silas. You know what he looks like. You know who he is. Catch up with him and kill him." Marcus stepped closer as he spoke, staring hard all the time.

"What about the Indians?"

"I'll handle them if they come back." Marcus allowed himself a smile he did not feel. He didn't think the dead things would come back too soon. Like anyone else, they needed to lick their wounds. That was why this was the best time to kill the gunslinger. He wouldn't be expecting it.

Silas finally nodded his head and went to get the others he'd need. It was time to get matters settled.

Marcus leaned against the wall of the stables and clenched his fists, fighting against the sudden pain that lanced through his chest. It was an excruciating heat, and all he could imagine in his mind was that it was coming from the pebble lodged in his skin.

For the briefest second he imagined a seedling taking root, driving tendrils into hard-packed soil. That was the only image that fit what he was feeling in his torso.

The pain abided but the image lingered.

Marcus wondered what was growing in him and shook the thought away. He wasn't entirely sure he wanted to know.

————

Moses Blake

Moses Blake watched the dead things stagger past him and hid himself away. His ears were ringing with his pulse, and his mouth was so dry he couldn't swallow.

He'd managed to push himself into the shadows next to the wall, and to slide deep behind some thick scrub grass that had grown long enough to conceal him with relative ease.

Somewhere along the way he'd lost the dead baby. That was okay. He could still hear the baby boy's wailing cries in his head and in his heart.

It seemed that hatred was not enough to guarantee him his revenge. That notion was enough to leave him on the verge of tears.

The air was still warm but he shivered, shock and blood loss stealing his body heat.

The bastards should have been dead. He'd killed them enough times to guarantee it. Still, they walked past him and took their new recruits with them.

Not long after the last of the dead things had gone past—he didn't think it was long, it was hard to tell with the way he kept drifting—more folks showed themselves and looked at the gates as if whatever was on the far side of it was both miraculous and frightening. He supposed that was the proper way to feel. Anger drove him harder than anything else, however. He wanted the white demons dead, truly dead, not moving around as if they had the right to live and breathe.

He shivered again and let his forehead rest against the thick blades of sawgrass that scraped along his brow and tickled his face with a threat to draw blood.

The voice from above him was soft and deep. "I know you. You're one of the settlers out by the westward trail. Buffalo soldiers, I believe."

"I am." His voice was weaker than he'd expected and he wondered if he was dying.

"Looks like you got yourself into a bind."

The damned fool was stating the obvious like it needed stating. "Reckon I'm probably dying." Even saying the words was painful.

"You could be saved. Your arm will never be the same. I can see the bone pieces sticking through. No surgeon I've ever seen would save it."

"Don't much need to live anymore, I don't reckon." His wife, his dreams, all destroyed by the nightmares he'd seen leave town.

"You sure about that?"

Moses stared at the ground and closed his eyes.

"Are you sure?" The man spoke again and this time he squatted down until he was close enough for Moses to feel the man's breath on his face. "Are you absolutely sure? Because I can fix you. I can heal your wounds and give you back your life."

Moses had grown up with stories of the Devil and the bargains he would make. Old Satan, he talked sweet and made promises in exchange for souls. Moses had never been to a proper white man's church, but he had been raised a Christian and heard plenty of tales.

"You trying to steal my soul, Old Scratch?" His words were slurred, but he managed to open his eyes and look up at the man. He was dressed in furs and he had a thick beard and mustache.

"I have no need of souls. I have one of my own." The man smiled, not unkindly, and leaned in closer. "I have need of a good shot, one who can help me take care of the dead things that just left this place."

Moses chuckled. "Now, see, I think I'd have given my soul to you to hear those words."

"No need." The man's hand touched his arm and pressed down hard on the broken bones and flesh. The gesture was unexpected, the pain so intense that he could not scream, could not even whimper.

A second later the pain was gone, replaced by an unexpected warm flow of blood into flesh that had been starved since he was shot.

"My name is Miles. We're going to be working together for a while." Strong hands pulled and Moses did not fight against the hands that helped him up. "Long enough to finish this insanity at least. Does that sound like a plan to you?"

Moses looked at Miles. He was a bear of a man, large and strong. He liked him, despite the fear that the man was Lucifer in disguise.

"Yessir, it does. It sounds like a fine plan to me."

"I have a room at the Piedmont. Let's get you a warm bath and a meal. And what is your name, my friend?"

He almost laughed at the idea of a white man calling him friend but decided against it. He'd met a few men he might have called a friend if he dared. "My name is Moses Blake."

"Moses, let's get you a good meal and a bath. Some sleep might do you good too."

"Ain't no hotel I ever heard of lets my kind stay on a bed."

Miles smiled through his shaggy beard and laughed softly. "We'll see about that." He spoke with such confidence that Moses let the subject drop.

He let the man lead him, still weak, still surprised to be alive. He thought for certain that he was a dead man and now, somehow, here he was walking and talking dealing with a man who wanted the same thing that he did, the destruction of the bastards that killed his family and friends.

"The Lord works in mysterious ways." He knew there was more to the saying but couldn't remember the words.

The trapper looked at him and patted his back as he smiled brightly. "That he does, my good man. That he does." The man kept the companionable arm across his Moses's broad back and they walked together toward the Piedmont. If anyone thought it strange for a white man to tend to the needs of a negro, they made no mention. Stranger things had already occurred that day.

Stranger things still were yet to show themselves.

The Skinwalker

The Skinwalker moved slowly around the town, his eyes narrowed in concentration. Where he walked the mud refused to spread, leaving his feet remarkably clean and dry. The cold was already creeping back into the area, but temperatures were not the sort of distractions he bothered with.

He camped close to the spot where Jonathan Crowley had been roped and dragged. The area was ripe with the echoes of violence and degradation and the atmosphere suited him and nourished his spirit as surely as the dead infant he'd found earlier fed his flesh.

He called out to his seeds and frowned when they answered.

The stones he'd used to create the seeds were common enough, but the ability to carve them properly and to nurture them, that was a special thing. In all his years walking the earth—which numbered longer than the Europeans had known of the land he dwelled on—he had only made seventeen of the seeds. They took time—which he had—and power—

which he also had—but they were a risk. The seeds were just what he called them, a chance for him to create more Skinwalkers, just as the Trickster had created him once upon a time. But like the spirit that had given him his new life, he was not a farmer or a nurturing being. He placed the seeds and watched them try to grow solely because it amused him. If too many of them took root, he risked making competition for his dominance. That would not be allowed. Still, for the time being he found the competition fascinating.

He whispered to the seeds and they whispered back. Their response left him puzzled. He spoke to them again louder, with more insistence and craned his head to listen.

They answered a second time and confirmed what he thought he had heard. There were too many responses. He had planted seven of the stones; six seeds he carefully settled in the skulls of the freshly dead. And now almost twice as many of the seeds responded. Their voices were not the same. They sang a different answer in words he had never heard before and the Skinwalker nodded as he realized the truth. These were not merely his seeds that returned his call. They belonged to another of his kind. He had seen others, of course. Not often but enough to know that he was not the only one of his kind. But this? To know that the others had learned how to create seeds as well?

He spoke a third time, calling out to the spirits that even now took root in human flesh, living and dead alike.

Satisfied with the response he received, the Skinwalker started back for his encampment. There were things he had not yet done with his women, and he wanted to complete his work with them.

The seeds were not quite ready to bear fruit, but they would soon, within days, not weeks. That thought amused him, and he intended to be ready when the time came.

Until then, he would wait and listen.

Skinwalkers always came into the world hungry. That much never changed. They were consumers, devourers. Best of all, they ate everything and took whatever was left into a storm of destruction when they were done with their feasts.

He would watch and he would wait, and when they were done he would welcome another of his kind into the world. Just one. More than that, and he would find other ways to handle the matter.

CHAPTER ELEVEN
DEAD MEN WALKING

Jonah Pratchett

When does a person know that everything has gone sour? When, exactly, can a soul know that there is no turning back from the bad things coming your way, no place to go, or to run, or to escape? It's probably different for every person.

For a few people in Carson's Point, the revelation came not long after dusk.

The sun set and the cold came back with the darkness. The odd heat of the day lasted exactly long enough to make people cringe when the frigid weather swept in. People who had taken off their thickest coats went to put them back on, and throughout the town fireplaces were lit to fight back the cold.

The winds that howled into the area brought a hard freeze with them that tried to bleach away every color with a thick layer of frost. They also brought the dead back to Carson's Point and the dead did not rest well.

Jonah Pratchett worked as a stable boy. The money didn't matter. The money went to his family to keep the bills paid. What Jonah cared about was being around the horses. Everything about the animals soothed him. At twelve, there was little about life in the town that he liked, but the horses made up for everything.

He stood in the stables and looked after his charges, preparing to head home as the cold intensified. The horses were fed, their stalls were cleaned, and he had earned a good night's sleep. There were four stables in town and two of them had already been attacked. No one knew what had happened to the horses taken, but they were definitely missing.

Alan Hopewell came into the stables carrying a shotgun. Hopewell was a big man, a good deal older than Jonah, and not much on conversation. He had been hired to watch the horses at night and keep them safe. Jonah didn't much care for the man or his disposition, but he was glad to see him there just the same.

Hopewell nodded his greeting, and Jonah waved sheepishly in return. That was the end of the conversation. They would never be friends. He wasn't sure Hopewell even had friends and wasn't about to ask to find out.

As he walked out into the bitter cold, Jonah took one look back at his charges. Normally he would talk to each of the horses and possibly even pet their faces, but with the older man in the room it didn't seem appropriate.

As he started turning back to the door something shifted in the darkness. Jonah tried to focus on it, caught by the sudden motion, but when he looked more closely there was nothing to see.

He left and in so doing saved himself from a very bad death.

The screams started two seconds after he exited the stables. There are certain sounds that are hard to forget. The sound of the first horse dying froze Jonah in place. It was not a noise he expected. They'd been fine a moment before.

Jonah sprinted toward the stable doors and stopped only when he heard Alan Hopewell's shotgun firing thunder into the air. The man yelled something incoherent at the same time, but the words were lost under the horse's dying shriek and the explosive fire from the weapon.

And something else, a hissing noise that was too loud by far, too violent. The ground shook even as the man watching the horses fired his weapon again. Oh, how he wanted to reach for the door, to save the animals that were his charges, but Jonah's hand refused to do as he told it.

Desperation can make a man or a boy do strange things. Fear can calm those impulses down. Rather than forcing his way into the stables and a pine box, Jonah called out in a voice that broke and strained. "Somebody! Anybody! Help!"

Not fifteen feet away he saw a man standing and looking in his direction. The man stared hard at him, a cold look in his eyes that Jonah could just see past the spectacles that hid them.

A sigh, soft as a lover's kiss, slipped past the man's lips and he shook his head. "I guess it was only a matter of time."

Jonathan Crowley moved fast, his feet sliding over the ground with unnatural grace. Jonah watched the stranger and tried to understand how it was that he crossed a mud puddle without getting filthy. It made no sense. In the long run that fact was hardly important, not in comparison to the horses, but it was decidedly peculiar and caught his attention.

The spectacled man reached out and grabbed Jonah's arm, pulling him off his feet as he moved toward the door to the barn.

"Nothing personal, boy, but you need to not be here any longer."

"It's the horses! Something's hurting them!"

"Yes, I have ears and they work just fine. Now go away." The man had an expression on his face that said he couldn't care less about the horses, or about Jonah, for that matter. He looked offended, as if someone had deliberately set out to insult him, rather than ask for his assistance.

Another scream from inside, this time from Hopewell, a sound so completely unexpected that it once again froze Jonah in his tracks.

The stranger was not as easily shocked. He pulled the door open and slipped inside, his long face pulling into a smile even as he stepped into the darkness.

Jonah was not brave enough to follow him. Instead, he slid closer to the wall and looked inside through a gap between the boards.

The lamps still burned in the stables, allowing him to see that most of the horses were uninjured and panicking. They reared and kicked at the walls and did everything they could to get away from the nightmare in the center of the room.

Through the boards, he saw the hole broken through the hard packed dirt. The pit was several feet across, and the thing that lifted from it was almost as thick. It was a massive, flabby thing that wavered in the air and shuddered, a high screaming noise coming from several gashes along its sides. They weren't cuts, he realized, but mouths. Every one of the screaming orifices had teeth, long and sharp and in a few cases bloodied.

The stranger crouched in front of it, his hands in motion, his eyes fixed on a part of the beast that was too high up for Jonah to see. There was no sign of either the horse that had screamed or of Mr. Hopewell. But there were patches of red splashed across the ground and the wood of the closest stable wall.

Jonah opened his mouth to call out to the stranger, to warn him to be careful. While he was preparing to speak, the first dead man reached him and grabbed at his face.

Jonathan Crowley

He resisted the urge to kill the boy, but it wasn't easy.

Jonathan Crowley was fully aware of the things going on in the town. He didn't know the cause of the dead people rising, but he was neither deaf nor blind. He heard people talking and had seen the last conflict from his window. That did not mean he wanted to deal with the situation. Hell, as far as he was concerned, the dead seemed advantageous. They had a passionate desire to kill the same people he wanted dead and were saving him the trouble, so by all means, they should have their way with the filthy swine.

And then, as he was walking around the town, and stretching his legs and his awareness, making sure that whatever was happening in the town didn't involve him directly, the boy just had to look his way and ask for help.

There was no obligation, not in any real sense of the word. He didn't know the youngster, and merely asking for his help didn't automatically force him to help a person in need. But, damn it, here he was walking past the boy and into a nightmare, just the same.

Maybe it was curiosity. Maybe he had a deep and abiding need to suffer for past transgressions. Whatever the case, the thing that slobbered from a dozen mouths as it swayed and hissed was decidedly willing to take him to task.

He had no idea what he was facing. That was rarer than most people knew.

It wasn't quite a single entity, though it seemed intent on looking like one. Several thick columns of wet meat had wrapped around each other and in most cases had grown together, thick ropes of flesh or streamers of arterial tubing fusing the uneven serpentine shapes. The mouths were uneven slashes, crooked lines filled with deathly sharp teeth, and though he could not call the things remotely human, they had features with each mouth that bore a passing resemblance. There were eyes, there were noses, but they were underdeveloped. The eyes were black, colorless masses that seemed incapable of sight—but he knew better because he could see them following his every motion. The nostrils flared and vented breaths, even as the mouths hissed and released ropes of thick saliva that flapped with each exhalation. What could have been arms, or half-formed limbs of some kind, were trying to grow out of the columns of meat, but so far had not succeeded. This nightmare was being born but had not finished forming.

"What the hell are you?"

The mouths moved, not all of them, but a few, and made noises. Two screamed, one hissed, another mumbled "dahullryuuu?" in a bad imitation of his words.

Crowley stopped moving, taken aback by the attempt at communication. A cavernous mouth split itself wider and vomited a column of wriggling flesh at him. Crowley jumped back, but not fast enough and felt the hot, wet meat slam into his leg. Teeth bit into his pants and tore past them, cutting his skin, his muscles and slamming against the bones of his calf.

Crowley screamed. The attack and the pain so fast that he had no time to prepare himself. He was thrown backward by the force of the blow. His body fell forward as his legs sailed back, knocked off kilter by the impact, and he caught himself on his hands against the vile thing that had attacked. The thick, grisly flesh shuddered under him and expanded, growing fatter as he recovered himself.

Despite the pain he vaulted himself up onto his hands and ripped his leg away from the mouth that tore and chewed. The pain was a living thing, a swarm of bees stinging at his leg, and he saw his blood spray through the air as the nightmare tried to catch his leg a second time.

"You bastard!" His teeth were bared and he flipped himself forward, sliding up the length of the growing snakelike trunk and twisting himself around in midair. The Greeks had their festivals, long gone now, for jumping over bulls, and he had seen more than one acrobat over the years. He tumbled and flipped and slid himself off of the bucking thing under him.

It should have worked better, but his leg gave out when he landed. Instead of smoothly sliding to the side he fell flat on his face, felt the skin scrape away, his teeth and mouth taking in the loose dirt that the worm-thing had disturbed.

The thing roared, every mouth opening and exhaling nauseating fumes into the air.

Crowley rolled over and scurried backward, looking at the thing as it swelled, expanded and continued to become more defined.

And, though he wished he could deny it, Crowley thrilled at the conflict.

The pain in his leg disappeared, replaced by a furious itch that signaled his body was healing itself again. The smile on his face grew wider and his eyes were alight with excitement. The adrenaline soared through him and, damn it, he felt good.

He felt alive.

It was the mystery, a new challenge, one he did not know how to handle with ease, and it was the danger, the chance that this new freakish thing could actually hurt him, perhaps even destroy him, that made him grin like a fool.

He hated his world. He loved his world.

Another mouth spit flesh at him, a thick writhing tongue that grew at a maddening speed until it didn't seem possible it had come from the maw that had released it. The base of the column obscured the previous mouth and then the full face. The tip grew a new mouth and fledgling features even as he drove himself to the left and narrowly avoided getting another chunk of his flesh removed.

The good thing about stables, aside from the fact that there were fewer people to see him fighting, was the array of weapons merely waiting to be used. Crowley grabbed a pitchfork used for cleaning the stalls and tossing in fresh hay. The tines were not as sharp as he'd have liked, but they would do the job.

He rammed the business end of the weapon into the fleshy limb and forced it in as hard as he could. The thing screamed again, this time in pain, as the four tines punctured flesh and drove through until they ripped past the mass and struck the ground.

Oh, how it screamed. The sound did his soul good.

The thing tried to free its stuck limb and when it failed, it ripped the flesh itself, tearing the newly grown meat away and leaving behind a bleeding stump.

Crowley pulled the pitchfork free and charged at the main mass, throwing his weight into the forward rush and driving the weapon home, impaling at least three of the columns as the nightmare roared and shuddered. The ground at its base ruptured as it heaved forward again and again, tearing itself from the soil like a bucking tree trying to uproot.

The good news was the damned thing could bleed. The bad news was that it didn't much seem bothered by the wounds. If anything, the demon was more enraged than hurt.

The black eyes of the abomination looked toward him and the mouths opened and spoke, the word clear, the meaning not merely mimicked. "Bastard!" It was learning, or worse, it already understood.

"Back away! Retreat, and I might let you live." Crowley made the offer already knowing what the response would be.

The thing roared again and he saw the trunk swell with pressure before the mouths exploded forth more fleshy pods. Streamers of meat came at him from every mouth, arcing through the air with intelligent malice. The thing was not playing, it wanted him dead.

Crowley grinned.

The feeling was mutual.

The tendrils caught him. Really, there was no chance to escape. The developing mouths bit deep, ripping into his flesh, tearing chunks of his body away and swallowing greedily. Crowley screamed again, the pain blinding him, ruining him.

Like a rabid cancer, the monster grew larger as it feasted.

The world sank down, faded to a distant murmur, almost lost behind the symphony of pain that the biting mouths became.

I've become lazy. I'm dying because I let myself relax. Stupid, foolish man.

Crowley opened his mouth and bit back. Not with his teeth, but with words. The sounds that broke past his lips were thunder and they summoned the lightning from above.

The roof of the barn exploded, cut open by a streak of electrical discharge that poured down from a clear sky and tore into the heaving mass of flesh that was still doing its best to devour Jonathan Crowley.

The air screamed. Forget the monster, the Hunter and the animals in the stables, the air screamed as the lightning ripped into the beast. Flesh boiled and exploded into blistered remains as the electrical stream ran directly down and into the thick columns of flesh still hidden beneath the ground. The same fire danced across Crowley, igniting hair, skin and clothes. The skin and hair regenerated at a furious speed, replenishing even as they were destroyed, and Crowley continued screaming long after the air had escaped his lungs.

The lifeless thing fell away, burnt and ruined, mouths and teeth drawing out of Crowley's body as it collapsed.

Crowley followed suit and slumped to the ground, his mind hearing nothing but white noise, his nerves blazing with furious pain, and waited. Cellular regeneration. His skin rebuilt itself, replaced the cooked meat with fresh, living matter. The heat of the strike had burned bones and they also healed themselves. The nerves that were fried recovered as well, and sent signals to his brain throughout the process. The agony was sublime, overwhelming conscious thought, dwarfing every sensation his mind tried to comprehend.

His eyes were good enough to repair themselves, giving him back sight enough to see the ruined beast that had been consuming him.

And Crowley grinned through his riotous agonies.

He rose slowly from the ground and looked around. The dirt around him was burned, glazed in blood and scorch marks; the hay closest to where he'd fallen was burnt, nearly incinerated.

Regeneration continued as he rose, muscles and flesh that had been destroyed knitted themselves together furiously. He looked around and noticed that the horses were unscathed. Terrified, rioting, but not injured by the blast.

Four quick words muttered softly past healing, blistered lips, and the horses quieted down instantly. No point in trying to save them if they tore themselves apart in an escape attempt.

The clothes he'd been wearing were ruined, little more than shreds of seared cotton. He shrugged them off and reached for one of several horse blankets. It was the least they could do to repay him.

And once he was wrapped in his new clothing, he stepped out of the barn without bothering to look back. The creature was dead. He recalled clearly what it looked like both before and after the destruction. Later, if he had the time, he'd investigate more completely.

Crowley walked out into the cold and looked for the nuisance who had asked for help. He found the boy struggling desperately against a dead man.

Jonah Pratchett

Rancid meat wrapped the fingers that scraped along Jonah's cheeks and smeared thick, dark fluids over his lips as he pulled back instinctively. The smell hit him and made him want to vomit. The taste that ran into his mouth guaranteed the reaction.

Jonah staggered back and fought against the gagging kick to his stomach. His eyes were wild, seeing less than he needed to, but seeing enough.

The man reaching for him was dead. There was no denying it. His clothes were crusted in muck, his hair plastered to his scalp, and his skin, Lord above, his skin was peeling away from the bones of his face, showing white skull and yellow fatty patches meshed with tendons. He only had one eye left and that one was leaking and obviously blind. Still, the dead man reached for him and belched a vile gas from inside its chest as it tried to speak or scream or maybe just roar.

Whatever the case, Jonah fell back again as the thing came for him. He tried to backpedal but panic had made him careless and instead of air his rear end ran into the wall of the barn.

Jonah screamed, an incoherent noise that was all he could manage as the dead man grabbed at him again and caught his jacket.

"Help me!" His voice broke as he called out and when he repeated the plea it was lost under a peal of thunder. The sky turned white and the dead man reared back, startled by whatever it could see through useless eyes, giving Jonah a chance to break free.

He slapped at the hands clenching his coat and felt gelid flesh splatter over his fingertips. His need to retch came back with a vengeance, and this time he couldn't fight away the gag reflex. He stumbled to his left, his chest heaving, and then felt the bile leave his body in a violent wave.

By the time he was done it seemed like every meal he'd ever had was torn from his guts. His body shook, his eyes watered, and his knees threatened to collapse.

And while all he could think about was the betrayal of his body, the dead man caught up with him again.

The hands grabbed tightly, snagging cloth and then catching the flesh beneath as well. Jonah screamed and threw his weight back as hard as he could, but to no avail. The grip was too strong.

He screamed for help again and a naked man answered.

"What is it with you, boy? You can't figure out how to run away from monsters?" The voice was ragged and angry. He looked to the source and saw the same man who'd walked into the stables. He was almost naked, wearing only a worn horse blanket for protection against the elements. The spectacles he'd been wearing were gone, but there were marks on his skin where they had been, like fresh burns. His hair was actually growing in spots at a speed that he could see, which by itself was unsettling—and almost as impossible as a walking dead man.

"I-What?" The man's words were accusatory and he couldn't decide how to answer. The dead man pulled harder and lifted Jonah from the ground. Flesh fell away from the gripping hands, but the corpse didn't notice. It merely leaned in closer to Jonah and bared its teeth, ready to bite at him.

Jonah shrieked.

And the monster's head exploded.

One instant it was going to eat his face and the next dead cold flesh and wetness washed over the object of the monster's attention. Rot and corruption spilled into his mouth, his nose, blanketed his eyes in burning darkness, and Jonah heaved again, overwhelmed by the filth that covered him.

He was distantly aware that a gun had been fired. It hardly seemed significant.

There was nothing left in his body to expel, and so he shook and suffered as his body tried to do the impossible and find more to vomit out. He knew he was dead. There was no way to avoid it. His body had betrayed him and now he was a dead man.

Only he didn't die.

He kept his eyes closed, not willing to look at the unholy thing again and kept them closed until he heard the man's voice.

"Are you done yet? Are you hurt or just being a baby?"

A brief flare of anger. He was old enough to help support his family. That counted for something.

"I'm not a baby." He meant to yell the words, but his voice was too quiet.

"Really?" He could barely understand how so much sarcasm could fit into one word. "Then why don't you start acting like a man and get to your damned feet?"

He opened his eyes and looked at the mostly naked man. The blistered flesh where his spectacles had been was pristine, showing no sign of injury. His hair was back to an even length. The only sign of change in the man was in his wardrobe, otherwise, he could have been unaffected by the madness that was trying to swallow Jonah's entire world.

The man scowled. "I said get up."

He held a revolver in his left hand. Then he shifted his wrist and the weapon vanished as surely as his clothes had.

Jonah rose on wobbling legs and the man looked him up and down with an expression best reserved for dead skunks and rotting chicken bones.

"What happened?" Jonah's voice shook. His mind felt fuzzy, lost in a wall of fog.

"You asked for my help and you got it." Oh, the voice was cold, filled with anger.

"Thank you." It was all he could think to say as the stranger continued staring at him, his mouth locked in a sneer, his eyes glittering darkly in the night.

"Go home. Get off the streets and out of the darkness. You hear me?"

"What about the horses?"

"They're alive. That thing won't bother them again."

"I should stay with them." It was his job to care for the animals and he took it seriously.

The man's face softened just a bit and only for a moment and then he nodded his head. "You do what you have to do. If you're wise, you don't mention this to anyone else."

Jonah stared back, trying to read the stranger, who offered him nothing.

"What happened to your clothes?"

"Some little brat called for my help and got it." The man turned and walked away with surprising dignity considering his wardrobe.

Jonah looked into the stables after the man disappeared and saw the gaping hole where the monster had come up. There was no sign of the monster itself, only a burned area where it had come up from Hell for all he knew.

Somewhere out in the darkness another of the dead men might be walking, or another of the things that had come up from below might well lurk just under the ground.

Jonah shivered at the thought and then closed the barn doors.

He did not stay the night. He preferred the comfort of home, where his mother and father waited.

Lucas Slate

Lucas Slate looked out into the darkness and watched his breath fog over the thick glass of his window. The air had been warm earlier. The return of the cold was not proper and it bothered him. He was unsettled and couldn't help but feel restless.

His arm hurt where the dead things had winged him when they shot Sheriff Meade. It was a small wound, a nuisance more than anything else. He would recover.

He believed in a peaceful existence, but he was also a realist. Being an albino in the south—really, anywhere, but especially in the political climate of his home—had taught him the need to be prepared. He also believed, unlike many people it seemed, in trusting his instincts.

He moved away from the window and walked over to his kitchen table. The wooden surface was covered with two shotguns and one rifle as well as gun oil, cleaning cloths and ammunition. The Winchester repeating rifle was well-cleaned and freshly oiled. The shotguns could both use a little work. It was easy to overlook that they needed maintenance too, because they were so much easier to kill with. Point, pull the trigger, and hold on tightly. Whatever they hit would likely be destroyed. He used shot. Slugs were too inaccurate for his tastes. And too violent. The end results of being struck with a slug were not pleasant to look at and impossible to hide. He preferred a corpse that could be viewed to allow a final chance for a goodbye.

Lucas sighed and began the task of cleaning the long barrel. The motions were automatic; they'd been performed many times before and likely would until the time came for his death.

Not that he was sure that would make much difference of late. The dead seemed determined to rise and walk and that was unsettling. He didn't feel panic exactly, but a definite sense of unease at the notion. The dead held remarkably few mysteries for him and he had heard stories and experienced a few occasions where people who should have been dead recovered. The sense of shock was long gone. His mind insisted that there had to be a rational explanation for the situation, no matter how absurd. That alone was what kept him from losing his mind as quickly as he was losing the bodies of the dead.

There had been a fellow from Louisiana that had come to work with his father when he was only a boy. A Cajun man with a thick accent and a terrible case of bad breath. That was what he remembered most. It took him a moment to recall the name, Gaston. Gaston had told him many a tale when the weather was horrid and he was stuck in the house. His skin didn't permit him to run outside on particularly sunny days and his mother would have never permitted him out on rainy days, so there were many times when the old Cajun had been his only company. He told tales of Voudoun and the sorceries the slaves worked. He told his tales with the understanding that Lucas never shared the stories with his parents. It was a small price for a little boy to pay for a bit of excitement. Of all the many stories he found fascinating, it was the tales of the zombies that held his attention the most. He remembered those stories while he cleaned his weapons. There had been something about how to incapacitate the walking dead—they were already dead so killing them was an impossibility—but he could not remember the methods to save his life.

The wind outside picked up and rattled along the sides of the house, whistled its way down the chimney.

He looked outside again and thought he might have seen movement out beyond the front yard of his home. Out where the darkness was complete enough to give only the smallest hints.

He was scared and he was lonely. Normally he was only lonely. Had he been feeling particularly brave he might have headed into the night and found himself a whore that could tolerate his dead white skin. But the stories he'd been told by Gaston were enough to guarantee he looked at the darkness with a coward's eyes.

Marcus Darby

Marcus Darby watched the men leave to handle business and laid back in a pile of hay that hadn't gone too sour. The pain in his chest was a knot of fire that twisted and fluttered around his ribs and sank needles into his heart every so often, just in case he started to feel a bit of comfort.

Urbancik, the youngest of their group, kept looking his way and gnawing on his lower lip. He was worried about Darby, which was both touching and annoying.

Something was happening to him. He knew that. He felt it inside his body and in his head, too. The pain started where the stone had punched into his muscle and it radiated out from there, but more importantly, the change was messing with his head. He saw better than he should have, and there were new noises—not sounds but like them—running through his fool head all the time.

He was changing, whether or not he wanted to. The good news was he was almost sure he wanted the changes. He felt like something he'd been missing for his entire life was coming home to him.

For just one moment, he wondered if that was how Silas felt about God. Then the next wave of pain came through, larger than the last one, a heaving violent wave that made his body twitch, and he forgot all about the good feelings for a while.

Silas

The Piedmont was a big hotel, bigger than a lot of them, at least, but hardly gigantic. It didn't take too long to find out what room the gunslinger was staying in. What took a while was managing to sneak into the place without being seen. For one man it might be easy, but for four it became a challenge.

The room was dark and while he could tell that they wanted to move around, the boys were behaving themselves properly. They'd spent a lot of time together on the road and they were seasoned veterans of long hunts and more combat than any of them wanted to remember.

The wind was strong enough to make the walls creak and somewhere outside someone was screaming. They'd already heard several gunshots and what sounded like an explosion earlier, but they didn't move to find out more. The only thing that mattered for now was killing Jonathan Crowley before he tried to kill any more of them. There were already nightmares waiting outside the town for them. They didn't need a madman coming for them while they were trying to deal with things that wouldn't stay dead. One slice of Hell was enough for anyone.

So this time they would strike first. Silas didn't much like it, he looked at the entire situation as the act of not one coward but several, but he understood it. He'd seen the man shooting earlier. Crowley was a scary bastard.

Hagarty cleared his throat as quietly as he could and Silas resisted the urge to shoot him. In the tense silence the sound was enough to fray his nerves.

He might have said something about the matter, might even have ruined their chances of ambushing the man they were after, but Crowley chose that moment to come back to his room.

The lock rattled for a moment and then the man came into the darkness, moving with unsettling confidence in the gloom. Silas took in a deep breath and slowly raised his revolver from where he had aimed it at the ground.

And Hagarty cried out, "Why in God's name is he naked?"

A flick of the eyes. Sure enough, their target stood without so much as a belt to hide behind. The closest he had to clothing was the tattered blanket he carried in his left hand.

A second later even that was removed. The man stepped out of the room and back into the hallway as he threw the blanket toward Hagarty.

Hagarty let out a yelp and tried to duck under the thick fabric. While he was busy avoiding the cloth, the target of their murderous plans moved back into the room, crouched low and following his blanket's trajectory.

Hagarty let out a grunt as the blanket slapped against him. While he was trying to get away, Crowley hit him across his skull with something that rang out like a cheap bell.

Hagarty hit the ground hard and did not get back up.

Silas took aim and fired, no longer willing to wait until the madman could be seen clearly. His shot missed and though the man made no sound, he saw Hagarty's body jump as the bullet slammed into him, but the darkness was too much and he couldn't see exactly where he'd hit his companion.

"You damned fool, you shot Will!" Parker called out angrily and told Crowley exactly where he was. Silas said a silent thanks as the gunslinger crouched again, still completely silent, and then fairly flew across the room. Parker fired at the dark shape and struck it dead on, and even as Crowley was struck, Silas aimed and fired, his bullet hitting the man in his lower extremity.

The man's head sailed in one direction and his body flailed in the air as if boneless, defying all reason.

Parker screamed again, no words this time, merely a loud volatile shriek, and tried to fire his weapon again.

Silas stared at the head where it had rolled, the shape completely wrong, and realized after a heartbeat that he'd been duped. They'd all been fooled, apparently. The head was a chamber pot, warped by bullets and by the impact with Hagarty's thick skull alike.

Parker's fumbling fingers finally managed to catch the hammer on his revolver at exactly the same time that the gunslinger rose behind him. The darkness had hidden him while he slipped through the room and let the whole lot of them shoot at a blanket and a piss pot.

Parker tried to scream again, this time with fright, but the man's hands on his throat cut his cry short.

In the darkness of the room Silas could barely make the man out, but he could see the face well enough to know the man was smiling as he broke Parker's neck with a series of wet pops.

Silas fired again, despite the tremble in his hands, and this time his bullet struck true. Crowley spun to the right, hissing in pain, and staggered back into the wall. He could see the blood splatter where the bullet exited.

And as the man was falling back against the wall and sliding down in a slick of blood, Booth decided to step into the game. He fired once, the bullet blasting into Crowley's midriff. Then he cocked the hammer again and fired. And again. Three new holes appeared in the naked gunslinger, who stayed where he was, unmoving save for the pool of blood that spread under him.

"Reckon that takes care of that." Booth looked at Crowley and Silas joined him, slowly nodding his head. There was nothing to be done about it now. Yes, they'd got the bastard but the getting had cost them two more of their team.

"Let's just get the hell out of here before someone sees us."

"Don't much matter if they do. The sheriff is dead and the deputy ain't exactly smart." Booth spat phlegm onto the rug and grinned. He was an optimist and always had been. Most times Silas admired that. Just at the moment, he was busy dealing with the deaths of two madmen he'd called friends for a long while.

"When did my world go so very sour?" He whispered the words, afraid that if anyone heard them, someone would give him an answer.

Rather than risk that, he made a simple gesture and the two of them left the room, moving quickly lest anyone come to investigate the sounds of murder.

CHAPTER TWELVE
LET THEM SUFFER

Molly Finnegan

The night was still growing colder, and the roar of the wind offered promises of more bitter cold to come. And in that atmosphere, the dead moved through town, drifting and shambling but not without purpose.

They were there to kill anyone they found, as ordered by the strange beings that had summoned their bodies from the cold ground. There was no remorse within them. They did not feel pity or anger, or pain. They simply moved.

Four prospectors who were planning to get out into the field with the first rays of light left the tent they'd pitched in search of food and encountered the shambling dead things. The first one spotted was not in the best of shape. The frozen ground, the warm deluge of rain and the wind had done horrid things to the body of Molly Finnegan. Even after almost a month without a woman's touch none of the men would have ever considered touching her willingly.

Her corpse had other ideas and she reached out thin, wasted arms, her nails clawing at flesh with sudden, violent fury.

The first of the men were dead before they even knew what was happening. The second had exactly long enough to take in that his friend was dead and bleeding on the ground before the dead woman sank her teeth into his face and ripped away half of a cheek and most of his nose.

While he was shrieking, she clawed at his eyes. Her fingertips plowed into eyes and forced their way through to the sockets underneath and pulled back, stealing his vision away.

The other two men tried to help. Despite the dark and the cold they moved in fast and tried to restrain the madwoman. When their hands plowed through rotting flesh to the bone beneath, they pulled back in revulsion, panic eating at their resolve.

And the dead woman killed them for their hesitance.

Many of the dead were not as successfully violent. Most merely staggered down the street and sought targets. When they found none, they continued their quest until they were called back to the woods at sunrise.

They felt no fear, nor pain or sorrow.

That was for the best. The dead should not be made to scream.

No one told that to Molly, who watched her body commit atrocities without recourse to stop it.

There was someone who could, however. And she intended to make him change his mind.

Jonathan Crowley

The darkness soothed him, drew him into its embrace and held him in sweet, peaceful silence.

He was dying, maybe even dead, and the notion pleased Jonathan Crowley. Or it would have, if he'd been capable of thought.

Instead, he merely let himself drift in the darkness, content to feel nothing.

Until Molly showed herself again. She was lovely, pale and shapely, her hair was down, a veil of dark tresses that half hid her breasts and face as it fell in a riot.

She came to him in the darkness and touched his face with hands that seemed too warm, though he couldn't have said why they felt wrong.

Her lips pressed to his, a dozen tiny kisses, and he felt the wetness of her tears as she adored him. "Come back to me Jonathan. Come back and help me."

He shook his head, frowning. There was something wrong with this. Her hands moved over his chest and stomach and lower, distracting him as surely as her kisses managed.

"Be with me Jonathan. Be mine." The words were a sweet invitation and he stirred, kissing her back at last, no longer wanting to resist. His hands moved to her body exploring her, discovering the beauty of her as she discovered him.

Had they touched this way before? Been intimate? He didn't know. He thought not, but she felt so very good, so right in his arms, over him as she moved with him, kissing, tasting, becoming one with him.

Crowley's eyes flew open in the darkness of his room and he coughed, spitting a wad of half-dried blood from his mouth.

The pain lanced through him, an overwhelming wave that left him staggered and half blinded. He fell to his side, his head striking the rough floorboards, and felt his body kick and twitch.

"Aaauuh..." The sound was involuntary, a side effect of his lungs pushing out the last breath he'd held as he died.

Molly's bare legs moved into his view. He could see her clearly and see the room behind her where the light did not touch her flesh.

"Jonathan, they've made me kill. Help me, please."

Hatred fired his heartbeat, gave him back the pulse that had faded away. He sucked in a lung full of breath and gasped it back out as he looked past the ghostly woman before him and saw the body of one of the men who'd been waiting for him.

"Unn...done. You hear me, you bastards? Done now. I'm coming for you." The threat was nearly hollow. He couldn't stand and even as he tried for a second breath, he coughed more blood from his throat and lungs. The pain in his body lessened, devoured by the vicious itching sensation of his flesh mending itself.

Molly reached out, tried to touch him, and he flinched as if she'd thrown boiling oil.

"No! Don't you touch me!" He spat the words, his eyes narrowed to slits in a face made terrifying by rage.

"Jonathan, I-"

"If you weren't already dead I'd kill you myself, you bitch!" He rose, his legs quaking, his skin cold and nearly as pale as her spectral form. Color came slowly as the blood he needed was replenished.

He stepped from the pool of his own blood and moved to the steamer trunk that held his recently purchased clothes.

"They're using me, Jonathan. They've made me a killer." Her voice shook and she reached for him again, begging for mercy or acceptance with a gesture. Her hands stopped before they touched him, and his eyes glared at them as if they might be contagious.

"It's *meat*, Molly. It's just skin and bone. That's not you. What's left of you is here, in my place, disturbing me."

"You were dying," her face was heavily shadowed, her eyes lost in the darkness of the place where her spirit dwelled. "I wanted to comfort you."

"You wanted my help. I told you before, I can't help you."

He ignored her as he grabbed clothes, pulling on pants and buttoning them hastily; a shirt, not bothering with the cuffs or the collar, he tucked it into the pants and reached for his vest, then his coat, a good piece for the harsh weather. He sat on the bed and pulled on boots that were too new to be comfortable.

"Where are you going Jonathan?"

"I've got a few men to kill." He flashed his smile at her and she shivered. "Don't be here when I come back, Molly. I've been forgiving and patient with you, but that's done. You've taken your last liberty with me."

"I was trying to help." Her voice had taken on a whining quality.

"I didn't want your damned help, woman! I wanted to be left alone!"

"You can't mean that. You were dying."

He stormed toward her, momentarily forgetting that she was already dead and grabbed at her arms. When he passed through her, she moaned, and he scowled.

"I'd still be dead if you'd have left me alone, Molly. I could have known peace for once. What makes you think life is so special?" He spoke the words, knowing she'd never understand.

She shook her head. "What else could ever be more important, Jonathan?"

Because he had no answer, he ignored the question and spun on his heel.

The dead men in the room did not move out of his way, so he stepped over them.

The hallway was dark, but not too dark to let him see. As an afterthought, he turned back to the room and Molly's ghost.

"Molly? If you want these men dead, you can show me where they are hiding." He could have found them himself, but it would have taken time he didn't feel like wasting and despite himself, he wanted to make the dead woman feel at least a small measure of justice. In the long run it would cost him nothing.

She flitted ahead of him, little more than a wisp of fog that looked like a woman, and he followed, his eyes taking in every detail of the area. There were dead things moving around in the night. He spotted one of them as it wandered toward the mercantile.

As he had managed for most of his time in Carson's Point, he ignored the thing and went about his business.

The stables were just up ahead. No guards barred the way.

The fools must have thought they were safe.

He intended to show them otherwise.

Marcus Darby

Marcus nodded his head and shivered feverishly. The news was good. That Crowley character was dead. One less obstacle between finishing their mission and getting paid a king's ransom.

He was in pain, but despite that fact he needed to be a leader. He stood up and took in a deep breath, trying to keep the room from spinning through pure force of will.

Whatever the hell had caught in his chest earlier, it wasn't done with him. He went from moment to moment, his body filled with pain or charged with unbelievable energy depending on the whim of the thing inside him that was still growing and had just recently started talking to him, whispering in the back of his head.

If he strained hard enough, he could almost understand the whispers. They spoke of transformation and growth, or just possibly of pain and eternal torment. Try though he might, the meaning just eluded him.

Silas had come back with only Booth by his side. Darby lowered his head and closed his eyes. Two more were dead. They were dwindling away into nothingness, brave soldiers once and now little more than animals, but they had trusted him.

"Silas."

"Yes?" His second came his way, a worried expression on his pinched face.

"We need to be ready to leave in the morning. We can't stay here."

"What about those things out in the woods?"

Marcus closed his eyes and felt the power in his body swell again, a tide growing stronger, a wave ready to crest and break.

"I'll take care of them when the time comes."

Silas opened his mouth to speak, but instead turned away as the door to the barn slammed open, rocking and creaking before it crashed into the interior wall.

They all looked and saw the pale shape of the gunslinger. He was sweating, his skin feverish, his eyes wild as they tried to look everywhere at once.

"Well, lookee here. Found me a whole nest of vipers, didn't I?" Despite the obvious pain and his weaponless state, the man smiled.

Silas stared, horrified, and crossed himself. "You're dead! I saw you die!"

The man looked his way and raised an empty hand in Silas's direction. Marcus watched it happen, saw the Peacekeeper appear out of thin air, and watched the man's thumb pull the hammer back even as he reached for the trigger of the gun that shouldn't have been there at all.

Silas tried to say something else, but his head exploded before he could finish his sentence.

"You go to hell." Crowley was still grinning, his pale face twisting into a grin worthy of the Grim Reaper.

Booth was next. The man reached for his weapons, fumbling them out of the belt he'd already taken off for the night. He never quite managed to draw before the bullet took him in the upper back, just below the neck.

Two men down and the bastard doing the firing seemed to be getting stronger each time one of his people died. Marcus forced himself to sit up and stared at the gunslinger, his eyes fairly bulging as he took in the details.

There were raw spots on the man, places where the skin was pink and fresh and hairless, but as he watched the hairs grew in and the flesh took on a different tone. No scars showed to prove the man had been shot, but Marcus knew, understood that he had been gravely wounded and recently. He was another monster, a thing that would not stay dead.

Marcus forced himself to stand up and reached for his own weapon. He'd see the bastard dead one last time before he gave up. To be sure, he might well die himself, but he'd kill the bastard again before that moment happened.

Crowley fired at Marcus's men, taking them down as they scurried for their weapons. He should have posted a guard, but he'd gotten sloppy and now it was costing them so very much.

Urbancik drew his piece, fired, and missed the man. Before he could draw back the hammer for a second shot, Crowley shot him in the throat. The man fell back with a dazed look in his eyes and then tried to catch a breath that refused to come for him. Before he could choke to death on his own blood, Crowley walked closer and shot him in the head. Marcus couldn't decide if the gesture was meant as mercy or if the gunslinger was simply trying to make sure his target was dead.

Grainger died while he was trying to stand up. Vincent got off a shot that punched a new hole in the gunslinger, but the man barely seemed to notice. Vincent never managed a second shot before he was blown backward, a hole in his chest that bubbled forth a pink froth. He fell back and writhed on the ground as good as dead from the lack of lung.

Crowley looked around at the dead, and then finally turned toward Marcus as if he were merely an afterthought.

"You bastard," his voice shook with outrage. "You killed them all."

Crowley came for him then, one smoking revolver in his right hand. He had surely fired all his rounds, but he didn't seem to care.

"Remember me? I remember you. A man pisses in your face, you don't forget him." Had he thought the gunslinger weak or pale? He seemed healthy now, with a rosy complexion and a dark, sadistic smile on his lean face.

Marcus took his time as he aimed. He didn't feel a need to hurry.

Crowley opened his mouth and whispered something. Marcus tried to hear the words, but they were lost in the sudden rushing noise that took all the air away and left him abruptly breathless.

Pain was already trying to drag Marcus down, but he focused himself and took aim. The gun seemed to weigh too much, and the air around the weapon blurred, distorted and warped as he concentrated.

Marcus pulled the trigger anyway.

The weapon exploded in his hand, sending white hot splinters of metal and wood through his palm, his fingers, his wrist.

No pain he'd ever experienced prepared him for the flaring agony that ran through his hand and arm. The impact shattered bones and flayed flesh from his fingers and Marcus shrieked, a victim of his ruined nerve endings.

"Never point a gun at me, boy." There was no change in the gunslinger's expression as he aimed at Marcus. His left hand this time, and another revolver that should not have been there.

He tried to raise his hands to block the bullet perhaps, or to plead for his life, but he moved too slowly and the pain weighed him down.

The bullet smashed into his cheek, directly below his left eye and mushroomed as it spun through his head.

Marcus Darby bled out across the stable floor, his life fading down to little more than white noise as Jonathan Crowley looked around the area for any survivors.

Booth struggled to move, his spine ruined by the single shot Crowley had fired earlier. The man's breaths were labored, his eyes rolled and sought any possible source of escape and found nothing.

Crowley squatted next to him and stared for a long moment, studying the pained expression on the face of a man he'd seen twice before. The first time he's been raping Molly Finnegan. The time after that, he'd been shooting Crowley himself in the chest and stomach.

"A merciful man would kill you. He'd understand the pain you're in and help you escape it." Crowley stood up a kicked the man's pistol just out of his reach. "I'm not merciful. You raped and murdered a good woman. Go to Hell."

He didn't bother to look back.

After Crowley had gone from the area Booth stared at the wall and felt the world dimming around him. He breathed slowly and shivered as the cold drew him in like a blanket.

This was sure death. He could accept that. He had lived a violent life for so long that peace seemed like a dream.

The woman who stood in front of him was naked and the light that shone off her pale skin did not match the light of the lanterns around the stables.

She reached for him as he was dying and her hand passed through his skin and caught at the stuff of his soul.

"He's done with you," she hissed, her eyes narrowed with hatred. "I am not. Not nearly."

Had Booth been capable of screaming, he surely would have.

———

Moses Blake

Moses Blake climbed out of bed and stretched, his muscles tight and aching. The day broke clear and cold and, despite his sour heart, his mind felt much like the morning outside his hotel room.

That thought brought a small smile that died before it got past his lips. Him in a hotel, like he was as good as a white man. He'd walked into the hotel, fully expecting to get invited to leave, but despite the look on the innkeeper's face, the company he was keeping had kept the man silent.

Albert Miles was in the next room, but he could hear the man walking around his room, the floorboards creaking, the tread of his heavy body enough to let Moses keep track of him.

It was only a few minutes before the man came to pound on the door of his room. "Time's wasting, Mr. Blake. We have business to attend to."

Moses called out his greeting and got himself dressed. The clothes he'd worn into town had been mended and laundered courtesy of his benefactor, and he put them on without reluctance.

This was to be the day. Whatever else happened, this was the day the damned things that had killed his family and friends came to an end. That was the promise of Albert Miles, who seemed very confident and frighteningly calm.

He had no reason not to believe the man who'd brought him back from near death.

He left his room fully loaded, his shotguns and his rifle strapped across his back and his pistol tight to his right thigh.

Everything about the town felt wrong. He intended to be ready for the vile things outside the town and for the people around him should they decide to cause troubles for a freed slave in their midst.

Miles watched him step into the hallway and nodded his approval. "Looks to me like you're ready for business."

"That I am." Moses's voice was scratchy from lack of use. He had no one he wanted or needed to speak to.

"Let's you and me eat a decent meal and then get to business."

Moses said nothing in response but followed the man down to the small dining area attached to the place. Several people were already eating, and they all stared as the trapper and he moved into the room.

"What do you think you're doing here, boy?" The man who spoke was lean and hard and sat at a table with four others who looked just as hungry.

Miles started to open his mouth and Moses took a step forward. "I'm coming in here to eat. You got a problem with that and think you can stop me, you best make your move or shut your mouth."

"Think you can take me?" The man was reaching for his sidearm as he spoke.

Miles spoke up. "Must have a death wish, fella." He pushed past Moses and leaned his thick hands on the table where the five men sat. "You have one revolver, and he has enough weapons to kill every last one of you."

"Mister, I have no problem with you, but I'll not sit in a room with a nigger."

The man's broad, bearded face grew thunderous, but he kept his voice low and calm. "Then I suggest you find another place to eat."

The standoff lasted all of ten seconds. The men decided to leave.

Moses sat down with the trapper and they ordered their food and ate. No one else considered debating whether or not a black man had the right to eat.

Lucas Slate

Lucas Slate had a busy morning. He wasn't alone. Pace Peabody was with him, carefully counting the bodies in the stables and trying to identify them. They had come into town together, and according to Peabody, the only other thing they had in common was a grudge with Jonathan

Crowley and with the dead white Indians that kept scaring up trouble.

Most of the men had been shot once. Most had died clean. A few had suffered dearly before they died.

Peabody was doing his best to be calm, but his nerves were stretched thin and his eyes had taken on a wild look.

Lucas kept his tongue. He didn't know the man well enough to offer advice that hadn't been asked for. It was always wise to know when to keep your peace, and in the current situation it seemed doubly sensible.

Two men were there helping him, both had earned their wages of late.

"It's that Crowley man. I need to bring him in."

Lucas said nothing though he was tempted.

Lawrence Hardy, one of the men working for him said what was on his mind instead. "Man killed five armed soldiers, Sheriff. Might be wise not to push him."

"Might be wise to wrangle up a posse."

Lucas pursed his lips but kept them sealed. Wise had nothing to do with it.

The next time Lawrence Hardy opened his mouth it was to scream. The sound was pure fear, untainted by anything else.

Slate looked toward the source of the scream and uttered one himself as one of the dead soldiers rose from his resting place. He was dead and there was no mistake about it. Half his face was pulped and a goodly portion of what should have been inside his head slopped out as he stood up stiffly.

Hardy did the sensible thing and ran, barely taking the time to push the stable door out of his way as he charged into the daylight.

The other man merely froze where he was, his hands inches from where he'd been ready to grab the cadaver's legs.

The dead man's mutilated face stretched into a wretched shape as he tried to speak. Lucas might well have waited around to hear what the corpse had to say, but Peabody grabbed his arm and yanked him half off his feet as he started running.

Whatever thoughts were going through the sheriff's head were kept to himself as he ran and dragged Lucas with him.

When they were safely outside the stables the men stood together as four of the dead men shuffled and moved slowly into the daylight.

Dean Carruthers, who ran the bank, stood by the door to his establishment and stared at the procession with open mouth and watery eyes, unable to look away as the oddly silent men headed for the gate to the town.

Peabody shook himself out of his stupor as the last of the men moved past him and walked over to where his horse stood ignoring the situation. He reached into the holster on the side of the saddle and pulled out a repeating rifle.

While Lucas watched, the man took careful aim and blew the back of the closest dead man's skull open. The corpse fell forward and hit the ground hard. A moment later it started trying to stand again and Peabody ignored it as he aimed for the next in line.

Feeling rather absurd and a little as if he were trapped in a dream, Lucas moved over to his wagon, drew aside the blankets he'd brought to cover the corpses, and pulled his shotgun from the bundle he'd set there earlier.

Between the two men they made short work of decimating the animated dead shapes. What was left still twitched, but seemed to lack the ability to do much else after they'd finished firing.

Peabody looked at him with wet eyes and nodded his thanks.

Instead of responding, Lucas pointed to the men he was paying. "Put them on the wagon."

"They're still moving, Mr. Slate."

"Then wrap them tightly. No sense in them escaping."

The men looked at him for a few heartbeats, and finally Lawrence nodded his head and did as he was told.

"What are you gonna do with them?" The sheriff's voice was surprisingly calm.

"I'm going to light a bonfire and burn them to cinders, Sheriff. I'm rather tired of burying bodies that refuse to stay down."

The man stared at him long and hard before he nodded. "I reckon that's for the best."

"I'll expect the same compensation either way, Sheriff. Burned or buried, I expect to be paid."

"Just keep a tally going."

"At the current rate, I might well need a new ledger to keep track of the numbers," he answered drily.

Peabody had no response. He stayed where he was until the last of the bodies was dragged onto the wagon. By then another problem had cropped up. A stable boy from down the road came and told him news that was not at all pleasant. A few poor souls had been caught after dark the night before and been torn apart. What was left of them had crawled from their trampled tents and made for the gates of the town. Lucas counted the shells for his shotgun and made a detour by Harding's mercantile before heading over to take care of the matter. He intended to bill the town for the extra shells as well.

They should have counted better. If they had, they'd have realized that one of the bodies did not join the others in the attempt to leave the barn.

Instead of leaving, the remains of Marcus Darby rolled away from the light and slid into the darkness of the closest layer of hay and dung, content to escape the sun's rays and continue to change. Death had not stopped the transformation, merely expedited it.

Avery Drake

Panic doesn't need much incentive. By the time most people were finishing with their breakfasts, the news of the dead rising was spreading through town. The results were not too shocking. A good number of the people in town decided to leave the area in a hurry, before whatever was happening could happen to them. Did it make sense? No. Not really. They ran because they were afraid of the unknown, but they also ran knowing that there were other forces outside of the town that could cause them just as much harm.

Some of them got lucky and got away from Carson's Point. Most did not.

The town was surrounded by woods, and just out of range of most decent firearms, not far from where the woods started, the oddly malformed shapes of six men in clothes or blankets either stood or rested on the backs of horses that looked almost as misshapen. They did not speak, nor did they offer any visible threat, but they inspired fear with their mere presence.

Four men who had come to town seeking gold and decided they could just as easily find their fortunes in California tried to get past the white Indians and failed to escape. They rode hard, driving their horses into a hard run, but the Indians were faster, even the ones who stood alone without a mount to carry them.

The men still had their horses, which made them luckier than a lot of the people in town, and they had worked out a plan. When the sun was up high enough, each of them split off to head in his own direction with plans to meet where the river forked two miles to the east of town.

As they rode they did their best not to get too close to the creatures that had moved themselves to different spots around the town. The first of the four died within seconds of making his break, taken down by a rifle shot that dropped him effortlessly. The next saw no weapons and thought he was safe, but learned otherwise when the shape under the heavy blanket dropped to all fours and charged him with unnatural speed. It was too far away for anyone to see clearly, but the thing that attacked him was hairless, still deathly white and covered with thick lumps that had little at all to do with flesh.

Whatever it was, it took the rider down with one pounce, knocking him several feet from his horse, which had the good sense to keep running. The thing looked at the man for several seconds as he recovered from his rough slam into the hard frozen earth. Then it proceeded to feast on his entrails, despite the man's screams and attempts to stop it.

The other two were no luckier. The hellish creatures killed them, though they were less visceral in their methods. With many of the townsfolk watching, the third man was torn into pieces until his skull could be removed mostly intact, and the thick thighbones were also pulled free. The shape was too far away to see clearly, but it managed to place the skull in a small sack. The thick bloodied bones from the legs were carried, one in each hand as the beast paced in the distance, waiting for the next person foolish enough to try leaving town.

The people inside the town's limits were justifiably horrified, at least those that were there to witness the violent murders. As always seems to be the case with tragedy, the news spread quickly.

Others never made it through the woods and the growing army of the dead that waited in silence among the trees.

There was no planning in the exodus, there was merely fear. The end result was not a good one.

Things changed a little after noon when one of the more cautious people in town wised up enough to try to hire help.

Avery Drake asked around and discovered the name and location of the gunslinger who'd made himself at home in Carson's Point and sought him out.

The stranger he found didn't look all that frightening, and didn't even appear to be carrying any firearms, but the barkeeper assured him that the man was in fact Jonathan Crowley, a very capable shootist, and then moved quickly behind his polished wooden bar. Dan Kaufmann had enough troubles of his own without getting the gunslinger's attention. The plate glass windows he'd ordered were going to cost him a small fortune and, in the meantime, he had used boards and nails to block off the worst of the bad weather, but the cold still crept in and the darkness in the place was almost impossible to escape.

Crowley sat at a table and stared at the wall with a sour expression on his face as Drake approached him. He barely turned his head when the man called out his name, but his eyes shifted and he stared hard at the man.

"What can I do for you?"

"Mister Crowley, I hear that you're a mean shot and currently I could use a good man to help me clear a few people from this town."

Crowley examined him from head to toe, his face expressionless, and then looked away. "Not much interested in leaving town just yet."

Drake was out of shape and squinted like he was staring at the sun. His thick muttonchops curled wildly along his jawline and twitched as he spoke. He looked nervous enough to rabbit at the first sign of trouble but held his ground instead of leaving. "I-I need your help, sir. I can pay you. Not much, maybe ten dollars, but I could probably work out something else to make up the difference in whatever you might charge."

"I don't intend to leave town." Crowley stared harder, speaking slowly enough to make clear that he was not amused by the continuing conversation.

"Mister, I'm begging here." Drake's voice broke as he continued talking. "I have a wife and two daughters here with me, and there's some awfully dangerous folks around these parts that might do bad things to womenfolk." He was sweating and he leaned toward Crowley and clasped his hands together. "If you could just get us out of the woods, take us as far as the river, we could make our own way, but my eyes ain't what they used to be, and I can't shoot worth a damn."

"Are you hard of hearing?" His voice cracked harshly as he leaned forward in his seat and placed his hands on the table in front of him. Several people who were paying attention to the conversation simply watched. A few chose to back away as carefully as they could.

Drake shook. He stood his ground, yes, but his entire body shivered as the man looked at him. "Got no choice but to ask, mister. There are dead things running around killing people here in town, and there's worse stuff outside the walls of the town, killing whatever tries to leave. What do you suppose I should do?"

"You should go back to your house, lock the doors, and stay there. The dead things are out there right now in those woods. What makes you so sure they won't kill you just as dead in the daylight?"

"We're going back east. We're going back to Boston, and we're never setting foot on this side of the country again, mister. This place is crazy bad!"

"Fine!" Crowley threw his hands up in a wild gesture. "That's a wonderful idea! But wait until the dead things go away before you leave."

"They aren't leaving!" Drake's voice broke as he yelled, then scaled up into a hysterical edge that was unpleasantly grating. "Mister, I know some of those people! I knew them when they were alive! They aren't going away! There's just going to be more of them until there's no town left!"

"You want to leave this town, you ride out on your own." Jonathan Crowley rose from his seat with his hands held out like they should have been reaching toward the holsters he wasn't carrying. "You want to stay here, you can wait with everyone else while I try to figure out how to handle the problem."

The door opened behind Avery Drake, and he looked over his shoulder to see Sheriff Peabody heading into the semidarkness of the bar with four men behind him. All of them were carrying firearms.

"Jonathan Crowley, you need to come with me." Pace's voice shook a bit, but he stood his ground.

Crowley's sour expression changed then. For one brief moment he looked confused and then a smile crept across his lean face. "Really? Why would that be, my good man?"

"You killed a few men last night. We don't take to that in Carson's Point."

Crowley laughed. His hand slammed into the table in front of him, and he roared laughter as he looked at the sheriff and the men behind him.

Pace and the others stared as if the man might well be mad, and Drake couldn't see a reason to disagree with that notion, but he still needed the gunslinger's help.

"Wait, Pace!" He held out his hands and moved four steps toward the sheriff. Peabody looked at him and held his nervous scowl.

"What is it, Avery? I'm a mite busy at the moment."

"Crowley, he was going to help me get Emma and Louise out of town."

The gunslinger shook his head. "No sir, I was not. What I was about to do was go with the new sheriff, to the cell he has waiting for me." Crowley held his hands over his head to show he had no weapons and looked at the man now in charge of keeping the peace. "I'm ready if you are, Sheriff."

"No!" Drake reached out his hands, grabbing for Crowley's jacket lapels. Despite rumors of the man's nearly unholy speed, he didn't stop the contact. Avery shook him for a moment, his eyes wide and wild. "You have to help me!"

Crowley's grin grew larger. "No sir. I don't have to do any such thing. You've got a sheriff right here who should be able to solve all of your problems."

Avery Drake let go of the man's coat and stepped back, crestfallen. "Pace, please...."

Peabody looked at him with an expression on his round face that said he had no idea exactly what was going on, but he was glad to be alive instead of fighting for his life.

"Let it be, Avery. This man is going to stand trial for murder."

Crowley kept grinning as the sheriff and his men led him away.

Avery Drake looked once around the saloon, and then shook his head in disgust before heading back to his small home. He wanted to leave the town, he wanted to keep his family safe and now his last hope had been dragged away by the sheriff.

There was nothing left for him and his in Carson's Point. He just couldn't find a way out of the trouble.

CHAPTER THIRTEEN
HUNGER

Albert Miles

While Jonathan Crowley was being wrangled into a cell at the sheriff's office, Miles, the trapper, was having a conversation with several men who wanted from him almost exactly what Avery Drake had sought from the gunslinger.

"We can pay you, Miles. We can pay you handsomely, and all you need to do is get us safely past those bastards outside of town."

The noonday sun was bright above the hotel, and Miles was sitting in the dining room again, eating a slab of roast beef and a loaf of bread that he shared with the freed slave he had taken into his care.

No one dared question his reasons, especially the ones who sought his aid.

"Gentlemen, I'm not sure if I'm ready to leave this town yet." He looked from one man to the next. They were the sort that could pay and would. They were the men who had the most money in town, and they wanted to be gone. He was amused by the idea and intrigued, but still uncertain if the circumstances would work to his benefit.

"You wouldn't have to leave." Hastings owned the hotel where Miles was staying and seemed determined to head out of town as quickly as he could. "If you can get us past those things, we can handle the rest of it ourselves."

"And what sort of compensation are we considering here, Mr. Hastings?" He crossed his burly arms over his chest and looked at the man, forgetting the meat he'd been eating only a moment before. The man with him didn't bother to look up. Instead, he continued eating with all the passion of a condemned man.

Hastings looked toward the men with him, and then licked his lips nervously. "We could probably manage a hundred dollars."

Miles nodded his head. "Double it."

Hastings looked uncomfortable but turned to his gaggle of cohorts and spoke quickly. "Two hundred dollars would be acceptable, Miles. But more than that would be impossible."

The trapper nodded his head. "When did you want to do this thing?"

"Immediately."

Miles smiled briefly and looked down at his food. It was a good piece of meat, but he could do much better with the money they offered.

He tore open his bread and shoved the remaining meat into the center of the loaf. "You've got a deal, gentlemen. Let's get your people ready. Me and my associate will meet you outside in fifteen minutes."

Hastings nodded his head, the relief obvious on his face.

When they had left the area, Moses Blake looked toward the man who had saved him and frowned. "You think we're ready to take them demons on?"

"Of course. I wouldn't have said yes otherwise."

"Then why were we waiting?"

"You heard the man. He wants to pay us money. And then he wants to work as a shield to help us get close enough to do what we have to in order to kill those things."

"How we gonna kill those bastards, Miles?" His voice was a low growl.

Miles patted the man's shoulder and smiled. He used his bread to sop up the blood from the roast and then took a hearty bite before answering.

"Have a little faith, Moses. I've had a chance to learn a few things. You're going to shoot those fellows with the bullets I give you, and they are going to oblige us by dying."

The man stared at him for several seconds, taking his measure. "You sure about that?"

"As long as you bring me their heads, they'll stay down this time. You can do that, can't you? You can bring me their heads?"

"I reckon I can." The man looked out toward the town gates in the distance. "What about the dead things?"

"They won't be a problem. They're puppets. Take away their masters and they should simply stand out there and rot."

Miles left the dining room, chewing on the roast beef sandwich as he went.

The Dead Men

They stood apart, but were united in their goals. The Nameless communicated without words, their desires easily crossing the distance that separated them, a new trick that they had only learned through the course of the night.

All of them had eaten. The foolish people in the town who tried to leave were taken down quickly and they ate, giving in to the ravenous hunger that had also become a part of their world since the Skinwalker had awakened them. Meat was the only sustenance that worked so far, though they suspected there were other foods that would work even better once their transformations were complete. They were changing, becoming something else, something glorious, though not a one of them could have said what it was they were becoming.

And none of them looked at all the same any longer. The one who had led them initially, and still did, no longer had skin. It had sloughed away during the night and a hide of thick scales had taken its place. His face still had two eyes and a mouth, and beyond that bore no resemblance to what he had once been.

He did not miss the things that were gone now, not even the genitals that had once seemed so important. The glands in his mouth salivated poison onto his tongue, and he spat a wad of phlegm that dissolved the crusted ice and burned the earth beneath it.

They once again had horses, all of them. The animals had panicked at first, but a few quick caresses from their new masters calmed the animals and started the changes within their bodies. The spirit that lived in each of the steeds died and was replaced by something else, something colder, more prepared for what the riders had become. It was for the best. The animals would have succumbed to fear or starvation too quickly, and their flesh would have been too savory to resist for long.

More of the humans were gathering at the gate entrance that led out of town. They communicated the news and came to a decision within seconds.

Without words, the riders gathered at the main entrance and prepared to deal with the humans coming their way.

They would feast again and welcome the new transformations offered by the sacrifice of new blood and meat.

All but one of the men they had come to town for was dead. The last one was hidden inside the town of Carson's Point, and they would not leave until that one came to them. Like them, the remaining target of their hatred was changing. He was one and they were many. They would have their way, and until then, they would feast, and they would change.

The Skinwalker

The dead stood and faced the town that some of them had once called home. They were not many, but they were enough to keep the people in Carson's Point terrified.

They did not think. The trapper was right about that. They merely stood and waited to be given orders. They did not feel, nor did their actions cause them reason to grieve.

The Skinwalker moved among them, nodding his head in satisfaction. They were serving the purpose for which he had created them. The saplings he had given life could issue commands, but in the long run, the dead answered to him.

He could hear their spirits wailing in sorrow and rage. The sounds were soothing and gave him reason to smile. He was still contemplating what to do with those wretched ghosts, if anything.

They, in turn, wished there was something more they could do to him. All save one, though he was unaware of her.

The spectre of Molly Finnegan stood close to her body's remains as if she could somehow stop the flesh from moving, from doing what it was told to do, merely because she had once inhabited that ruined shell. She could no more move the body than she could force Jonathan Crowley's hands despite her best efforts.

She knew that now and hated that she could do so very little. That hatred gave her a certain edge over the other dead around her, and she was only just beginning to understand that.

Earlier a ghost had come to her, its shape wavering and distorted. It had pled with her to help it somehow and after several minutes of explaining that she could do nothing, and having it ignore her words, Molly had lost her temper and attacked. Her fingers sank into the thin, watery flesh of the other ghost and broke through the shape as if it were merely smoke. Her anger was not sated by the change, but merely increased. As she pulled her hands back, the ghost came with her, sticking to her hands like a hundred cobwebs, insubstantial but there, and impossible to ignore.

And, as she felt her anger grow, she felt something else as well, a revitalization of her essence that made her look to her hands where the feeling emanated from.

And she watched as the wavering, wailing spirit that had offended her was drawn into her, absorbed into the shape of her body like kerosene consumed by fire.

Before the wretched thing she had attacked could escape, she dragged the rest of it into her arms and held it until it disappeared and her very being hummed with unexpected power.

The feeling was finer than her first kiss.

She contemplated that fact as the Skinwalker moved among the dead and watched the forces he had created prepare to face off against the Europeans who had come to claim the place as their own.

He could feel the gathering storm of emotions and desires and he allowed himself a small grin of pleasure.

One way or another, blood would soon be flowing. He looked forward to the coming conflagration, for unlike his saplings he understood that meat would feed a body, but conflict and death would always be the best sustenance for a hungry soul.

Albert Miles

Miles looked at the wagons gathered together in front of the gates and shook his head. They wanted to take everything with them. They wanted to carry every last possession of worth, and if he'd had to guess, they brought nowhere near enough food for even a short trip.

That was fine with him. He didn't care if they survived, so long as they paid him and helped him clear away the nuisances that had come to Carson's Point.

Stomper pranced lightly under him. The animal treated him exactly as it had his son, which made perfect sense for, despite the change of the mind controlling the body, the memories from the trapper were still accessible to Albert Miles. For so massive a horse the animal was incredibly nimble. He petted his mount's neck and leaned down to whisper in the ear to the left of Stomper's mane. "Don't let me down, Stomper. We're not going far but we have to get there quickly."

The horse snorted, a plume of steam coming from his broad nostrils, and stamped with one hoof.

Miles looked up at the wall near the gate and the platform that Moses stood on. His rifles were loaded and the man's hands were steady.

"Are you ready, Moses?"

"You say the word and they all die." His voice was steady and calm. His dark eyes were slits against the glare from the bright day.

Miles looked out to where the six figures stood in plain sight. They were a sizable distance away, far enough to stop most weapons. Blake's rifle, however, was designed for long-range firing, and the man had a steady hand and a good eye.

"Kill them, Moses. For your family."

Moses nodded once and settled in to aim.

The first of the things standing beyond the gates twitched as the bullet blew through its chest. It looked down at the wound and then back at the gate and the miniscule puff of smoke from Moses's weapon and then it howled in pain as it fell from the horse forced to carry it.

Miles smiled and nodded to himself as he pulled the saber from his waist.

The things looked at their fallen brethren and realized slowly that it was not already rising from where it had fallen. This time there would be no recovery.

Before that realization struck home, Moses had fired two more times and blown massive holes into another couple of riders.

Miles smiled and tapped Stomper's sides gently. "Let's go, boy. We have prizes to collect."

The fourth of the things roared, its head thrown back and every muscle in the neck and chest strained into new shapes. The sound was not human, but then, neither was the creature itself, not anymore.

It looked toward Miles with deep and abiding hatred, and charged forward on its mount. The animal moved in a rush and Stomper snorted before he tore across the ground toward the rider and mount.

And the bullet from Moses's rifle blew half the chest of the rider away and sent the thing sailing backward onto the frozen ground. The shot wasn't perfect, the thing was still alive and the sounds it made were weaker, but no less hatred filled.

The last two riders tried to break away, realizing, perhaps, that they would be targeted.

Moses had no desire to let them escape. He took careful aim, cocked his rifle again and fired. The shot was clean and took out the midsection of the reptilian thing that tried to get away.

The last one that Moses shot was the same thing that had earlier chewed most of the face from a man trying to escape.

Even as the lumpy thing fell to the ground the crowd of people seeking to leave the area cheered their approval. Black or white, Miles had little doubt the shooter was a hero for the next few hours at the very least.

Miles himself took care of hacking the heads from the dead and dying things. They were trying to recover from their wounds, but he had crafted the bullets very carefully. They did not kill, per se, but they stopped the restoration of form that the pale riders had come to depend on.

Beheading, on the other hand, that killed. Or at least it killed the bodies. Surprisingly strong muscles flexed, and the blade of Miles's saber cut deep, hacking through the necks of the things until the misshapen heads could be removed. The heads still moved, their mouths twisting with rage and trying to make noises despite the lack of vocal cords.

He gathered the heads together and slipped them into a heavy leather sack. Stomper, who was usually the most stoic of animals—if he could be called an animal at all anymore—eyed the bag uneasily but did not shy away.

Long chords tied the sack to the pommel of the saddle and Miles mounted his horse and looked around at the surrounding woods. The dead people were still there, still standing, but they did not move nor show any indication that they wanted to do anything else.

To make his point, Miles moved toward the woods and used a thick length of rope to drag the closest of the walking dead closer to the town's gate. The thing barely struggled as it was dragged closer and did not try to stand when he was done hauling it to his destination. Large chunks of flesh and bone were torn away over the rough terrain.

Miles looked at Hastings and smiled tightly. "They don't seem to care if you're here or not, and the ones that led them are dead. I'll be taking my money now."

The man reached into his purse and pulled out the appropriate cash, albeit reluctantly.

"I can't thank you enough, Miles."

"Business is business." He counted the money and separated out half of it for Moses. "Don't think for a moment this was anything else. I'm not the sort to do for others from the goodness of my heart."

The words shocked the hotel owner. "I'll remember that, sir." His tone was stiff and formal.

"See that you do. You want to thank someone, thank Moses Blake. He's the fellow that did the shooting."

"Why did you take the heads?"

Miles smiled and looked the man over again. "Now and then a man has to answer to his own curiosity. I am most curious about what made those things what they are, and I suspect the heads will tell me."

Hastings stared at him with open distaste and shook his head slowly from side to side. "Sometimes it might be best not to know."

"It's always better to understand what causes sorrow, Mr. Hastings. How else can you defend against it?"

The man rode on, not answering, perhaps not able to answer.

Miles watched him go and then rode back into Carson's Point.

There were prizes to be examined. More importantly, there was something else out in the woods that was watching him and considering his actions carefully.

He did not know exactly what that something was, but he wanted to know. He needed to know. Knowledge was power, and Albert Miles had a long history of seeking power.

Pace Peabody

The prisoner sat in his cell and stared at him. That was all he did. He didn't try to talk about being innocent, he didn't ask for food or for a blanket to fight back the bitter cold. He just stared with his plain brown eyes.

Pace Peabody wanted to scream. Jonathan Crowley was worrying him something fierce, and there was nothing he could do about it.

Because the man made him feel a mite nervous, Pace stood up and walked from the room. He walked along the boardwalk in front of the office for a good ten minutes and then came back inside. After a long pause, he peered into the back room with the cells, and sure enough, Crowley was staring at him. The man hadn't so much as moved a muscle as far as he could tell, but his eyes were still staring, still looking at Pace and maybe even looking through him.

"Why'd you kill them five men?"

"Eight."

"What?"

"I killed eight. Three in my hotel room."

"Well, why?"

"You ever have a bunch of men sneak into your room with guns in their hands?"

It wasn't really something he had to ponder for long. "Can't say as I have. No."

"Well, after you do, you can come ask me why you killed 'em all."

"What about the ones in the barn?"

Crowley's smile spread slowly across his face, and his eyes glittered. "Three in my room out of the five that were there. I followed the last ones back to the barn, recognized the men who tried to kill me in the woods and showed them how to do it the right way."

Pace looked at the man for several seconds, swallowing his nervousness. "Shows how much you know."

"What's that, Deputy?"

"I'm the sheriff." He puffed his chest out.

"For now." Crowley shrugged. "Way I hear it, you were the deputy before the new sheriff got here and afterward, too."

"Well, you don't know everything, do you? There were only four bodies in the barn. That makes seven dead."

Crowley leaned back on the narrow cot where he had been leaning forward. "Really?"

"Yep." Pace couldn't help but feel a bit smug.

"Town full of people that won't stay dead, and you aren't worried about one getting away from you?"

"What?"

"I killed five. You missed one." Crowley's grin grew broader.

"How the hell am I supposed to kill dead people?"

Crowley chuckled. "All sorts of dead people can get up and walk around, Deputy. I suppose you'd have to know what made them get up in the first place, wouldn't you?"

"Well how am I supposed to know that?" The conversation wasn't going at all the way he wanted it to.

Crowley chuckled again and closed his eyes. "I suppose you'll have to ask around...."

At least the man wasn't staring at him anymore. That had to count for something.

He looked at the man for a few moments and shrugged before he left the room. When he came back five minutes later, Crowley was staring at him again.

Marcus Darby

His head ached. Not surprising really, as half of it had been blown away from his skull earlier.

The pain was dull, hardly worth noticing. He ignored it easily enough as he forced his body to move, half dragging himself across the stable floor and burrowing under the thick hay.

The changes were happening, and there seemed little he could do about it. Muscles shifted under his skin and bones twisted with slow, deliberate motion. In comparison to those agonies, the headache was barely even an inconvenience.

His mind didn't feel like it was his alone anymore. There was something else inside of him that crooned and mumbled to him in a different language, something that almost made sense, but not quite.

He wasn't completely sure he wanted to understand the words. Partly, he expected that knowledge would do him harm, though he'd have been hard-pressed to say why he believed that. Instinct, perhaps, or a well-honed sense of self-preservation.

All of them were dead. Every last person he had come to depend on in the last two years, gone, killed by that bastard with the deadly aim.

He paused in his trek as something shivered through his body, moving through his insides as if he were filled with water instead of meat and bones. He couldn't have screamed if his life had depended on it, the pain was simply too large.

And then he was looking at the ceiling, and the light was drastically different. He must have lost consciousness, though it seemed like he'd barely even closed his eyes.

The words of the damnable song were starting to make sense and much as the notion scared him, he was also delighted by the idea. The song, he suspected, would explain what he was becoming and tell him secrets that could help him achieve his goals, if only he could decide what they should be now. One look at the distorted fingers of his left hand told him he could never go back home. He should have been terrified, but instead he was…well, he was simply curious.

The fingers were long and thin and seemed far too pale in color. He was as white as the snow falling outside. His hand clenched into a fist, and he felt strength in that flesh. To test that theory, he reached for the closest support and squeezed the wood harshly. His fingers sank into the seasoned timber as if he were grabbing an infant's flesh, leaving angry dents as a reminder of how strong he'd become.

Marcus Darby was no longer human. He couldn't deny it anymore.

He wasn't sure if he wanted to.

The worst part of it was he knew there was another like him not far away and that the thing out there was as aware of him he was aware of it.

Worse still, the thing out there beyond the edge of the town and halfway lost in the woods was angry. It demanded blood and as surely as he was a different man than he used to be, he knew the thing would have that blood.

The Skinwalker

The Skinwalker paced slowly around the perimeter of Carson's Point. Words could not possibly explain the sense of loss, of outrage. The seeds were not toys to be stolen, they were a part of the Skinwalker, his chance to have progeny, to be more than a solitary figure lost in a world of other, lesser beings.

He had watched the stranger on the massive horse as he rode across the field and took heads from dead and dying bodies, and he had known fear for the first time in a thousand moons.

Even as mere saplings his children should have healed from the damage done by the Europeans and their weapons. He had watched them recover from far greater injuries without concern. But today was different. They were struck down by a single rifle, a single shooter, and they fell and stayed down.

He walked the battlefield, ignoring the fools who fled the area. They were cattle, and if he had need of them, he could find them easily. They did not see him. He did not want to be seen, and he knew the right rituals to protect himself from human eyes.

One by one he walked to the remains of his children and searched them, examined them until he understood the truth behind their deaths.

The bullets that struck them were not merely lead. They had been enchanted as surely as his seeds were more than mere pebbles by the time he was done with them.

He held the ruined metal pellets in his hand and studied them carefully, examined the magic that was still wrapped around them and coursing through them. They were not the incantations of his kind, or even of the shamans he had encountered in his time. They were as alien to him as the Europeans themselves.

Still, they could possibly prove useful before he was done. He merely had to decipher how to use these new tools, and interpret the wizardry that made them unique and deadly to his kind.

When he had gathered the last of the bullets into his hand he moved toward the open gate of the town. He needed to be closer to the creature that had created these deadly weapons if he wanted to understand them completely.

Then, when he understood the power he was up against, he would make his move.

His children had been destroyed, but more importantly, the seeds he could have used to recreate them had been stolen and no one, living or dead, would steal from him without suffering for their insolence.

The Skinwalker moved in the shadows and took his time, reminding himself to be cautious. Care and secrecy would win this unusual battle for him, as they had helped him time and again since he was reborn.

A family of hungry fools moved past him, mother holding baby close to her breast and doing all she could to shield the child from the bitter cold. He reached out with a hand that didn't even cast a shadow and plucked the infant's soul from its body. The bright, vibrant spirit wailed as he devoured it. Another five minutes passed before the mother joined her own voice to the distant echoes of her child's painful death.

He would have his seeds back and he would have his revenge for the ruination of his plans. And he would see the man who had sent his children to their deaths destroyed for his troubles, or he would see the very town of Carson's Point leveled.

Lucas Slate

Lucas Slate dared the unusual and ate at a restaurant for a change of pace. He was too tired to cook and even if he were so inclined there was nothing in his larder that he wanted to consume. So, a treat. He savored every bite of the lamb stew the restaurant was offering along with a thick, crusty slab of bread.

His mother had managed far better, but the meal was superior to his own cooking and after the last few days no one seemed overly unsettled when they looked at his pasty skin.

The negro he'd seen ride into town only a few days before also ate at the restaurant and he marveled at that. No one in his home state would have tolerated the notion of a black man eating in a white man's establishment, no matter how threatening the man's attitude. They'd have dragged the man behind a herd of horses long before that occurred. And that would be if they were in a forgiving mood.

Yet there the man sat, accepting a meal and listening to several different people praising him for his heroism. Of course, Lucas had heard all about the deaths of the dead Indians who refused to die. It was all anyone could talk about, and even for an outcast like him, news had a way of coming around.

The trapper, Miles, sat with the Negro. As he owed the man money, Lucas rose from his chair and slipped across the room as soon as the worst of the crowd had thinned out and he'd finished most of the first decent meal he'd allowed himself in the last week.

"Mr. Miles, I believe I have something for you." He nodded to the rifleman and to the trapper alike as he came closer. Miles looked at him and smiled that soft, warm smile he showed at odd times. The black man eyed him warily, no doubt alerted by his accent as surely as by his pallid skin.

Miles raised a hand to stop him as he reached for the small purse he kept in his vest. "No need for that, Mr. Slate."

"We had an arrangement, sir. I prefer to honor that arrangement."

"I have come into a substantial reward, my good man, and I know that you have been working very hard of late. For the present I suggest we suspend our previous agreement."

He prepared to protest, but Miles rose from his seat and patted him on his shoulder with one of his oversized paws.

"Perhaps I'll simply keep the funds for you then, should you have a sudden turn in your fortunes."

"Much obliged, Mr. Slate." The man looked at him for several seconds with that odd smile of his, and then reached into a small tin he pulled from his coat. "I have something for you, then. Call it a marker if you will."

He held out an intricately carved stone, only slightly larger than a shelled pea, and Lucas picked it up, studying the detailed lines and curls that wrapped the piece. He couldn't quite decipher what the images were, but they were unsettling, like the vestiges of a dream that sometimes remained after he awoke.

"I don't know what to say, Mr. Miles...."

"Take it. I have a few more." He smiled and said softly, "Consider it a reminder of the tales Gaston used to tell you. I suspect there are similar roots."

Lucas blinked and nodded his head. He could not resist staring hard at the trapper. He couldn't think of a time when he had told the burly man anything about his childhood.

Before he could make a statement to that fact, the trapper was heading back toward his seat and his meal. Rather than appear rude, Lucas nodded his head and moved back to his own repast.

He ate slowly, his eyes taking in the fine images on the stone. They seemed to shift, to change ever so subtly, but he couldn't be sure. Either way, he lost himself in the stone for a while, barely breathing as he examined the unsettling piece of work.

When he looked up again, the trapper and the rifleman had left the restaurant.

He hastily paid for his meal and headed for home. He had work to do, just as soon as he was done studying his new trinket.

He forgot about the work as he worried the pebble between his fingers and studied the images again and again, convinced they were changing, and far more important, that they were trying to tell him something.

He just had to understand how to listen.

CHAPTER FOURTEEN

Molly Finnegan

The hunger didn't abate. It grew, even as she feasted. Molly moved among the dead and found those unfortunates who had attached themselves to their bodies, trying to regain what had been taken from them. They looked to her as she moved from one body to the next some nearly mindless, others merely sick with hope.

She found the ruin of her old flesh and knew nothing but disgust at the notion. She had never been a vain woman, though she knew she was attractive enough, but the rot had taken most of her features and torn them away, and what was left still stood, a hollow thing waiting for a voice to give it orders. It would not listen to her demands and so she divorced herself from the lifeless thing.

The spirits, the ghosts that surrounded the area and surely haunted the town itself, were unaware of much beyond themselves and she wondered if it that was the natural order of things. She tried speaking with them and they did not acknowledge her until she once again reached out to touch them and make them her own. It was the touch, you see, that showed her the way to her newfound abilities. Her hand had but to touch and the process began, they drained into her like water into a reservoir, spilling into her but never filling the emptiness that grew inside her depths.

Jonathan Crowley had slighted her, and that simple fact caused her no end of frustration. He wanted her, he had made that very clear, and yet he refused her when she offered herself, when she could have given him some minor comfort and taken the same for herself.

She understood his reasons: What good was a mere ghost that could do little but tantalize when he wanted flesh?

But she was learning, wasn't she? Oh, yes! She fed on the other, weaker spirits, and in the process she learned about them. She could have studied their lives, their deaths, the experiences of a handful of people already and more to come, but she didn't want to know their lives. She wanted to understand what they had learned after death. There were secrets to understand, mysteries of the world around her that she wanted to comprehend, and that simple fact was enough to drive her on, to keep her hungry when she should have long since been sated.

She touched a soul and learned that it had been a fighting man. She recognized him easily enough: he was one of the pigs who had raped her.

Molly gladly returned the favor, tearing his essences apart and feasting, casting aside his memories of life, save for the knowledge of how he died. That she savored like a fine feast.

When that memory no longer held her attention, Molly quickly sought the next of the dead to catch her attention and pulled it into herself, ripping through memories of a wife that died, a mother who used a belt at the smallest offense and a father who left home never to return. They were not important memories, not to Molly. Instead, she focused on the things that mattered most to her, the manipulation of…what? She didn't have a name for it. The stuff she and the others were made of, the unique energies that made up the soul. This one had the knowledge she wanted: as the second of them had known that there were things that could be done with the soul-stuff. This one knew how to use the very same energy to create a new form.

Jonathan Crowley would not scorn her again, and if he did, she'd fix the situation.

Her hand lashed out and grabbed at another of the dead, draining away power and storing it within her incorporeal form.

Each one she grabbed and fed on brought her relief from the emptiness inside her, and added to the brilliance of the light that glowed within her. She cast no shadow, she had no weight, but for those who could see her, she was nearly a beacon.

Oh yes, he'd be with her, just as soon as she had finished feeding.

———

Dan Kaufmann

Daniel Kaufmann should have been relaxing. The dead things seemed to be dead this time, and thank the Lord for that. None of the corpses had risen again after that rough tracker and his black man had finished their work. People were clearing out of town and none too soon for his tastes, thanks just the same, and the gunslinger was locked away. All was well, and he'd received a telegram that his new window would be coming his way in a week's time instead of in a month's.

He should have been happy as a lark. Instead he stood behind his bar and watched the patrons on his establishment with a wary eye. Maybe he was just gun shy after the last few days, but he couldn't make himself relax. There were too many people around that he didn't know and even the ones he did know weren't the sort he'd have preferred as patrons.

That idiot Peabody sat at the center table of his restaurant and chewed noisily at a steak. He should have been trying to restore order, but as far as the new sheriff was concerned, everything was fine now that the Crowley fellow was locked away.

He couldn't agree with that assessment. Not a chance. The people around him, stranger and familiar alike, looked like they were recovering from a nightmare. He half expected them to pinch themselves for reassurance.

Peabody waved to him and pointed to the mug he'd been drinking from, and Dan ground his teeth behind thin-pressed lips. The damned fool intended to get drunk. That was his entire reason for coming in. The steak dinner was just an excuse.

"You thinking you maybe should feed that man you have locked away? Or do you suppose he'll manage that all by himself?" The words came past his lips without warning, but he didn't feel the least bit of guilt over saying them. Sometimes words needed saying.

The damned fool looked around sheepishly. "I hadn't thought about that."

"So I can see."

"Well you don't have to be nasty about it." He pushed his emptied plate away as if he were making a statement. At least he wasn't asking for seconds again.

"Man sitting in that cell isn't the sort you should be riling, Pace. I'll get you a plate for him while you settle your bill."

Sure enough, he looked shocked that he would have to pay. "I thought meals were included in my pay."

Dan shook his head and scowled. "Do I look like the mayor of Carson's Point to you? It might be that he will pay you for the pleasure of eating, but he doesn't pay me to feed you, and that means you have to pay."

"I don't have any money on me…"

"Get your damned fool self out of my place before I drag you out!" Dan's blood pressure soared at the thought of the deputy's stupidity. He wanted to throttle the man.

Pace stood up and glared.

"Go on you fool, I'll have the food sent to your prisoner. And I'll send you the tab for today and for his meal." His voice calmed down a bit.

Peabody made a show of stomping his way out of the room while most of the people around them did their best to pretend they weren't watching an idiot having a debate with the owner. It wasn't that Pace wasn't well liked, because he was, but he lacked the common sense to come in out of the rain, or to even not stare at the falling raindrops with his mouth hanging open.

Ten minutes later Dan packed up the meal himself and told Annie, one of the hookers who roomed up above the main bar, to watch the place for him. She was honest enough and properly scared of him, so it wasn't an issue.

The cold hadn't gotten any better outside and he huddled inside his thickest coat as he walked the distance between tavern and jail.

Pace wasn't in, but the main door was left unlocked. Dan shook his head and made a noise of disgust. What? People were supposed to leave the fool a note if they had a situation? There were plenty of hungry people around who would have gladly taken a job as deputy, but apparently he was too busy looking for free meals to consider that.

The back of the place was easily accessed. Though it wasn't all that often that Dan had worked as a cook for the town, he'd done it in a pinch before. He remembered the way to the cells.

There were three small rooms with bars instead of walls or doors at the front. Only one of them was occupied.

Jonathan Crowley sat on his narrow cot and looked toward Dan with the slightest curl of a grin on his mouth.

"If you've come to collect on my tab, it might be a bit difficult to pay you just now."

"No sir." He shook his head and held out the plate of food. "Town's gonna lock you up, they have to feed you."

"I'm surprised Peabody could figure that part out."

Dan snickered. "He didn't. I'll be sending a bill for this to the mayor's office."

"There's a mayor here?"

"Not so you'd know. He doesn't much like leaving his office."

Crowley rose from his seat and took the offered plate of food through the small opening just wide enough to let the plate slide through. Two rolls, boiled potatoes and three slices of roast mutton were the items he inspected.

"Much obliged." He tore the rolls open and shoved the cold meat into the middle of them. A moment later he was feasting.

Dan watched the man eat with a sort of sick fascination. He was less of a slob than a lot of people, but after watching Crowley meticulously eat with a fork and a knife, seeing him using his fingers was almost unsettling.

When he finally came up for air, the gunslinger looked at him with less amusement. "Have you ever been to a zoo, Mr. Kaufmann?"

"A zoo?" He shook his head.

"It's a place where men of science get together to study animals. They feed them, observe them, from time to time cut them open. And in order to make other people interested in their work, they put these animals on display for the public."

He nodded his head though he had no idea where the conversation was going.

"I have been to zoos in Paris, in London and in a few more exotic places." Crowley wiped his mouth on his sleeve, as Dan hadn't thought to bring a napkin. "While I understand the notion of studying animals better than most people would imagine, I've never been much for leaving them on public display. They can't eat, mate, sleep or defecate without somebody watching and that lack of privacy might become uncomfortable after a while. Certain things are best left in the privacy of one's home. Would you agree?"

"Oh yeah, absolutely."

The pleasant demeanor faded in an instant and the look of fury on the man's face had Dan backpedaling quickly. "Then kindly do me the courtesy of not staring at me like I'm a monkey on display!"

"I'm very sorry." His face flushed with embarrassment. "I just-I wanted to ask you a question."

Crowley rose from his seat and moved closer to the bars. His eyes glittered and his smile was decidedly unpleasant.

"Then ask."

"Those Indians are dead. They all got killed by a couple of guns for hire."

Crowley looked at him hard, his head slightly tilted to the left. "Really?"

"Yes. Oh my yes. I watched the whole thing with my eyes and watched the trapper cut their heads off as trophies." He blanched a bit at the very notion.

"So what's your question?"

"I've watched you." He hastily put his hands up in the air. "Not to be rude, but in my business I have to watch people or I end up burned out or dead." Crowley nodded and he continued. "I watched when those fellas came at you the first time and I saw you take them down. And I saw you stop that damned fool Morris Biggs when he tried to draw a gun on you." He swallowed. "I also saw his gun explode when you pointed at it. You never drew a weapon. You just pointed."

Crowley nodded his head silently, neither confirming nor denying.

"If you have a point, get to it Mr. Kaufmann."

"I don't know if I have a point. Except I know you aren't quite normal. You're a mean shot and you blew a man's hands to pieces by pointing, so I reckon maybe you know a little something about the strange events around here. Am I right?"

The eyes that looked him over were frightening things. How had he ever thought the gunslinger a plain looking man when all he had to do was look into those eyes to suddenly fear Crowley? "Let's say you are for the sake of argument. What of it?"

"Do you think it's safe in this town, Mr. Crowley?"

Crowley shook his head, but his eyes never left Dan's. "Not in the least."

"Why?"

He might have been discussing the weather with a casual acquaintance. "There are other things working here, Mr. Kaufmann. There are other creatures moving in this town and they've been drawn here for a reason."

"What sort of creatures?"

"I don't know." Crowley shrugged. "I've never encountered the sort before. Then again, that's why I'm out in this miserable area, isn't it? To learn about other creatures."

Dan nodded his head and swallowed hard.

"Were there other questions, Mr. Kaufmann?" The look on the man's plain face was mocking. It had to be. He knew why Dan was there, but he wasn't making it easy on him.

"Mr. Crowley, if I was to ask your pay rate, would you be able to take care of these problems?"

Crowley shook his head. "I don't want for money. I have plenty. You have to ask for help, not ask how much help will cost."

Dan stared at the man for several seconds, trying to fathom if he was being had or if the man was sincere.

"Mr. Crowley, will you help make this town safe again?"

Crowley walked back to his cot and settled in, his arms moving behind his head, giving him some meager cushioning against the rough wall. "First there's the problem of me being behind bars."

"I could get you out, I suppose."

Crowley nodded his head. "Get me out. Then I'll help you."

Dan looked long and hard and remembered the ruin of Morris Bigg's hands, the bleeding shattered stumps of his fingers.

"You could get yourself out, couldn't you?"

That little flash of a smile, like lightning peeking through gathering storm clouds. "Yes I could. But I rather like the idea of you having to put Peabody in his place for me."

Albert Miles

Albert Miles stared at his companion for a long moment. Moses continued looking out the window into the cold winter sky.

"What's on your mind, Moses?"

"I kilt 'em. They're dead. But I still don't feel complete." His voice was low and lost, the mourning he'd delayed had come for him at last. and he was hollowed out by grief.

"That will get better in time." He placed a heavy hand on the man's shoulder and felt the coiled muscles under the shirt that covered him. "My wife was murdered a long time ago. I understand your grief."

"I killed them, Albert. It should feel better but all I feel is…is…."

"Nothing?"

The man nodded slowly, his eyes looking out beyond what they could see, searching for something that had been taken from him. "Yeah. Nothing."

"Maybe we can find a way to fix that in time."

"We had us a settlement. Had the land fair and proper. Had cattle and had more of them coming. And now that's all gone."

"No, Moses. It isn't gone at all." He leaned in closer and whispered softly in the man's ear. "It's just waiting for you. Go back to the homestead and see if I'm wrong. They'll be waiting for you."

The light in the man's eyes broke apart, shattered by the tears that started to fall.

"Oh, Albert…. Oh they're waiting for me." His voice cracked and trembled and from the ashes of his sorrow the sound of joy slowly rose, a cinder of hope among the ruin and destruction.

He patted the man's shoulder one last time. "Go to them. Go be with your wife, your friends."

Moses scrambled quickly, grabbing his battered old coat and his hat before he gathered his rifles and his weapons and headed for the door, barely even bothering to look back.

Miles watched him go and nodded his head. It was better this way. Moses Blake was not a happy man, would likely never be happy again. His heart and soul were back on a lot of land he'd fought hard for, with the lives of the people who'd been stolen away from him.

The woman he loved was dead and while Miles could manage many things, bringing the dead back was still beyond him.

He sighed and pulled out his pipe, tamping the tobacco in without conscious thought. Resurrection was beyond him, but he could tell lies, couldn't he? He could make those lies very convincing, too.

Moses Blake left Carson's Point fifteen minutes later, sitting on a wagon that was ready to fall apart, drawn by an ox that had seen its best days five years earlier.

He left in search of a dream that had been stolen from him. Miles gave him back the dream, insubstantial and hollow, yes, but good enough to make the man happy for as long as he might live.

Moses Blake left town before the final days of Carson's Point. It was a small kindness, but the best the Albert Miles could offer.

The Skinwalker

The sun settled itself behind the closest mountain and the town was lost in the growing darkness. The Skinwalker preferred it that way. He moved from one shadow to the next with ease, not seen but most definitely felt. Those who came too close to him shivered and thought it merely the cold that chilled them to the core. Sometimes ignorance is bliss.

The cold still held no surprises for the Skinwalker. Before the Europeans had ever come to the land he'd been here, creeping into the minds and nightmares of the people and taking what he wanted. His had been a very long existence, and he intended to live quite a while longer.

But for all of that, he could barely contain his rage.

Seven of his seeds had been planted in this very area, and each had been drawn here, to this foul-smelling place of Europeans and their maddening structures, and why? Because there was something about this place that called to the foolish. He understood the nature of man well enough to know that race mattered very little when it came to the darker desires. This town drew the Europeans as surely as a good fire drew the flies and other flittering insects. And their desperation, their endless need for more, was what drew him to this place. He had no idea what they sought, but he wanted to know it better if it meant he could draw still more of them to this blighted waste and feed on still more misery.

That same desire had drawn his seeds into the town and led to their destruction. The deaths of his children were not his motivation for entering the town, and he could have fed on the desperation and woe of the town from a distance and never once entered the area, but there was something else, he had to consider.

The children he had created were dead, but the seeds were still alive, still calling to him, seeking information and wisdom and he wanted the seeds back or at least to see what they were being used for. Trickster had created his kind with a curiosity that was both quiet and insatiable. He would know who or what was collecting the seeds.

And then, like as not, he'd kill the possessor.

The Skinwalker closed his eyes and stood perfectly still in the shadows. There was one voice that was stronger, angrier than the rest. It called out a song that was close to one of his but different. The seed of another of his kind had taken root and that, oh, that was a problem. He was not sure about leaving any of the seeds alive if they were not his.

Marcus Darby

Something was wrong with his hands. Even in the darkness of the barn, in the hole he'd dug for himself in the frozen earth, he could tell that there was something wrong with his hands.

They didn't feel right. The fingers were too long, and there seemed too many joints to each of them.

He turned slowly in his makeshift haven, the wetness of the slicked walls allowing him to reposition himself with relative ease.

How was it that he ever thought the area cold, when he was so unbelievably warm? It had been an eternity since he ate, but there was no hunger inside of him. There was just a vast emptiness.

He didn't want to think about what his body looked like. The only certainty he had left was that he could no longer recognize his hands. That was enough to unsettle him.

The darkness around him felt too small, too tightly woven, and he felt panic trying to crawl into his mind. Before it could take root he let his unfamiliar hands catch the edges of the tunnel he'd carved with those strange new limbs, and felt his fingers dig past the wetness to the silky lining beneath. He pulled and lifted himself into a new position, then stretched his body toward the opening above him.

Dried out hay fell into his haven as he slipped out. The impacts from the falling debris were minor enough that he barely felt them.

Somewhere out in the darkness something called to him. He could feel it, hear it, almost taste the summons. He didn't want to listen, but there didn't seem to be a choice in the matter. Despite his desire to stay where he was and rest, his legs moved, taking one tentative step and then another.

Marcus tried to open his mouth and felt a distant panic bloom inside his chest.

He couldn't feel his mouth.

Hands that felt completely wrong reached up to touch his face and the echo of fear grew a bit larger. He couldn't feel his mouth and he couldn't find it, either. Where his lips, his teeth, his jaw should have been, there was instead a thick column of bone that ran down from below his eyes and angled down along his chest.

It was too much to tolerate. He lashed out with his hands and felt them claw first at the air and then at the wood of the doorway leading from the barn into the cold. He slashed the wood with his unfamiliar hands and felt the threshold break into a new shape beneath his fingers.

He tried to run, but his legs betrayed him and buckled. He collapsed to the frozen ground and shuddered as something happened under his clothes, under his skin.

Something shifted.

Something grew.

Deep within his body wet sloshing noises gurgled and groaned and if he'd had the mouth to do so, Marcus Darby would have screamed.

He lay where he fell and clutched at the ground with his improper hands as more changes wracked his insides.

Off in the distance the same something called for him. Much as part of him wanted to listen he could not. His body was not done changing.

Lucas Slate

"I won't do it."

Pace Peabody looked at him and shook his head. "Well, why not? It's your job, ain't it?" His voice was had a whining quality that Lucas did not like in the least.

He looked out into the woods where the dead stood still, some of them covered in ice and others frosted white, and shook his head again.

"No, sir. It most decidedly is not my job. My job is to bury the dead. I buried every last one of those wretches at least once before and I haven't been paid yet. I'll surely not do it a second time without recompense."

The sheriff looked at him and let his mouth hang open in the bitter cold. "Well, what do you expect me to do about them then?"

Lucas's eyes looked away and back out at the dead who still stood in the woods around Carson's Point. They did not move. They did not breathe. They were very obviously dead, and yet they stood, resisting the forces of nature that should have had them down on the ground and rotting away.

"You're the sheriff. Perhaps you should arrest them?"

"What? What the hell for?" Pace looked out at the dead and shook his head and Lucas could almost see him trying to figure out the logistics of getting the corpses into his jail cells.

"You're the sheriff, Pace Peabody. I suspect you'll have to come up with something."

Without another word the undertaker turned on his heel and started back for his home. Pace would have to do his own dirty work.

"Maybe I ought to arrest you then!" Pace's voice was shrill.

Sometimes keeping his composure was more challenging than others. Lucas closed his eyes and counted slowly to ten, as his mother had taught him to do when the bullying children made him want to lash out in his youth.

"You have less reason to arrest me than to detain the corpses, Deputy. Consider that carefully before you threaten me with incarceration."

"It's sheriff."

"No, sir. I do not believe you have yet been appointed to that particular station, despite the circumstances."

Peabody muttered something under his breath and then stomped an irritated foot into the hard-packed frozen ground. Lucas continued walking.

There was something he needed to do, but exactly what that was seemed to be eluding him.

Where were you going, Lucas? Where were you going and who had called you out into the cold?

He shoved the thoughts aside hastily. He'd been on his way somewhere when the deputy had called to him and all but dragged him over to look at the corpses standing in the woods. As if there was any doubt that he knew about them. As if, as the man had assumed, he might feel a sudden compulsion to escort each of them back to the holes they'd crawled out of.

In his lifetime there were many things that Lucas could fault about his world, but the one thing he'd always prided himself on was his mind. And now, for the first time ever, he began to doubt whether that last precious commodity was working as well as it should. He strained to remember where he'd been going, what he'd been up to when Peabody called to him and there was nothing. The lack of memory wasn't merely unsettling, it was frustrating as well.

"Damn it all to hell, Slate, what am I supposed to do with them?" Pace's voice was a wasp buzzing in his ear and Lucas turned fast as he looked at the man.

"I don't care!" His anger flared and his voice cracked as he took two steps toward the deputy. "Do whatever you have to do, but leave me out of it. How hard is that for you to get into your fool head?"

Pace stared at him hard, shocked, no doubt, to hear the soft-spoken albino dare to talk back.

"I've no desire to look at those damned things, Pace! Do you understand me? They aren't natural. They're abominations in the eyes of God above!" He shook his head and then did the nearly unthinkable and spat a wad of phlegm on the ground. His mother would surely have fainted dead away at the very thought if she weren't already dead and buried. "Call that preacher you go see every Sunday when you're recovering from your latest drunken night and see if he can do something with them, but leave me out of it!"

Pace stared hard at him for a moment and Lucas began to wonder if he'd pushed his luck too far. It was always a possibility.

"Well, maybe I will! Maybe there's one decent person left in this town!"

"If there's a decent man in this town he'll likely have nothing to do with you, Peabody." The rage that he'd been trying to suppress was growing hotter in his mind, surging like the fires of a furnace that gets a fresh gust of air and another hundred pounds of coal.

Peabody's face took on a crimson color that was unpleasant. Rather than continue to look at the man he turned on his heel for the second time and walked away.

Something to do with a pebble. Had that been it? Had there been an unusual stone or bead that he wanted to do something with, or about?

He couldn't remember and in the long run he started back for his home.

And in the distance, something sang and seemed to call for him.

CHAPTER FIFTEEN

Pace Peabody

The preacher shook his head. "No, my son. I don't believe I can assist you."

Pace stared at the man and clenched his fists. "Can't you say a prayer or something?"

"I've said several prayers already, and if the Lord plans on answering he's not done so yet."

He was about to say something more when Dan Kaufmann came storming toward them in the cold. The sun was setting and the shadows had grown long and the man looked truly, deeply annoyed.

The preacher took one look at Dan and started walking away, his lips already forming an excuse of some sort that was drowned out by Dan's booming voice.

"You want to tell me why there are dead people over there instead of in their graves?"

He wasn't looking at the preacher. He was looking at Pace.

"Well I'm trying to work that out right now, ain't I?" He bristled. He'd had about enough of the nonsense from everyone expecting him to work miracles.

"You should talk to Jonathan Crowley about that while you're letting him out of his cell."

Pace snorted. "That's not likely to happen."

"It should. He says he can fix all of this."

"He's good with a gun. Don't mean he can work miracles."

Kaufmann pointed at the preacher who was doing his best to slink away without being seen. "That damned fool can't even find a place to stay or food to eat without charity from the likes of me. What the hell makes you think he's gonna do the least bit of good?"

"He's a man of God?"

"He's a fast-talking snake oil man."

The preacher looked over with a wounded expression on his face and started to say something but one look at the barkeeper's face shut him up.

"Let Crowley out of his cell so he can fix this."

"What if I don't?"

"Then I'll tell everyone you're the reason all the dead people out there are standing up."

"Like they'd listen."

"I give them a few free whiskeys and they'll listen to whatever I tell 'em, you damned fool."

"You wouldn't." He said the words but he had his doubts.

The man sucked in a deep breath and scowled even harder, his brown hair falling in front of his face and his jowls quivering. "You damned fool, I live here and I intend to keep living here. I need to make a living to do that, and no one can buy from me if they've all left town. So you fix this, Pace Peabody, or I'll do everything I can to make your life miserable. You hear me?"

Pace threw his hands up in the air. "Fine! I'll let him out! But there's a catch, you loud-mouthed bear! He kills anyone else I'm gonna blame you for it and lock you in the cell next to him!"

Kaufmann crossed his arms over his broad chest and smiled thinly. "You go right ahead. And if he should get out of that cell and actually handle what you have not, I'll even have a word on your behalf with the mayor when it comes time to pick a new sheriff."

He jabbed a finger into the man's gut. "See that you have yourself ready, Kaufmann. I'm finished with you and everyone else telling me how to do my duties."

Kaufmann didn't say anything else. Instead, he waved a hand in the direction of the sheriff's offices. "After you, Pace. Let's go get this situation fixed."

Pace looked at the man for a long second and resisted the urge to just shoot him in his head and be done with the matter. Then he started walking, his strides long and furious enough to burn off some of the anger he was feeling.

He made it to the jail faster than he would have under almost any other circumstances, fueled by his frustration.

Pace Peabody thought he understood what being inconvenienced and frustrated was all about. He was wrong, as is often the case.

But he was about to learn.

Molly Finnegan

The power sang inside her. She couldn't exactly say that she had form, but she knew she could with practice. Her rage was a monumental thing, but it was dwarfed by the energies she had stolen from the dead around her. They were gone, all of them, but she remained, stronger for the experiences.

Jonathan Crowley had scorned her, but she would fix that. She would make him want her. Had she still been rational she might have pondered exactly why it was important for the man who was nearly a stranger to love her and want her, but death had been unkind to Molly and her sudden growing hunger had only made matters worse.

So rather than contemplate why she wanted the man who had been a stranger only passing through her life, she decided to handle the matter once and for all.

As she walked, she drew the power into her form, coalescing, condensing herself back into a familiar shape.

Only two beings saw her as she manifested. One was a young man who had only recently come to understand how much larger the world was than he had expected. Jonah Pratchett had watched the horse eating monster crawl from the ground, and he had dealt with the walking dead, and now, as he stood outside of the barn and paced in the cold weather, he saw a white cloud of mists spiraling down from the night sky and swirling into a more solid form. The shape took on feminine curves and as he watched the thin tower of mist grew limbs and a body that made more sense than what had been there only seconds before. As he watched, mouth open and eyes bulging, the form became solid. Not just a cloud that took the momentary shape of something vaguely familiar, but the solid, graceful shape of a woman. She was older than him by at least five years, at a guess, with autumn hair and snow pale skin. Lots of pale skin. She did not manifest wearing clothes, but as naked as the day she was born, which made a certain sense as he was almost sure he'd seen her get born before his eyes.

He watched the entire thing with a mixture of dread, wonder, and lust. Dread because she was surely not a natural thing, wonder for the very same reason—she was fair to the eyes and there was a part of him that was almost sure he must be seeing an angel manifest on earth—and lust because she was the first woman he had ever seen who was naked, and the wonders revealed before his eyes were of the sort he'd been trying to decipher since the first hair grew around his nethers.

Jonah held his breath as she moved closer, her eyes—so dark that they seemed a part of the night itself—did not see him, but looked past him as she took bold steps toward the very spot where he stood transfixed.

She stepped closer still and he closed his eyes. Much as he wanted to see the way her body moved, the way gravity played with her parts and, oh, much as the notion of touching the wonders her body promised appealed to him, fear and awe won over desire. Perhaps she was an angel, and if so, perhaps she could see any sin in his heart and surely lust was a sin, like the Pastor kept saying.

He trembled, not because of the cold that he had already adjusted to, but because he feared damnation even more than the nightmare he'd seen the previous evening.

"What a sweet young man you are." Her voice was ephemeral, a distant whisper that was exactly loud enough to catch his attention. He dared open one eye and saw her standing before him, her breasts bared and just below the level of his eyes. He looked quickly toward her face, his terror growing even more profound. Hellfire and worse must surely wait for the man who had such notions about an angel of the Lord!

Jonah shook his head. "I'm sorry I looked! I didn't mean to!"

"Shhhh, sweet boy." Her hand reached out and caressed his face. The long, delicate fingers were so very cold, so much worse than the freezing weather and Jonah tried to take in a breath, but the wintry caress seemed to steal even his ability to breathe.

Where her fingers stroked the skin of Jonah's face blazed with a cold so bitter it burned. The pain was strong enough to remove his paralysis and he tried to step back, tried to scream, but that frigid agony spread from her touch, rippled under his skin and exploded through his skull, his neck and then the rest of his body.

He stepped back exactly one pace as he opened his mouth to scream. Then he died.

Jonah's body fell lifelessly to the ground.

Molly stared at the body for a moment and marveled at the feel of the soul she held in her fingers, at the warmth that soul spread into her.

This was unexpected. This was...this was so much more powerful than she had imagined.

She walked quickly toward the cell that held Jonathan Crowley. She would show him the error of his ways.

Only a short distance away, Albert Miles watched as she walked, as she forced her rebirth upon the world, and as she destroyed the boy from the stables with a mere touch.

He said nothing, did nothing to stop her or to get her attention. His fingers felt the small leather sack that carried his prizes, the odd pebbles that held so much power within them. Each was carefully carved, meticulously designed, and bore a strong resemblance to a small seed. Each held a secret, and he would have the answers to those secrets one way or another. There were other issues at hand, other beings of power around him and that was something fairly new in his experience. There were other forces at play, and he had no desire to get involved in what was happening.

He had other matters to attend to.

Like the albino.

The undertaker fought against what was happening to him with all his willpower and struggled to hold on to what made him an individual.

And Albert paid attention to that struggle as it occurred, curious as to which was stronger, the seed he had given the man, the man himself, or the alterations he had made to the seed before he gave it over.

The night was promising to be an interesting one, and Albert had every intention of letting it become as interesting as it wanted to. He had learned many things during his time on the world, but surely the greatest lesson he'd mastered so far was how to be patient.

He merely had to wait. The answers he sought would come to him when the time was right.

The Preacher

Out in the woods the dead stood motionless, uncaring, unfeeling. They had no concerns, no needs that had to be satisfied. They were beyond pleasure and pain, hatred and happiness. They were, after all, dead.

They did not rest.

Several different people had come to investigate them earlier, and most had left quickly, too frightened by what they saw to stay.

The preacher was the only exception.

The deputy and the bartender had their little debate, and the preacher moved away from them, grateful for the chance to escape from Peabody's demands and the menacing stare of Kaufmann, who had grown frustrated with the preacher's attempts at free meals.

And the damnedest thing happened as he was slinking away. He had an epiphany. He was a man of God and as such he should not have been afraid of a deputy or a whoremonger. That notion came into his head and settled inside of him with a power that surely had to come from the Lord himself. His fear, his uncertainty, both evaporated before the thought.

He had planned to find a place to sleep, a place to get a meal. Instead, he turned and looked toward the dead where they stood at the edge of the woods and walked slowly in their direction, his eyes fiery with his growing outrage at their existence. The dead were meant to rest, to rot back into the earth that birthed them, ashes to ashes, dust to dust. And these…Abominations defied the will of the Lord and surrounded Carson's Point, sapping the faith from the weak and making even the bravest men and women afraid for their lives and possibly even their very souls.

And that, brothers and sisters, would not be allowed.

He stared at one of the bodies. The man was unknown to him, but the elements had ruined him. Skin sloughed away from the bones of the face, and muscles rotted into a frozen slop beneath the same decomposing flesh.

His heart thudded deep in his chest and he shook his head. "You need to lie yourself down in the ground. You hear me?"

The dead man did not answer, nor did the bleached, milky eyes look away from the town and toward him. The preacher stared hard, damned near willing the flesh to move, but nothing happened.

And then, not too far off, he saw a movement to the left. He turned his eyes in that direction but the heavy snows were almost enough to hide anything in the first place. The darkness and the snow hid whatever he had seen.

Rather than rant at a dead man, he closed his eyes and held his hands out in supplication. Fear nibbled at the edges of his heart, but instead of giving in to that growing sense of dread, the preacher called to Heaven above. "Dear Lord, your children have been taken from you, stolen away by the unclean and the unrighteous. I ask of you that you put their bodies to rest. I ask that you grant them the peace of your embrace. I ask-"

He spoke no more as he felt the cold intensify behind him.

Though he wanted little more than to put the dead to rest, he stopped his prayer and turned to the cold that threatened to freeze his flesh solid.

And saw the Skinwalker for the first time. The flesh that was as white as purest snow, the eyes that were surely as black as a murderer's soul. The Skinwalker looked at him, his head turned slightly, the unreadable eyes locked on his.

"No," the Skinwalker's voice was creaky with lack of use. "Do not pray to your god. Pray to me." The accent was thick, but the words were still clear enough.

"G-Get thee behind me Satan." He could barely manage the words. The creature was not like the dead things that stood before him. They were unnatural, true, but they held no malevolence. This thing, however, had an air of wickedness that made him want to run screaming back into Carson's Point to hide himself away. This thing, this demon, was surely an agent of the Lord of Lies.

The Skinwalker stared at him for several heartbeats, neither of them moving. Then he shook his head. "You are nothing, European man. You are less than nothing, just like your god."

The preacher's blood nearly boiled. Without thinking, he swung a hand toward the demon. "Blasphemy!" His palm slapped across the cold, hard skin of the white beast, but the only noticeable reaction was that his fingers stung from the impact.

Powerful hands reached out and grabbed the preacher's face. Before he could do more than blink the Skinwalker held his skull as easily as a man can hold a newborn, and no matter how much he wanted to struggle to free himself, the grip was too strong for him to break.

He opened his mouth to protest, but his tongue refused to move. "No more prayers, foolish man." The Skinwalker's expression did not change. Ancient, withered skin remained in a scowl of disapproval, and those impossible eyes glittered darkly.

Much as he tried to beg, to pray for his life, the creature continued to hold onto him. And then, when he thought he might go mad merely from staring into the soulless night held within those eyes, the Skinwalker acted. He leaned forward until his lips were pressed to the preacher's. The lips that kissed his were colder than ice, hard as stone and tasted of ash and death.

And when he thought the worst must surely already be happening, the Skinwalker drew in a deep breath, pulling all the air from his mouth, from his lungs, stealing his oxygen, and so very much more. There was no physical pain, but there was a growing understanding, a deep, resonating knowledge. His soul, his very spirit was pulled away, drawn into the abyss inside the Skinwalker's flesh.

He could not scream. He could not fight. In the end he couldn't even manage a last prayer to the Lord before he was consumed.

And when he was dead, his body continued to stand, motionless and cooling in the wintry air. His heart did not beat, his blood did not pump, and his lungs no longer drew in breath. He was dead, just like the hellish sentinels that looked toward Carson's Point.

And though his body began to slowly decompose, his form did not rest. As the Skinwalker moved back into Carson's Point, the preacher's body slowly turned to face the town proper. And like the other dead around him, he waited.

Jonathan Crowley

Crowley sat in his cell and smiled as the deputy came into the room, his round face torn between unease and frustration.

The bartender stepped in behind him, his thick arms crossed over his chest.

Crowley did not move. He had no intention of making anything easier for the idiot.

When no one spoke for several awkward moments—awkward for Peabody, Crowley was fine with the silence—Kaufmann cleared his throat. "I brought him."

Crowley shot him a hard look. "And yet, here I sit behind a locked door."

The barman pushed a thick hand into the deputy's back and staggered him. "Come on, Pace! Let's get this done."

Crowley allowed himself a smile. Peabody looked back at the bigger man and then thought hard about protesting, but in the long run he fished the cell door key from his pocket and unlocked it.

"You're free to go."

Crowley stood, a leisurely, fluid motion that most people would have sworn was impossible, and walked toward the opened door. He barely acknowledged the deputy's existence, and that, more than anything else, was what started the troubles.

"You could at least say thank you," the man mumbled.

Crowley looked back at the man and skewered him with a glare. "For what?"

"For letting you go!"

"You really are as stupid as you look. I wouldn't have thought that was possible." Crowley kept walking while the deputy stared at him with an open mouth and Kaufmann did his best not to laugh out loud.

"You miserable bastard."

Peabody reached for his weapon.

Crowley heard the sound of leather and metal scraping and turned, his eyes focusing on the man and watching as the hand drew the revolver.

The deputy was fast.

Crowley was faster. His foot landed against the deputy's shoulder and sent him sprawling backward. The weapon sailed away from his hand and bounced and skittered across the floor.

Crowley followed the man and hit him with the palm of his hand across the face. As Peabody fell, Crowley hit him again and a third time.

Peabody might have protested the rough treatment had he been conscious.

Jonathan Crowley looked at the unconscious man and dragged him to the cell where he'd been kept. Without a word he closed the door and locked it. The key went with him. So did the deputy's revolver.

"Now, where were we?"

"You just gonna leave him there?"

"He threatened me with a loaded weapon." Crowley stared hard at Kaufmann until the man looked skittish. "He's lucky I didn't leave him hanging by the neck until dead."

Lucas Slate

Lucas Slate shivered. His entire body felt feverish.

He'd been dreaming about his mother and his father and the many, many people who knew the family shame. He had been an embarrassment at best, but his folks had shown their love in a hundred odd ways.

The pain in his chest blossomed and moved, sliding through muscles and bones and nerves inside of him. His pasty white skin was covered in a thick caul of sweat and he moved as carefully as he could, trying to make his body stand with very little success.

Every muscle he could think of hurt. Every tendon creaked. His entire body shook with effort as he walked and then he fell forward and caught himself on his arms.

What had he been doing? He couldn't clearly remember. He'd gotten up to make food, perhaps, but something about that wasn't right. It didn't resolve itself properly in his head. There was something about food. But he wasn't even remotely hungry.

The recollection came quickly, and Lucas tried once more to force his fingers down his throat and make his system give up whatever he had eaten.

He gagged and retched, but nothing came out of him. With his eyes closed and his body doing its absolute best to reject what he'd put into himself, he remembered the moment clearly for the first time. He'd been given a small bead, scarcely larger than a pea and for some reason—a compulsion, he'd had no choice—he'd popped the damned thing into his mouth and swallowed it.

Lucas forced himself to his hands and knees and looked down at his floor, blinking furiously. Inside his body something moved, twisted and turned, and more importantly spread through him. He had once watched ivy over the course of a year, examining it every day and marking how far it had grown. It was seldom impressive to see on a daily basis, but this? He could feel the tendrils sliding deeper into his essence.

"Aauuggh!" the pain was sudden, a flash fire moving through his body. Lucas fell again, this time scraping a few layers of flesh from his brow as he slammed himself into the hardwood.

Every muscle in his body twitched, and a few of them moved against his will, pulling him flat to the floor. His stomach muscles pumped. His back muscles knotted. He arched off the ground in a seizure, his head thrown back, and the cords of his neck muscles standing out in hard relief.

The worst of it was the change in his bones. As if the muscles were merely there to distract him from the pain his bones tried to sneak their transformation through, as they grew longer. He felt his shirt tear at the seams, heard the purring noise past the low grunts of agony forcing themselves from his body.

How long did it take? Eternity, or a few seconds. Who could say? The fire was still burning in the stove. The sun had not completely gone down, or shifted at all that he could tell. Still, his body was exhausted and he felt like he'd been dragged behind a wagon.

He sat up as carefully as he could, as if the very bones in his body might be made of thinnest glass, but the pain was better now.

Lucas Slate looked at his arms and then his legs. His shirt was torn apart, but he could see where the cuffs of his sleeves ended too soon. He could see that his pants were too short, by several inches.

Somehow he had grown.

Standing took a few tries, not because he was too weak, but because his muscles seemed completely off from where they belonged.

"What did you do to me, Mister…?" There was a name in his head, but it refused to reveal itself. He could see the man with his eyes closed, a big man, burly with a heavy beard, he was a trapper, but the name eluded him.

He ran his hands across his face and felt the bony contours. His flesh was drawn too tightly. His face, always on the effeminate side, felt made of angles and ridges. The skin was as soft as sunbaked leather.

Somewhere in the depths of his mind a song was playing. The notes made no sense and he could not hear it with his ears no matter how hard he tried. The effect was maddening.

As calmly as he could Lucas Slate walked to the wardrobe where he hid his shotguns and rifle. The Winchester would do just fine. He thought for a moment and then took one of the shotguns as well.

He had no idea what had been done to him, what was being done to him even then, but he intended to work out the details after he settled the matter once and for all.

CHAPTER SIXTEEN

The Skinwalker

The night was growing long.

The Skinwalker sat on the cold ground outside of Carson's Point and contemplated what he wanted to do next. There was little left for him in the area. He would gather his seeds, oh, yes, but first he had to collect them. He had to find them within the town, and to do that, he had to enter the area properly. If he did that, he would have to face not one, but two separate creatures that were, at the very least, capable of destroying his progeny.

That was a rarity. In the time he'd been alive, the most dangerous creatures he had ever encountered were other Skinwalkers, and these creatures were different. The sorceries they used were unknown to him.

More importantly, both of them had died and come back. He wanted to know how that worked. He wanted that power for himself. He would tear them apart slowly if he had to, in order to learn their secrets.

The dead had served their purpose, but he used them anyway. With a simple nod of his head the corpses he'd animated moved toward the town, some walking easily and others jerking as rotting muscles and tendons did their best to hold together. In a few cases the rot had gone too far and the corpses simply fell apart as they tried to move. The rotted remains shuddered and jumped, but to no true avail.

He did not count the number of dead things. Ultimately, they did not matter. They were only a distraction.

Deep within the confines of the town, locked in the ground and struggling to break free, a spawn of his seed twisted and moaned as the changes continued.

The Skinwalker reached into the satchel he wore at his hip and moved his fingers until he found the long bone he was looking for.

It was a thin bone, one part of a forearm, but now carved into a new shape, altered until it suited his needs. He had hollowed the bone out and carved the holes necessary to make music.

He listened to the song that had been a part of him since, so very long ago, another of his kind had planted the seed within him and let it grow. The song was a personal thing, a deeply religious thing for a creature that had no religion. He played the notes of the song as his mind heard them and the notes carried across the still air and drifted into Carson's Point.

The average person heard nothing. The animals, however, heard and responded. Throughout the town, dogs went into barking frenzies and cats yowled their fear into the air. Horses, those left unharmed by the creature Jonathan Crowley had already dealt with, grew nervous and whinnied their concerns to the air. Birds in the area took flight, glad to escape the song.

Of the people in town, few heard anything. Those that did had been infected by the stones the Skinwalker, or others like him, had created in the past.

Lucas Slate grew angrier still as he marched slowly through the streets of the town, looking for someone he could no longer remember, intent on causing grievous bodily harm.

The music played on, heard only by a select few, but it had an impact on nearly every person in Carson's Point.

Albert Miles

The cut of meat was nearly perfectly cooked and that was a rare thing. The bread was hearty and the potatoes were young and fresh despite the miserable weather. Albert Miles understood why it was that his son had liked the hotel so much. The cook they employed managed what was very nearly miraculous in a shithole of a town. He ate the meal with enthusiasm he seldom managed for any aspect of his life and that decidedly included food.

Albert Miles closed his eyes and heard the music clearly. It was a flute playing, but the sounds were identical to the imperceptible tunes played by his collection of stones.

They were fascinating things. Each was different, most bore powerful resemblance to the others, but each was as different as the waves that crashed along a stormy shoreline. No matter how closely they resembled each other, they could never quite be the same.

Still, they all played the same music, or rather parts of the same song. He believed that each was connected to the others. Whatever they were, whatever the source of their power, they were smaller parts of a whole that was beyond his comprehension. At least for now. That suited him just fine, especially since he'd made adjustments to most of them. He could not alter them, not really, but he could add to them, even if he could not subtract. The enchantments he wove into the things were each different. All he had done to the stone he gave the undertaker was to make him want to own the thing completely. Though he was unsure exactly how that manifested itself, the man would covet that stone with all of his being until he found a way to make sure it was his and his alone.

Miles listened to the music but was unaffected by it. The sounds were pleasant, but not compelling. He imagined they would have a different effect on anyone who was infested with the stones.

He wondered how many of the infected were still around. Perhaps Lucas Slate. Certainly one or two of the men who'd been around long enough had managed to catch one of the things along the way.

Miles closed his eyes and concentrated. There were three. He could tell that one was Slate. The man was actively looking for him, but he would not find him. The first thing he did was make certain that whoever he tainted with the sorceries involved would not see him. They could look at him a hundred times and their gaze would bend elsewhere. One was changing a man even now, warping him, reworking him into something else. The changes seemed nothing at all like what was happening to Slate. They were as different as night and day, just as with the dead red men that he'd seen moving around and infested with some of the stones he now possessed.

And the last of them was-

"Well, now. That's a very different story isn't it?"

He set down his cutlery and took a drink of the pale red wine that the kitchen served. The wine was a failing, to be sure.

Albert Miles had lived a long time. He had walked the world since the very first English settlers had come to this country and he had lived in many, many places. But the thing out there? The last of the beings living with one of the stones? That creature was older by far than he. That thing was very possibly close to a thousand years old and the notion was intimidating.

For the first time since he'd brought himself to Carson's Point, Albert Miles worried.

He had power, but there was very little he could do to outmatch experience. One of the reasons that Albert Miles had lived as long as he had was simply that he did his best to predict every possible outcome and work out contingencies. He had played loose with that rule since coming to Carson's Point because, frankly, he was deeply curious about the things he saw since arriving, and curiosity was always his weakness.

Curiosity, however, could be a deadly distraction. Miles wiped his face with his napkin, rose from his seat and headed for his room.

There was a very real chance that the time had come for him to leave the area. He had collected what he'd come for, and further studies could be done elsewhere.

A few of the locals were running down the street and screaming about the dead walking again. Miles frowned. The last he'd heard they were outside the town's walls and unmoving.

One glimpse through a window told him all he needed to know. The dead moved, staring at nothing as they stumbled and walked through the streets.

That was just fine. They would make a nice distraction.

Still, his glimpse outside of the hotel showed him more than he'd expected. A woman walked through the darkness, naked and pale. It only took a moment to recognize that she was a spectre. Not merely a ghost but something more now. She'd been feeding on the spirits of the dead, and taking their energies into herself. He'd heard of such things but never seen one before.

The dead ignored her and she returned the favor as she stalked the dark streets, obviously looking for something or someone.

This was too good an opportunity. There were secrets he did not yet understand about the dead, about the life force of a person and about what lay beyond death's domain. The spectre before him might well hold the answers he needed and so he stepped outside without considering his actions too carefully, once again letting his curiosity get the better of him.

She had likely been beautiful in life, if the shape she took now was a reflection of what she had once been. Not that he concerned himself with such matters.

"Who do you seek, miss?" He spoke softly, and directly to her, locking his gaze on the pools of shadow where her eyes hid away.

She did not look real. She was light and shadow, black and white, and though she looked solid and could likely touch flesh, she had no true weight, no real substance. She was the stuff of ghosts, flesh made of spirits, and illusion made reality.

She stared at him, and her mouth moved into a scowl. "You are not Jonathan. I am looking for Jonathan."

"Perhaps I can help you find him."

His hand reached for one of the stones he had altered to suit his needs. "Do you even know who he is?"

Without giving any other answer, Albert Miles threw the stone toward her and watched as it made contact with her spectral flesh.

Molly Finnegan

The need to find Jonathan Crowley had not abated. If anything, her rage was growing more and more concrete the longer that she looked for him.

The man before her was large, to be sure, likely one of the biggest men she had ever seen. Despite his air of kindness, she sensed he was more than the image he presented. There were things about him that were hidden, locked away and kept from view for good reasons, of that she had no doubt.

Had she been alive, she would have thought simply that he was not a man to be trusted around a lady. She was dead, and so her perceptions were darker than that. He was a man who simply should not be trusted. His heart was surely black.

He threw a small object at her. It was no larger than a bead from a necklace, but when it arced out and touched her, it struck as if it weighed as much as a boulder.

All the power she had taken into herself, all the essence she had consumed from the other dead, seethed and boiled within her as the stone touched her spectral flesh.

For one more moment Molly had the delusion that she was powerful, that she could alter her world, and then the stone pulled at her, ripped away layer after layer of all she had taken from others and, let her feel what it must have been like for her victims.

She cried out as best she could, and tried to pull away but to no avail. The form she had created dissolved and Molly screamed again, this time in blind fury, but nothing changed.

A few seconds later she stood and shivered, suddenly cold again, and alone. She saw the man who had attacked her reach down and touch the stone he had struck her with.

After a moment he smiled.

"Well, I have no idea who Jonathan might be, unless he's the man Crowley I keep hearing about. If so, you could likely find him at the sheriff's office. Last I heard he'd been arrested."

He looked right at her, saw her despite the fact that her physical form had been torn away. "Good luck to you. And thank you for this. I've been needing exactly this for some time."

With that he turned away and left her to her own devices.

Molly fell to her knees and wept, howling her frustrations out into the cold night.

No one noticed. No one at all.

Marcus Darby

The dead moved through the town. They did not attack anyone; they did not need to. Their mere presence was enough to send people scrambling from their tents and lean-tos in an effort to escape the rot and corruption that walked among them.

The people who ran were desperate and afraid, and the Skinwalker walked among them, unseen, and feasted on their fear.

He did not need to touch them to feast, merely to be among them. The emotional tides spilling from them were as rare and delicious as any physical meal he might have considered. His gaunt face pulled into a grin that hurt his cheeks, but still he smiled as he savored his feast.

Not far away from him the seedling he sought was finished with his transformation. The man pushed his way from the ground and shivered in the cold as he tried to understand what had become of him. His face was wrong. His vision was a confusing blast of images that crossed over each other and came from too many directions at once. Had the poor wretch had a mirror, he might have seen the bulging eyes, the many facets of them, so like those of a fly.

Marcus Darby tried to scream his frustration and fear into the night and instead heard a warbling note, too deep and loud to have ever come from him. It spilled from the bony protuberance that had replaced his mouth. The thing ran from where his mouth and nose had been down to the center of his chest. Where it ended several barbs moved and twitched. They vibrated as he attempted to scream and added to the cacophony.

His body was altered, too. His legs had split themselves into three long, multi-jointed things that seemed spindly and should not have possibly carried him, but managed just the same. Walking was a challenge for the first few minutes, and even with six limbs to work with, he fell down a few times.

It was instinct that made the difference. When he fought to understand his new legs, they became uncoordinated. When he left them be, and thought of moving, they did what they were supposed to do.

The body he had known his entire life was gone, replaced by a hard carapace. There were sections to the thing. Several holes pushed through the hide and he understood instinctively that those openings replaced his lungs.

He should have been terrified. Nothing about his new form made sense. Instead, he was ecstatic. He had become something new, something deadly, and something that reflected how little he felt he belonged to the human race.

Darby let loose another sound and moved from the barn with exactly one plan in mind. He wanted to kill the bastard that had destroyed his friends. Again. He wanted to make Jonathan Crowley suffer dearly before he died, but ultimately he wanted the man dead.

The street outside the barn was frozen mud and little else. He did not care. He walked for several feet before stopping as his body made still more adjustments. The cold did not matter. He was strong enough to withstand the wind and the chill with ease. But he needed to know where his prey was and that was an imperative he could not resist. His eyes saw so much more than they had before, but taking in all of the information was a task. He saw in all directions and making sure that he saw what he needed to see was disorienting.

For three minutes he stood perfectly still in the cold night air and sniffed the air, looked around did all he could so understand where the man he'd killed twice might be hiding.

And then he found him.

The wings unfolded from his back, hard shells that flexed with the wind and moved at a speed nearly impossible to see. He caught the breeze and lifted into the air, the sound of his wings like a low thunderous note moving through the air.

He hadn't even known he had wings until they moved.

There was so much he did not yet know about his new body. So much that he looked forward to discovering. He should have been horrified, traumatized by the transformation, but truly he saw all that had happened to his form as a blessing.

A cadaverously thin, pale man stood on the ground not far from where he'd been standing. The man looked at him with a serene expression.

For a moment he knew a blend of hatred and fear as he stared at the shape, and then it was gone.

He would consider the new player soon enough, but first he needed to kill Jonathan Crowley.

The Skinwalker

The Skinwalker stared at the seedling that rose into the air and considered the endless possibilities. In all of his time he'd never made a new shape, only used the shapes that nature provided. He had, on many occasions, become a bear or a wolf or even a bison, but he had never thought to make up new forms.

When this was done he would consider the possibilities. But for now, he did not have the time to teach himself a new skill. There were things that needed to die, including the one that had just flown away from him.

He watched it move away into the cold night air and then he followed, moving at a slow pace. There was no reason to hurry. He had learned patience a long, long time ago.

The dead he'd sent to move through the town had done their part, and a good number of the living had run from their homes and fled into the darkness, or moved to places where they could easily be found.

When he was done with the creatures he planned to destroy, he would have his way with the rest. First the oddities and the threats had to be eliminated.

The seedling he followed descended from the skies and dropped toward one of the buildings toward the center of Carson's Point.

A moment later the screaming began.

Dan Kaufmann

Kaufmann stared at Crowley and felt a deep and abiding unease spread through him. The man was smiling a great deal, and there was nothing kind about that expression. He was having second thoughts about the man being the possible salvation of the town.

Those thoughts were shoved away when the giant bug dropped from the sky. He'd seen plenty of insects in his life and always found them fascinating, but none of them were at all like what he saw now. The thing had four long legs and it used them as it settled in the road. Those legs looked like tree branches, gray and straight and heavy. Above them was a body that made little sense to him. There was an abdomen that was heavy and round, and a smaller section above that which looked almost like a ball. Above that was a shape similar to a man's torso, but as with the rest of the shape, it was covered in a thick plate armor most akin to the crawfish he'd captured in the rivers as a child. It was a bug, surely, but far larger than any could possibly be.

The face of the thing was the worst. There were bulging eyes, nearly as round as that abdomen, they were black as the night and seemed nearly liquid in their texture, he half expected them to wobble and move like dew drops on a branch. Below that, the face was little more than a heavy tube that ran down the underside of the torso.

Vast moth-like wings blurred and then slowed down as the thing landed. It looked toward him and past him, and Kaufmann was fine with that.

No, that was a blatant lie. He wasn't okay with any part of what he was seeing. Kaufmann's heart slammed noisily in his chest as he licked at his lips in the frigid weather, as he shook his head and took four steps backward.

"That can't be real."

Crowley snorted. "Of course it's real, you fool. Everything you've seen lately, and an oversized insect is what sends you wanting to run to your mother?"

Kaufmann turned to look at the man, his eyebrows knitting together. He knew what the man was doing. Crowley was insulting him to get him back to the reality of the situation, but he still resented it.

Then it saw Crowley and let out a sound that would never be human. The noise was too loud and ranged through multiple octaves at once in a cacophony that nearly deafened.

Crowley looked at the thing and his smile grew a fraction larger as he tilted his head slightly to the left. "Well now," Crowley purred, "What in the name of Hell are you?"

The head of the thing jerked and twitched, and the hands of the far too human looking arms spread impossibly long fingers as the thing, well, it seemed like it was trying to speak and couldn't find a way to make words known. The creature chattered and then screeched as it lunged toward Crowley.

Crowley did not stay in the same spot but moved very quickly out of the way, shoving Kaufmann aside in the process.

There was no outrage to be had about that. Kaufmann knew that the man had just saved him from his own frozen fear. He staggered sideways and landed on the street over a yard from where he'd been standing. In that spot the thing now stood, its hands curled into thorny nightmares as it let out another inhuman noise and then turned its oddly shaped head to look at Crowley.

Crowley had his Peacekeepers drawn. He had not been wearing them a moment ago.

Kaufmann flinched as the weapons were fired, blowing holes into the hide of the thing. Pieces of shell, and what passed for flesh beneath that shell, exploded away from the nightmarish body. Large chunks of gore sailed away, but the thing only roared again and launched itself into the air.

Instead of doing the proper thing and falling down dead, the bug monster reached toward Crowley with those impossible hands and caught the man before he could move a second time.

Crowley thrashed and struggled but to no avail. The hands crushed in tighter on him and long fingernails dug deep, puncturing cloth and like as not the flesh beneath.

The smile never left the man's face as he planted one foot on the creature's chest and then kicked as hard as he could with the other, smashing his heel into the bony protuberance that was most of the nightmarish face. His boot drove the thing's face back, breaking the hard shell with the impact.

The thing dropped him and staggered, impossible hands reaching to cover the obscene face. Fluids ran down between overly long fingers and painted the torso of the thing with glistening tracks of wetness.

Crowley hit the ground when he was dropped and then stood awkwardly, blood flowing from both arms. He stepped back and reached for the ground before him, his fingers clawing at the dirt, drawing markings that made no sense to Kaufmann. Looking at them was as bad as looking at the bug creature. It hurt his mind to see the symbols.

Crowley stepped back and called out to the thing, "Is that the best you can do? I'd have expected more from you."

Kaufmann wasn't sure the beast could understand a word the man said, but it responded as if it could and lurched forward, its bulging, insect-like eyes staring from between the fingers of its hands. Once again it made odd noises as if it were trying to speak, and Crowley grinned as he stepped back.

Whatever words he said were whispered. The marks he'd made on the ground grew bright, bled a deep red light like blood, and when that light touched the bug thing, it burned.

The creature let out a noise loud enough to make the bones in his chest vibrate and to make his vision blur as its hide blackened and then curled up in strips, baring the insides that were never meant to be seen. The legs collapsed, the wings of the thing caught fire, and the body fell toward the burning light before striking the ground and bursting in a wash of dark fluids.

It died in seconds, but the sound seemed to go on forever, and Kaufmann looked on as the body rotted and burned, as that unholy light faded away.

The smell that hit him left Kaufmann gagging, repulsed.

He shook his head and backed away, looking toward Crowley as if the man might possibly have answers.

He could see the wounds through the tears in man's clothes, which meant he could see them as they healed at a frightening speed.

Crowley was grinning at him and he stepped away, shaking his head. Too much. It was too much. The monster, the way it died, and now the madman smiling at him as his wounds vanished.

"I know that look," Crowley said. "If I meant to hurt you, Kaufmann, you'd already be hurt. So you can calm yourself. You asked for my help, and I'm giving it."

"What the hell is wrong with this town? Why are these things happening?" He could feel himself breaking apart in his head. Nothing made sense anymore. The world was not supposed to work this way and he wasn't sure if he could handle it any longer.

Crowley shook his head, still grinning and reached for his pistols where they lay on the ground. "May as well ask why the wind blows or why it snows. Some things aren't meant to be understood by people. They just are."

"'Some things just are.' I like that." Kaufmann turned to the man speaking and stepped back, surprised. It was the trapper, Miles. The man hadn't been there three seconds earlier, he'd have sworn it.

Miles was wearing his thick fur coat and leading his oversized horse by the reins. He almost looked like the same man who'd come into town not that long ago, but he carried himself differently and his expression was off. Kaufmann had trusted the man once, but didn't feel it likely he'd do so now.

Miles watched Crowley gathering his things. "I'm leaving this town. If you gentlemen are wise, you'll do the same."

Crowley chuckled, never even looking at Miles. "I've seldom been accused of wisdom."

Crowley pointed with his chin to where a gaunt, pale man stood in the shadows, barely noticeable. "Besides, I don't think I'm done here just yet."

The stranger stepped out of the shadows, and Kaufmann stared for a long, long moment as he tried to register the changes that had taken place in Lucas Slate.

The man had been several inches shorter only a day earlier. His hair was still long, but currently was not drawn back into a ponytail; instead it was free and blowing in the cold air. He was wearing his usual outfit, but it was too small for him. His legs showed clearly in the cold air, from just above the middle of his calf. His arms showed in much the same way, straining against the too small fabric of both shirt and jacket. He was wearing his undertaker's hat and doing his very best to look dignified, but considering the rest of the changes, it was not working very well.

Lucas Slate was a small man, and his face was soft, positively feminine, but to look at him now? Not at all. His cheeks were gaunt, his lips thinned to the point where they barely seemed to exist. His nose was the same, but seemed too small on the rest of his elongated face. He looked like a corpse left too long in dry heat; withered and drawn. The problem with that was simply that the man was still alive and had changed drastically in the last day.

"What the hell happened to you, Mister Slate?" He spoke without being aware that he was going to talk.

Slate looked his way and shook his head. "I have no idea." His eyes turned to where Miles should have been standing. The man was gone. "I'd planned on asking Mister Miles, but he is not here." He shook his head. "Not any longer, at least."

Crowley was staring at the man, and his eyes were narrowed. His smile remained, but it had slimmed down to a look that bordered on a sneer.

Slate turned toward him. His oddly gaunt face taking on a different expression. His eyes narrowed, too. "Is there a reason you're staring at me?"

"You don't look the same as you did before."

"As I have just been discussing with Mister Kaufmann. And you are?"

Crowley's smile grew. "Just passing through your town, Mister Slate."

Before the albino could respond, the thing that Crowley had destroyed came up again. It had been little but ashes and blackened carcass, but now it moved. It surged forward, a black tide of thick fluids, and before he could fully take in what was happening, Kaufmann let out a scream of pain. The blackness that reached for him hardened as it moved, and became a pointed skewer that was surely as hard as bone. The business end of that spear punched through Kaufmann's chest and out through his back before he could draw in a proper breath to scream.

The pain exploded through him and Kaufmann reached for Crowley, trying to beg his help, trying to warn him. The point erupting from his back pushed harder and split bone and meat alike.

He never made a sound larger than a gasp before he died.

Lucas Slate

Lucas Slate did not like the man in front of him. There was something about the stranger that left him nervous and sure he was going to regret the encounter.

The man's smile made him twitchy. It was not a warm greeting, but a promise of pain and suffering as surely as the grin on a skull was a sign of death.

He was about to tell the man to stay away from him when the ashes of the thing the stranger had killed moved forward and killed poor Kaufmann.

Kaufmann had always been one of the few people in town who treated him with any semblance of dignity. Didn't matter to the barkeep that Slate was an albino, or that he was from the Confederate side of the war between the states. He'd always greeted him with kindness.

And now he was dead. Just that fast, the man was lying on the ground and bleeding from a hole large enough to move Slate's arm through with the greatest of ease.

Crowley let out a stream of obscenities and moved, sliding between Slate and the black, formless mass.

No, not formless. There were very fine tendrils moving through the thing. They shifted and danced as the thing rearranged itself into new forms, each as fluid as the last.

The stranger moved his hands and spoke so softly that Slate could not hear the words, not truly. He could feel them, however. Each syllable uttered changed the pressure in the air, and each gesture of his fingers and hands caused faint trails of light that moved like reminders of where his hands had been. Whatever he was doing caused the stranger effort. His arms shook and muscles and tendons in his neck corded with strain.

The fluid thing rose higher, until it stood as tall as Slate himself, and wavered, shivering as if it were a wave ready to crash along the shoreline. He'd grown up with the ocean near his house and had spent many an evening watching as the waves rose and fell, still, this offered nothing like homesickness. This was a vile, hellish thing that was not kind or innocent in any way.

And to prove that point it slammed forward and crashed into the man trying to protect him.

If he had not been watching out for Slate the man might have survived. Instead that blackness hit him hard and shattered bones and flesh alike as it crashed into him and blasted him backward as surely as if he'd been kicked by a mule.

Skin peeled back from bone. Cloth was shredded. The man surely died then and there and the thing that had killed Kaufmann claimed a second life as it surged around the body and moved toward Slate himself.

Slate felt it then, that impossible tug within his body. This thing, this wave of black filth, was connected to what was happening to him. He could feel it. He could sense it as surely the plants that follow the light of the sun know where their sustenance comes from. But this was different. He drew nothing from the dark, formless nightmare. He just sensed a twisted sort of kinship.

"You don't want to do this." He was barely aware of speaking. There was a growing sense of unease, but it wasn't fear exactly. It was more akin to hatred. In his life there had been few times that Lucas Slate allowed himself to get angry and fewer still when he considered the notion of hatred, but now both of those dark sensations crawled under the surface of his skin and seethed.

Something welled inside of him; the darkness growing, moving much like the shapeless thing in front of him, surging, roaring overwhelming his senses with a powerful, gravitational pull.

His hatred was drawn toward the amorphous form.

The shape surged toward him and he reached out, his teeth bared, his lips moving, and spoke words that meant nothing to him as his hand and the blackness connected.

The black fluids washed over his hand and sloshed up his wrist, his forearm, moving up his arm and down his body in complete defiance of the laws of physics and gravity. The stuff seared his skin where it touched, and the fine tendrils throughout it moved, trying to worm their way under his burning skin.

Slate fell backward, a scream peeling past his teeth. The pain was only a fraction of the problem. Along with the agonies dancing through his nerve endings, a song tried to burn its way into his mind. The notes were different than the song already pushing into his brain, causing a discordant cacophony to echo through his five senses and his thoughts alike.

Slate staggered and fell backward as the black wave covered him, tried to crawl through his nostrils, his eye sockets, his ears and his mouth.

He could not breathe. He could not scream. He could only burn and drown in thick, hellish water.

The fluids filled his eyes, crushed him under an unbearable weight, and try though he might, he could not lift himself from the ground.

This then, thought Lucas Slate, is how I die.

He closed his eyes and felt himself surrendering.

And then the hatred was back, stronger than before, a song within him, a high, keening song of rage, of missed chances, of possible pasts and futures lost because of the dark thing that drowned him and tried to fill him.

He opened his mouth and gasped out one last breath and in that breath were the first syllables of the song within his body.

The power of those unknown words made itself clear when the black fluids were forced away from his body, exploding off him in waves and droplets that danced and shimmered across the frozen ground.

Slate sat up and coughed the vile blackness from his lungs. His hands clenched into fists and his eyes watered.

He stood, moving on legs that did not quite want to do their part. His body shook, his muscles threatened treasonous failure, but he did not allow it.

The song was everything. He was aware. He could think, but the song crushed his personal thoughts under a weight of hatred.

He opened his mouth and the song continued. The black watery thing rippled and moved, trying to collect itself again. His words hit each droplet with oppressive weight. As he watched the fine filaments that wavered throughout the mass started to glow and burn within that darkness. Each of them lit up as bright as the sun at noon and flared white before fading away completely. Whatever it was that truly held the thing together, those fine stands burned and died away, and, as they died, the blackness lost cohesion and collapsed to the frozen soil.

The song faded down in his head until it was only a distant sound, much like the tide in Savannah.

Lucas Slate leaned forward and rested his hands on his knees as he gasped and tried to regain his breath and pull his thoughts back together.

This was madness, surely. This could not be his life.

The battered, broken thing that had been the stranger who tried to save him was still moving. The man rolled onto his hands and knees and tried to push himself up into a standing position, but he failed. Slate stared at him, horrified. Nothing, no one, should be that ruined and continue to move. Had the man been a horse, a kind soul would have put him down.

"Stay down, man. I think it's dead." Despite his trepidations, he moved toward the dying man and froze as he saw the way his body repaired itself. Flesh grew back together, strands of torn meat and skin pulling toward the parts that had been shredded away, like ivy moving from one tree to another.

The blood that had spilled from the man stayed where it was, but where a moment earlier his blood had flowed poorly it ran bright and warm again and pulsed with a strong heartbeat.

"N..N..hhhhahh…." Whatever the man was trying to say was lost on Slate as he looked at the poor bastard moving, trying his best to stand.

From around him he heard whispered voices, not quite the same as the song inside his head, but a similar sort of noise, and Lucas Slate looked around to find the dead were on the move again, shambling toward him and the man who was healing as he watched.

The man fell on his face and groaned deep in his chest. Lucas looked around, marveling at both the fact that the dead were moving and the very notion that he hadn't pissed himself while noting the first fact. They moved, and that should have been impossible. They were, after all, very dead.

They did not attack, but stumbled and stepped, making no real sounds except the whispers of flesh on cold, frozen earth. No, the other sounds were in his head, echoes of something else. Perhaps their souls cried out. Perhaps their spirits were discontent with their treatment. Whatever the case he heard them and knew they were in their own special miseries.

The song that filled his mind changed as it acknowledged the suffering of the dead. It became joyous, and he, in turn, was repulsed by the very notion. No one should take pleasure from another's suffering and surely not the suffering of the dead who had already lost all that mattered in the world.

As one, the dead stopped, their bodies standing a bit taller, and then they collapsed. The muscles that shouldn't have worked in the first place gave up their impossible fight and bodies dropped where they were, gracelessly.

Something shifted in the air as the forms collapsed. He felt it as surely as he saw it. Whatever had made the bodies roam had been taken back and moved from each corpse in a streamer of barely seen energies, much like watching dust caught by a breeze. He saw those streamers and followed them with his eyes, until they coalesced around a single form standing down the road a bit.

It was not a mirror image of what he was becoming, but there were similarities. The creature was gaunt and tall, and at first glimpse was so pale as to resemble a corpse. No, paler than that. As pale as snow.

The long frame and limbs seemed too thin by far, but he could feel the power moving within that body. The face was turned to the right and looked at him askance even as the thin lips pulled back in a smile that was without mirth or kindness of any sort. Eyes as black as a moonless night regarded him, and dark hair whipped about the thing's head in tendrils long and filthy.

This, he knew, was his kin. This was what he was becoming. The other things? The nightmares that had surrounded the town and the obsidian pool that had come for him? They were the preamble to this, echoes of the sort of power he knew enough to dread.

It spoke with words that made no sense, but his mind translated the meaning easily enough. "You have taken your new form quickly. You are stronger than I expected."

"Mister? What in the name of God are you?" His voice was a husky whisper. His hands shook. His mind screamed that this was his enemy, this was the surest threat he had ever encountered, and his body responded with a desire to either flee or to kill this abomination before him.

That smile grew, baring yellowed teeth in receding, blackened gums. This was not like the corpses. The creature in front of him was alive, but not in the sense that he knew or easily understood.

"You could not hope to understand me. You would have to live for a thousand seasons or more, and you will not live past this day." The eyes looked him over, and he sensed the amusement the thing felt. "You are not one of mine. What a pity. You could have been magnificent."

"One of yours? What do you mean?" The words made no sense. The thing spoke gibberish and his mind interpreted but this time the translation was off.

The pale creature moved forward, and one long arm reached out to touch his forehead. Slate tried to pull back, but he underestimated the reach of the creature. The fingertip that touched his forehead was hard and cold. The connection felt hot, as if a firebrand had been shoved against his skull, but he could not move, could not flinch. The pain grew like a flame, brighter and more intense with each beat of his heart.

For a moment, the song that was constantly haunting him was gone, lost to him, and at that moment, panic set in.

The silence was overwhelming, worse even than the burning pain.

Slate reached for the bone-white hand and grabbed at the other creature's wrist, planning to force the grip away from him but without success.

That damnable smile grew broader and those black eyes glistened wetly. The creature opened its mouth to speak again and then let out a gasp of pain.

The finger touching Slate's forehead fell away and the mountain of pain vanished with the broken contact.

Slate fell back and gasped, unaware that he'd been holding his breath, uncertain for how long he'd been struggling.

The gasp repeated itself when he saw the stranger was back on his feet and had managed to mend himself somehow, his clothes remained damaged and soiled but the flesh beneath was intact, and the smile was gone from the man's face, replaced with a cold fury.

His fingers clutched at the back of the pale nightmare's neck, and dug into flesh.

"I don't know what the hell you are, but we're done here." The stranger's voice was a low purr.

The pale thing drove an elbow back and struck the man in the side of his head. The move was so fast that Slate had to replay the images in his mind to get them to make sense.

The man dropped back and shook his head, obviously disoriented.

It turned toward him again, the grin coming back, and reached out to strike a second time.

Slate pulled the trigger on his shotgun and shot the thing square in its chest. The kick was immense, and his arms jerked at the force from the weapon. His enemy, on the other hand was blown completely off his feet and knocked back a dozen feet.

Rather than wait to see if the damned thing was dead, Slate moved forward, pumped another round into the chamber and fired again, blasting meat and flesh away from overly long bones. A hole large enough to fit a human head in was the result. There were blackened organs inside that hole, but none of them seemed to work, and blood pooled on the hard ground, underneath the thing.

He loomed over the dead thing and stared at the wound, and then at the cadaverous face.

Those black eyes glared at him, and the hellish thing sat up, ignoring the massive wound in its chest and the pieces that fell away.

"You cannot kill me. I am eternal."

Lucas Slate backed away, screaming his head off.

Albert Miles

Miles had no idea what the two things said to each other. Truth be told, he almost ran from the scene instead of merely hiding, but watching what had happened to the undertaker overwhelmed his sense of self-preservation and enflamed his curiosity.

He stood perfectly still and did not let himself shift. So long as he managed that, he would be safe from detection. Still, one hand held a long skinning knife and the other held a revolver.

He watched when the thing that he suspected had caused most of the mayhem walked out of the woods and into town. He kept watching while it called forth the dead and then stole whatever power had let them move. The stones he kept on his person vibrated as the two abominations fought each other. He was pleased with his new toys, but he craved the chance to study them better.

But for now, he would watch and see what happened when one of the creatures had to fight another of its ilk.

The damned thing stood up. It should have been dead, or at least beyond the ability to move, but it rose just the same, ignoring the catastrophic damage it had received. He could see where the severed spine of the thing dangled in shreds of meat and gristle. By all rights it should have at least been paralyzed he'd certainly vivisectionalized enough people to understand the way the human body worked and knew the laws of physics were being discarded.

Of course, he had defied death several times himself, but this? This was different. This was a new mystery he wanted to solve.

The best way to do that, however, was to stay alive, and so Miles remained where he was and watched as the wounded creature lunged for what had been Lucas Slate.

Jonathan Crowley did not stand still. He uttered something under his breath and threw a handful of what looked like ashes at the creature. The ashes soared like buckshot and caught the thing across the back of its shoulders and head. Where they touched flames erupted.

It turned around and roared, even as the long black hair on its head caught ablaze. The long, lean face grew longer still as it screamed, the sound louder than should have been possible. Despite the flames, the thing walked toward Crowley, its shape changing as it moved.

The form twisted on itself. The legs split in half and the body grew, until the pale thing walked on four legs and sported a body as heavy as a horse's though it was hairless. The feet had become hooves, and the torso of the creature grew thicker, heavy with muscles as it strode toward Crowley.

The hair kept burning but seemed to cause no pain or injury.

Crowley grinned. Then he crouched, preparing for whatever might happen next.

The thing reached for him as fast as a striking rattlesnake, and Crowley, despite his best efforts, was caught and held by the massive hands that had replaced the earlier thinner shape.

From his hiding place, Miles heard the bones in the Hunter's arms crackle and then break, and Crowley let out a scream of pain.

It's possible, truly, that the Hunter would have died at that moment, but instead the albino he'd altered with the shapechanger's magic seed recovered from whatever had happened to him and unloaded a round from his shotgun into the thing.

The shot tore flesh and punctured one eye. The creature roared again and threw Crowley as if he were tossing a small stone. The undertaker ducked, and pumped another round into his shotgun.

He pulled the trigger and fired, bracing himself properly, and as he did so, he spoke words that Miles could not hear. He could, however, feel the power that rippled through the air as the words jumped.

The second blast of shot tore flesh again.

The words, however, did far worse. Each syllable sent ripples of power through the air, and though Miles could feel them as if they were the bass beat of a large drum, they caused him no harm.

The shapechanger could not say the same. Each sound hit the creature like a hard slap, rippling flesh and rocking the thing back further.

The thing let out a snarl and returned to its previous form, the flesh of its face and torso battered and bruised by the noises.

Miles did not dare move. Whatever he was seeing was different from anything he'd ever experienced when it came to magic, and he wanted to know more, *needed* to know, else he would have left long before.

The attack staggered the pale creature, but only for a moment. Even though flesh had been torn and muscles shredded, the thing lashed out again. It spoke words and gestured, and the undertaker staggered, his eyes wide and his mouth drawn in an O of shock. Whatever force the creature employed, it caused a great deal of pain and made the poor bastard weep blood. Surely he'd be dead if not for the alterations Miles had made.

The experiment was worth his invested time. He was learning so much already and there was much, much more to study, if the undertaker survived, of course.

The two pale things fought harder, standing against each other and using their odd sorceries that made no sense to him. Inevitably, however, Miles knew how it had to end. The old, withered, creature would win. It had experience, and it had a greater grasp of what it could do.

Of course, now and then providence lent a hand.

The Hunter was alive, and he seemed in perfect condition. He also seemed extremely angry. Or insane, depending on one's perspective. The man was grinning but there was nothing of mirth in the expression. It was a baring of fangs, really. His teeth were clenched, his gums bared, his eyes narrowed with fury. His Peacemakers were in his hands and he took the time to aim carefully.

The first bullet took out the gaunt creature's right eye and removed a portion of his skull. He flew backward and landed on the hard, cold earth, his body shuddering. By rights he should have been dead and would have been if he were human. Even Miles, with all his abilities, would have been a goner.

The thing lay flat for several seconds, breathing vast bellows of hot breath into the cold air. The energies around the thing's body never wavered. It was not dead, and it was not dying. It was merely injured.

It sat up to prove his point. From his perspective he could see the road on the other side of the wound in the creature's head. There was blood, though it was thick and black.

When it spoke, the power in the words was obvious. It started to say something and the air changed, shifted, grew pregnant with a promise of violence.

Four syllables in, Crowley blew out the thing's other eye. It crashed back to the ground and writhed, mouth open in a wordless moan as it flopped and tried to find a position where it was not blind, and half its skull was not lying in the dirt.

Crowley stepped closer. Keeping both weapons drawn. His eyes were still narrowed as he stared at the remains of the thing.

Had he not been watching carefully, Miles would have missed the sight. There wasn't much forehead left to the damned thing, but there was enough and when the pale creature rose up again, the skin above the eyes, between the eyebrows, moved enough to let him see what looked like a small third eye.

Crowley shot the thing in the chest four times. Holes appeared and took with them large pieces of deathly white flesh and the bone beneath.

The damned thing fell down again and stayed down. Crowley started to walk closer to it and the undertaker spoke up, his voice a hoarse whisper.

"It isn't dead. I can feel it. Its mind is squirming around, and it's still there."

Crowley nodded his head. "I thought as much." His eyes studied the albino, and it took everything Miles had not to move, to intervene. He wanted to learn so much more from his latest project.

He was saved the effort by the spectral woman he'd dealt with earlier. She was barely there any longer. Where before she had manifested a physical form, all that remained of her now was a weak, fading wraith.

She called out to Crowley, and he turned his head toward her, once again baring his teeth in that raging smile of his.

"We're done, Molly. Go to your peace before I have to cast you away."

Whatever she said was too faint for Miles to hear. It was for Crowley alone. Instead of dealing with her he turned his back, dismissing her again. She wept, that wretched remnant. It was almost enough to make him feel pity for her.

Pity was a luxury he could ill afford.

The dying thing on the ground did something to the world, or to the players in their little battle, including Miles. One moment it was still dark out and a heartbeat later, the sun was rising.

He wasn't the only one that noticed, either. Crowley and the pasty undertaker both looked around, surprised. They should have had hours of darkness. But instead they were blinking against the early morning glare.

"The hell...?" Crowley looked at the easy to follow path and shook his head. "Too easy..."

The gaunt, cadaverous thing was gone, but it was easy enough to follow the trail of where he had been. There was a trail of mostly dried gore that headed to the west, toward the gates of the wall around Carson's Point.

The undertaker, Slate, shook his head. "He was mostly dead. Might still be. If he's trying to escape, he might not have enough left in him to hide his path."

Crowley shook his head again. "Whatever that thing is, it just made the sun rise early or put a spell on the both of us to make us stand still long enough for the day to come around again. Either way, it has power."

"I intend to find that thing and finish this."

"Well, that would be the both of us." Crowley sneered.

"Might I suggest we do so together? Injured or not, it has power."

Miles needed to find a way out of his current circumstances, and he needed it soon. Eventually he would move his hand, or that annoying twitch in his calf would become a cramp and he would break his concentration. When that happened, when he moved, they would notice him and when they did, he was as good as dead.

Albert Miles closed his eyes and concentrated, spreading his senses across Carson's Point. He could feel the power of the ancient thing that Crowley had wounded so heavily. It was in fact, heading west.

What he needed was a proper distraction.

Finding the right sort of diversion took all of two minutes.

Oliver Harding

The people in Carson's Point, with very few exceptions, were in town for the sole purpose of trying to find a fortune in gold. At the present time that wasn't happening very much. Most everyone was stuck, or rather they had been, while the dead walked.

The dead, finally, had done the right thing and fallen right and properly dead.

The word spread quickly and though no one came out to celebrate, a few did come out to get about the business of striking it rich. To that end, there was a run on the Harding's mercantile.

Oliver Harding was a businessman, and though times had recently grown rather lean, he was ready to handle what needed handling. He was also no longer taking promises as payment from the many people who had come in before the current dilemmas had started, and that was a point of contention for many of his would-be customers.

Harding, along with his sons Louis and young Curtis, were busy trying to handle the numerous requests for supplies. The gathered people were getting a touch unruly.

On the best of days he was not exactly an intimidating man, but Harding could make himself heard when he needed and his two boys, who took after his wife's side of the family, were larger than he was and better shaped in general, which is to say neither suffered from narrow shoulders or a large belly.

Rather than risk the patrons of his establishment getting worse about it, he called out as Luther Updike tried to reach across the counter and help himself to a satchel of hard tack.

"Enough!" Even Updike listened, and slowly pulled his hand back where it belonged.

"That's enough," he continued at a lower volume. "I know that everyone wants to get back to their business, and I respect that, but this is my business and I am no longer offering credit to anyone who hasn't paid me as yet for their last loan."

Updike started to speak and Harding silenced him with a glare. "I know, I know that all of you intend to pay me just as soon as you strike it rich. I know this winter has been harsh, but I cannot continue to order supplies I am not getting paid for and I will no longer allow anyone without cash or gold on their person to purchase anything in my establishment."

Several people thought about protesting, but one look at him and his two sons was enough for most of them. The mercantile very nearly emptied out within moments of his declaration.

Carl Jessup was the first one to reach him with a wallet that was not empty. Jessup was one of the early claims in the area and had already made a decent amount of money from his mining efforts. He was also wise enough not to waste his time drinking and whoring, which meant he still had most of what he'd earned.

Jessup was a tall, lean man with a mutton chop mustache and hair that was both receding from the top of his head and gray rapidly. He was known to smile about as often as the moon was known to outshine the sun at high noon, but he was mostly of pleasant disposition.

"What can I for you today, Carl?"

The man nodded slowly and considered his words. "A while back I asked you about procuring a few sticks of dynamite. Needed to see if they'd come in."

Harding nodded, glad that the man had waited until most everyone was gone before asking. "They did, and I still have them for you."

Carl nodded his head. "I'd like to go ahead and collect those along with two pounds of beans, and if it hasn't gone sour I'd like some dried beef."

"Bit cold for going back out, isn't it?"

Carl Jessup stared at him for a long moment, as if he might have grown a second head. "We're in the mountains, Oliver. It tends to be cold here in the winter. But I have work to do."

Harding nodded quickly. "Fair enough. I'll just gather those things for you." It was always best to know when conversation was wasted.

While he went into the back of the shop and located the requested supplies, Jessup continued his perusal up front. By the time Harding made it back, the man had gathered another two pounds of dried stock and decided to purchase a box of shells for his Winchester as well.

It was the best sale Harding had managed in over a week.

Carl Jessup left with a dozen sticks of dynamite secured in a wooden crate. The sole purpose of that dynamite, to Carl's way of thinking, was to blow open a rich vein of ore that he intended to exploit to the absolute fullest.

Albert Miles, who was currently witch riding along in the man's body, had a different purpose in mind.

The Skinwalker

The Skinwalker made it most of the way to the gates leading away from Carson's Point before he collapsed.

The damage he'd suffered was enough to kill nearly anything alive. His head was broken, his chest was open, and most of his internal organs had fallen away as he walked.

He would heal, but he needed time, and most of his stored power had gone to suspending the fledgling Skinwalker and the sorcerous nightmare with the revolvers.

Bullets should not have wounded him. They should not have broken his skin, let alone caused damage enough to leave him ruined. The man who carried the weapons had done something to them, and whatever that something was, it caused damage he could not heal easily. He was a shapechanger; in most cases, he could simply will the damage away and his body would recover, but he was not changing shape. He was not healing.

He was closer to death than he had been in centuries and that meant that he was also afraid for the first time in just as long.

In times long past, he might have recovered from this by switching bodies, by taking the seed from his head and planting it elsewhere, in another body, but that was a trick for younger Skinwalkers and not one he could ever do again. This was his only form and he had to understand what had been done to him. In time, yes, he would recover, but if he wanted to survive another fight, he had to fix what had been broken inside of him.

The Skinwalker crawled, hiding in shadows as best he could. If the wrong person spotted him, he would surely be dead.

He would not accept that possibility.

Slowly, carefully, he made himself grow calm. Little could be accomplished if he let fear rule him.

There had to be a way to repair what had been done.

He would find it.

If nothing else had been learned in his long life, he had come to understand the value of patience.

CHAPTER SEVENTEEN

Jonathan Crowley

Crowley finally decided to follow the trail. Whatever else the damned thing might be, it was crafty. He could find no sense of where it was hiding except the marks moving across the area and heading for the gates. If it got away from Carson's Point he might never find it again and for now, at least, it was vulnerable.

There were many, many forms of shapechanger in the world, and as a rule if you took away that ability, they were that much closer to death. There were a dozen different spells he knew that limited the ability to transform. He hadn't expected a simple casting to work as well as it did, but he'd take it.

Walking next to him, the man whose clothes he'd taken when he woke up in Carson's Point was trying to look everywhere at once and scowling as he checked his shotgun again. He had a good rifle strapped to his shoulder, but for close range combat the shotgun was likely a better bet.

"What's your name, son?" Crowley heard his voice. It was softer than it should have been.

"My name is Lucas Slate, sir."

"Mister Slate, where are you from, originally?"

"I'm from Savannah, Georgia." The man turned slightly to look at him, his eyes scrutinizing Crowley very, very carefully.

"Mister Slate, my name is Jonathan Crowley, and I am currently here to hunt and kill monsters."

Slate nodded and Crowley noticed the way his hands gripped the shotgun a small bit tighter.

Crowley's lips curled up a bit, but he forced his smile down. Best not to aggravate the man with the loaded weapon.

"I point that out because I am very, very good at what I do. I am also not quite certain what to do with you."

"Kindly clarify that, sir." The man did not stop walking. He also did not stop staring hard at Crowley.

"You and the thing we're hunting may or may not be the same things, but you are definitely related. I've seen enough of these damned creatures of late to know that much."

The voice was low and soft, sepulchral. "Are you considering whether or not I'm a threat, Mister Crowley?"

"I am indeed."

"And where am I in your considerations, presently?"

Crowley's smile crept out again as he looked into the pale, blue eyes and their heavy eyelids.

"Currently we are talking and you are alive. I would say that's a positive sign in your favor, if I'm being completely honest."

Slate nodded slowly. "I have killed no one, and I am guilty only of defending myself."

Crowley reached over and put his hand on the shotgun's barrels. He urged the weapon down with his hand until it was pointed toward the ground. Not far off several people were looking at the two of them as they continued to walk, and not a single one of those people was looking particularly relaxed. "At the moment we share the same goal, Mister Slate."

Slate nodded, slowly. He also let the gun be pushed to a lower position instead of pulling the trigger.

"I suggest we come back to this discussion when we are finished with the current business. I just felt it was important to be forthright with you."

Slate's eyes, already halfway lidded, became slits. "Much obliged."

"There is no reason to start an issue with you before I have to, Mister Slate. I just wanted to make sure you understood the situation."

"My situation is simple, Mister Crowley." His accent was soft and subtle, an aristocratic drawl. "I find I have no particular desire to die today, or to be killed for that matter. I rather prefer a long, peaceful life."

Crowley nodded. "Peaceful I can certainly understand."

Slate turned his head and pointed with his chin. "That way. I can feel him."

"I think we can safely assume that he feels you, too."

Slate nodded. "I know that he does, Mister Crowley. I can feel it. And he is surely coming our way."

"You can feel that too?"

Slate closed his eyes for a second, still walking as if there were no cares inside of him. "I can. He intends to kill us. Mostly, I think, he intends to kill you."

Crowley nodded. "It won't be the first time."

Slate offered a laconic smile. "That someone has tried or actually done it?"

"Both."

That one made the pale man look nervous, which amused Crowley to no end.

When the thing came for them, it came fast and hard, and it screamed its fury into the air.

A dozen people on the street did exactly what any sane person should have done. They took one look at the demon, and they started running away.

The creature was in horrible shape. Its wounds were still there. Half of its head was missing, but still it came for them. It had no eyes, but it moved unerringly. The arms of the pale abomination held items clenched in long-fingered hands.

There was a small effigy in one hand. It was human-shaped and the arms and legs bobbed and jittered as the man came towards them. The head of the thing, if it had one, was clutched in the death grip.

In the other hand was what looked like a small flute carved from bone.

The doll sailed through the air, hurled at Crowley as he came closer.

The mouth of the nearly headless shape opened and despite several large holes in the damned creature's chest, it managed to utter words.

Crowley tried to step back, but he was too late.

The effigy struck him across the side of his head and bounced to the ground.

Crowley looked down at it a frowned. Where it had touched, his skin felt as if it had been scoured with gravel.

He looked at the thing, noticing for the first time what appeared to be a small, dark eye in the remains of its forehead.

He might well have done something about blinding that eye, too, but the sudden attack stopped him.

The effigy grew as it lunged for him. The simple cloth and wood arms exploded into hardened skin and bone, and the mitten-like hands of the thing expanded, grew into articulated, heavily clawed and fully functional paws. Those deadly appendages came connected to a beast the likes of which he had never seen before.

The thing was bigger than a bear and broader, too, but more humanoid in shape. The face of the creature was a nightmare of teeth in a muzzle that opened wide enough to swallow his head if he wasn't careful.

Crowley stepped back as quickly as he could and narrowly avoided getting crushed in those powerful arms. The stench of the thing was a wild musky odor mingled with the rot of a carrion eater.

Whatever it was, the beast didn't seem interested in waiting patiently for Crowley to die before it attacked.

Lucas Slate

Jonathan Crowley, who had told him only a few minutes earlier that he wasn't sure if he'd let Lucas Slate live, got a panicked expression on his face and began dancing and weaving in the middle of the street, his eyes wide and his face drawn into an expression somewhere between proper anger and a deep, abiding fear.

Lucas Slate stepped back quickly as the creature came for him. It had paused long enough to hit the man with him in the face with a ragdoll and then stopped moving. That was when Crowley started acting as if he were trying his best to avoid getting killed by something much larger than he was. As pantomimes went the entire affair was rather interesting but not something with which he could truly concern himself.

Instead of attacking him, it reached up with long, nimble-fingered hands and placed a bone-flute to its withered lips.

The music that came forth hit him like a wall freight train. The pain was immediate. Somewhere deep on his chest something was going very, very wrong. His heart felt like it would explode from his body. The tension that ran through him started at the center of his chest and grew outward. He could feel it like a root system, a fine series of traceable lines moving from the center of him and creeping outward.

The creature came closer to him, still playing the flute. Slate looked on, trying to understand what was happening, wishing that the song within his head would respond to the new notes instead of going silent.

That song. That endless music that had become a part of his reality, it should have been there, should have been playing on and soothing his mind, his soul, but instead there was the new song coming from the flute, that overshadowed or actually destroyed what he had been hearing.

Slate's vision grew blurry and he felt his knees buckle, felt the skin on his knees scraped raw as he fell forward.

The shotgun was there. Still in his hands, still held tightly, but his fingers refused to move.

He opened his mouth to scream but gasped instead. There was no strength left in him.

Towering above him the dead thing kept playing, and the thin lips playing into the bone flute pulled into a smile. The world started to fade down into a tunnel of darkness. Even the sound of the damnable flute started to go soft.

His heart was stopping. He could feel it happening.

Lucas Slate was dying, and that thought made him sad for a moment.

And then it made him very, very angry.

He grew angrier still, and then he pulled the trigger on his shotgun.

And then the pain went away.

Jonathan Crowley

The thing caught him. That was inevitable. Crowley grunted and then let out a deep groan as the powerful arms of the creature drew him closer and then constricted around his chest. He felt the blood in his body pushed into different places as the creature squeezed down on his chest. He wanted to scream but all the air was forced from him as the pressure grew.

It wasn't possible. He could feel himself breaking, but the usual irritant, the damnable itching that told him his body was already trying to recover from the effects of sorcery, was missing.

He should have been healing, but instead bones creaked, his right arm bent into an unnatural position and he prepared himself for the pain of being crushed. His ribs were bending inward.

If he was going to die, he'd do his best to take the damned thing with him.

Jonathan Crowley opened his mouth and started whispering words never before heard on the continent where he was dying.

The creature killing him did not respond, and that, too, was an oddity. The pain should have been immediate and strong enough to make the thing flinch, unless it felt no pain at all.

The muzzle of the thing peeled away from teeth large enough to carve trenches in his skull.

Crowley kept speaking, gathering the power he'd need to burn the abomination away.

Four more words and his death would remove the thing from existence.

And then the damned thing vanished.

One second he was held in the air, easily four feet off the ground, and the next he was standing in the middle of the main road in Carson's Point, close to the western wall of the place. His hands were free, his body was untouched, and Lucas Slate was on the ground, gasping, moaning, and crawling, his eyes bulging from his head, and his skin flushed enough to look almost normal.

Standing above him were the remains of the thing they'd both been hunting. It was screaming, holding its ruined right hand in the palm of the left, and calling out in whatever tongue it spoke. Fragments of bone were scattered over its chest and the remains of its face.

Crowley reached forward and drove two fingers into the half-closed remaining eye that adorned its forehead. The fingers pushed deep and ruptured the dark organ.

And the thing fell to the ground as surely as if he'd cut its head away completely.

It made no sound, but instead lay on the frozen soil and slowly stopped moving.

Lucas Slate groaned and crawled on his hands and knees as if he were a hundred years old. No, Crowley had met people that old who were spryer.

While the pale man did that, he thought over what had just occurred. It was an illusion. He shook his head, surprised that he could have been so readily fooled.

It had been a very, very long time since he'd fallen for a spell that confused his senses. Mostly he was able to see through any form of mind tricks if he took the time.

"Cocky. Too confident by far."

He was talking to himself, but Slate answered him. "No. I was lucky. Didn't even know I'd aimed the damned shotgun at it."

Crowley looked at the cadaverous man. He was standing now, and his eyes were looking particularly bloodshot though his skin was once more as pale as a corpse's.

Crowley was just thinking about what to say to the man when the first explosion went off.

He couldn't say where it was, but not far away a building went up in flames and thunder. Shards of wood launched through the air in every possible direction, and Crowley ducked instinctively as a piece of board caught Lucas Slate in the arm and knocked his shotgun spinning.

Slate let out a scream. Crowley saw his mouth open and his throat working in a bellow of pain, but he heard nothing beyond the roar of detonation. Hot air pushed his hair and knocked his hat aside.

He turned and looked at the cloud of flames and smoke rising into the frigid sky.

"What the hell was that?" He couldn't even hear his own words.

He took two steps toward the ruined building—not even sure which building it was as yet—and then paused long enough to look at the thing he believed he'd killed. It remained perfectly still.

Slate moved closer and shook his head. The expression on his face said all he had to know. It was not dead. It was likely very close, but not dead yet.

He crouched over the ruined form and placed both hands on the shredded remains of the torso. The skin was cold. The heart did not beat.

His fingers drew lines across the bloodied remains and he concentrated. Sometimes a single word was enough.

"Burn."

Where he touched, the skin blackened quickly, smoking for a moment and then catching ablaze. The fire was bright enough to be seen despite the sunlight above, and grew brighter still as the flames spread.

Whatever it was that kept the thing animated it shrieked as it died. The mouth did not move, the body did not fight, but something deep inside those remains screamed and shrieked and, if noise alone had been enough to extinguish the fire, it might still have gotten away.

Slate looked from the burning remains to Crowley and back again several times as the body died once and for all.

He looked like he wanted to ask a question, but he never got the chance.

The next explosion was close enough to knock them both off their feet and send them into a stunned darkness.

Albert Miles

Albert Miles sat on Stomper's back and waited until his pawn did what needed doing. The first explosion was too far away. The second knocked the Hunter into a stupor and gave him enough time to flee.

He did not take any extra supplies with him, only the horse, his fortune and his collection of…seeds for lack of a better term.

He rode past Crowley and Slate, and he rode hard, his heels digging at the big horse and compelling it to move faster than it was used to. There were a few people who were in his way as he moved. He did not move around them. Stomper was a very large horse. He won each of the encounters with ease.

There had been a time, oh, so long ago, when Albert Miles had been a good man. He had loved his wife, loved his neighbors, and believed in the genuine goodness of people.

He could barely remember those times.

What he knew now was that there were ways to survive and ways to make sure that you were not remembered. To that end he had made certain Carl Jessup was prepared for what he wanted done.

The mercantile was a good business. Good people ran it. It carried supplies aplenty for the miners and the locals. It was also the only place in town with the supplies to arm a rifle or a handgun.

He had no idea how much gunpowder might be in the place and he did not care. Sorcery had its ways.

While Carl Jessup carefully set his remaining ten sticks of dynamite against the back of the very building from which he had purchased it—convinced that he was clearing away the obstacles between him and his silver mine—Albert Miles recited the spell he'd learned over fifty years earlier from a French thaumaturgist. The incantation had one simple purpose: it increased the magnitude of flames. The fool who taught him used it to expedite fires he was making to cook or to keep himself warm.

Albert chose a slightly different end result.

When the dynamite detonated the explosion was far greater than the sum of its parts.

The mercantile exploded and so did the closest fifteen buildings in a town that had exactly twenty-seven structures worth noticing.

The tents and wagons that made up the rest of the town were inconsequential. Flames roared into the sky, and every building within Carson's Point was knocked flat as if God Almighty had stomped down on them in a fury.

By the time the detonation, occurred Miles and his steed were almost half a mile away.

He felt the heat from even that distance and the noise was great enough to startle Stomper, who simply did not startle.

Miles found himself on his back in the snow, staring up at the clear blue skies as the thunderous roar of Carson's Point's death bounced off trees and from the sides of mountains.

By the time he stood up and dusted himself off, the worst of the damage was done. The wall around the town, built to withstand any sort of attack by the red man, was shattered along with the town itself and most of the structures were gutted and burned.

He found Stomper only a half mile away, looking at him with bulging eyes. The horse might have known he was different from what he had been before Albert stole his son's body, but the familiar was still a comfort. The great beast moved over to him and snorted a few times as he patted its thick neck.

"Sorry old boy. Sometimes a town needs to die."

Were they all dead? Was the Hunter gone? Not likely. People were more resilient than buildings. They tended to bend instead of break.

He closed his eyes and sensed that Lucas Slate was still among the living. He could not tell if the man was wounded, not without risking revealing himself, and he could always find out later when he had time to prepare himself.

Still, he was safely away and doubted the man called Jonathan Crowley would be following him any time soon.

That was enough for the present time.

He had so many wonders to examine, and all the time in the world.

Jonathan Crowley

When he came to, Jonathan Crowley was furious. He cursed, he screamed, he walked around the remains of Carson's Point and cursed some more, enraged that he let someone, or something destroy so much and so many.

"I don't think you could have stopped that, Mister Crowley." Lucas Slate walked with him his long, gaunt face drawn into an expression that was more sad than angry. Crowley could not understand that notion, not really. He preferred rage to sorrow. It burned brighter, and it burned away, leaving little behind but the occasional corpse.

Sorrow lasted longer and tended to linger in the darkest corners of the soul.

"This wasn't that damned dead thing. This was something else. It reeks of sorceries." His voice was almost as soft as Slate's which was usually a sign that he was close to snapping. Not that anyone around him knew that particular fact.

Slate continued to look around, searching for living people. So far he'd found a dozen corpses, but that was all.

"I believe I'll be leaving town, Mister Slate."

"Where will you go?"

"West, I think. And for the time being I will go south. It's far too cold."

Slate nodded, but said nothing.

"I make that point because I'd like you to go with me."

Slate looked his way and frowned. "Good Lord, man, why would you want that?"

Crowley looked toward the remains of the jail. The walls had blown apart and if Pace Peabody was anywhere in there, he was very likely dead.

"I'll be honest. I'm not sure if I can trust you on your own."

"What do you mean?"

"Whatever that thing was, whatever those things were that came before it, you are connected to them. By all rights, the safest thing to do would be to kill you."

Slate opened his mouth, but Crowley silenced him with a gesture.

"Yes, I know. If I'd truly wanted you dead, I could have done that before you woke up. I could have decided not to protect you from the explosion. I let you live for the same reason I want you with me. I'm not sure about you yet."

Slate considered those words and sighed, then nodded. "Fair enough."

"We'll find horses."

"You seem confident."

"I am. I'll make sure of it."

"And if I decide not to ride with you, Mister Crowley?"

"Your weapons are gone. Mine are not."

Slate looked him over very slowly and finally he nodded. "I rather like the idea of a companion to travel with. The territories can be lawless places, and I'd rather not walk alone if I don't have to."

Crowley nodded his head. The air was cold, but he didn't mind. The smell of smoke was still strong, and the wind was ruffling his hair.

"I've never much cared for company."

"Why is that if I might ask?" Slate looked genuinely interested.

"People tend to die, Mister Slate. And then you have to stop and bury a body, or if you've been foolish enough to care, you have to mourn the passing of a fellow traveler."

Slate nodded. "I am an undertaker, Mister Crowley. Or at least I was. I reckon I can handle the occasional corpse if you aren't up to it."

Crowley smiled and nodded his head. "Fair enough. For now. But remember, Mister Slate, that I'll be watching you. Do not disappoint me. I'd rather not have to kill you any time soon."

Slate nodded. "That works well for both of us, Mister Crowley, as I would rather not have to die."

250 / James A. Moore

They spent several hours looking for survivors in Carson's Point, and they even found a few. The next day they found horses, just as Crowley promised they would.

The day after that, when the wounded had been tended and given shelter, Jonathan Crowley and his new companion left the area.

For his part, Jonathan Crowley did not look back.

He seldom did.

About the Author

JAMES A. MOORE authored more than forty novels. The first decades of his career focused on his love for horror, as seen in many novels including the critically acclaimed *Fireworks*, *Under the Overtree*, *Blood Red*, and the Serenity Falls trilogy. Later, Jim earned a reputation as the "prince of grimdark fantasy" with his hugely popular Seven Forges series as well as the Tides of War trilogy. The author loved collaborating with other writers, most frequently with Christopher Golden on the Bloodstained Worlds trilogy and with Charles R. Rutledge on the Griffin & Price series, among others. Nominated for the Bram Stoker Award twice, Moore won the Shirley Jackson Award for co-editing *The Twisted Book of Shadows*. He first came to prominence as one of the principal world-builders involved in the World of Darkness from White Wolf Games, most famously Vampire: The Masquerade and Werewolf: The Apocalypse. At the time of his passing, Moore left behind one completed solo fantasy novel, as well as completed collaborations with Charles R. Rutledge and Mary SanGiovanni. Plans are afoot to bring those to readers soon.

Bibliography

NOVELS

The Black Stone Bay Series
Blood Red (with "Blood Tide")
Blood Harvest
Bloodlines

The Bloodstained Series (w/Christopher Golden)
Bloodstained Oz
Bloodstained Wonderland
Bloodstained Neverland

The Tides of War Series
The Last Sacrifice
Fallen Gods
Gates of the Dead

Standalone Novels
Deeper
Fireworks
Harvest Moon
The Haunted Forest Tour (w/ Jeff Strand)

NOVELLAS
Dear Diary: Run Like Hell
Homestead
The Wild Hunt

SHORT STORY COLLECTIONS
Slices
This is Halloween

Curious about other Crossroad Press books? Stop by our website:
http://crossroadpress.com
We offer quality writing
in digital, audio, and print formats.

Subscribe to our newsletter on the website homepage and receive a free
eBook.

www.ingramcontent.com/pod-product-compliance
Lightning Source LLC
Chambersburg PA
CBHW031942240626
47153CB00003B/829